Dakota Blues

By
LYNNE M. SPREEN

Copyright © 2012 Lynne M.Spreen
All rights reserved.

ISBN: 1475191332
ISBN 13: 9781475191332

PRAISE FOR
Dakota Blues

Dakota Blues captures a woman's mid-life crisis and blends it into a remarkable novel. First-time novelist Lynne Spreen takes a woman whose life is coming apart at the seams and weaves a remarkable recovery. Every woman in her middle earlies will identify with and accompany Karen Grace on her journey to resolution.

—-RAYMOND STRAIT,
Author and celebrity biographer

Dakota Blues is a real winner. The people who inhabit the novel are flesh and blood, and the journey of the protagonist makes for captivating reading. Few first novels are as satisfying as this.

—-JAMES HITT,
Author of *Carny, A Novel in Stories*,
Grand Prize Winner for Fiction – 2011
Next Generation Indie Book Award

In vivid prose, Lynne Spreen's debut novel, Dakota Blues, presents questions painfully familiar to today's readers: What have we lost in this modern, fast-paced frenzy we call living? What if we could turn back the clock to a time and place where personal connections outweigh profit, where the land itself can both challenge and make us whole again? Dakota Blues is a novel to make you laugh, cry and revel in being human. You won't put it down.

—-KATHRYN JORDAN,
Author of *Hot Water* (Berkley/Penguin, NY)

Insightful and extremely poignant! In Dakota Blues, Lynne Spreen has created a character to love, one who will have you cheering her on as she discovers the richest treasures of life are sometimes the simplest. A debut novel that is an absolute must-read!

—-Bette Lee Crosby,
Award-winning author of *Spare Change*

Dakota Blues

By
LYNNE M. SPREEN

For Bill — my husband, my mentor, my friend

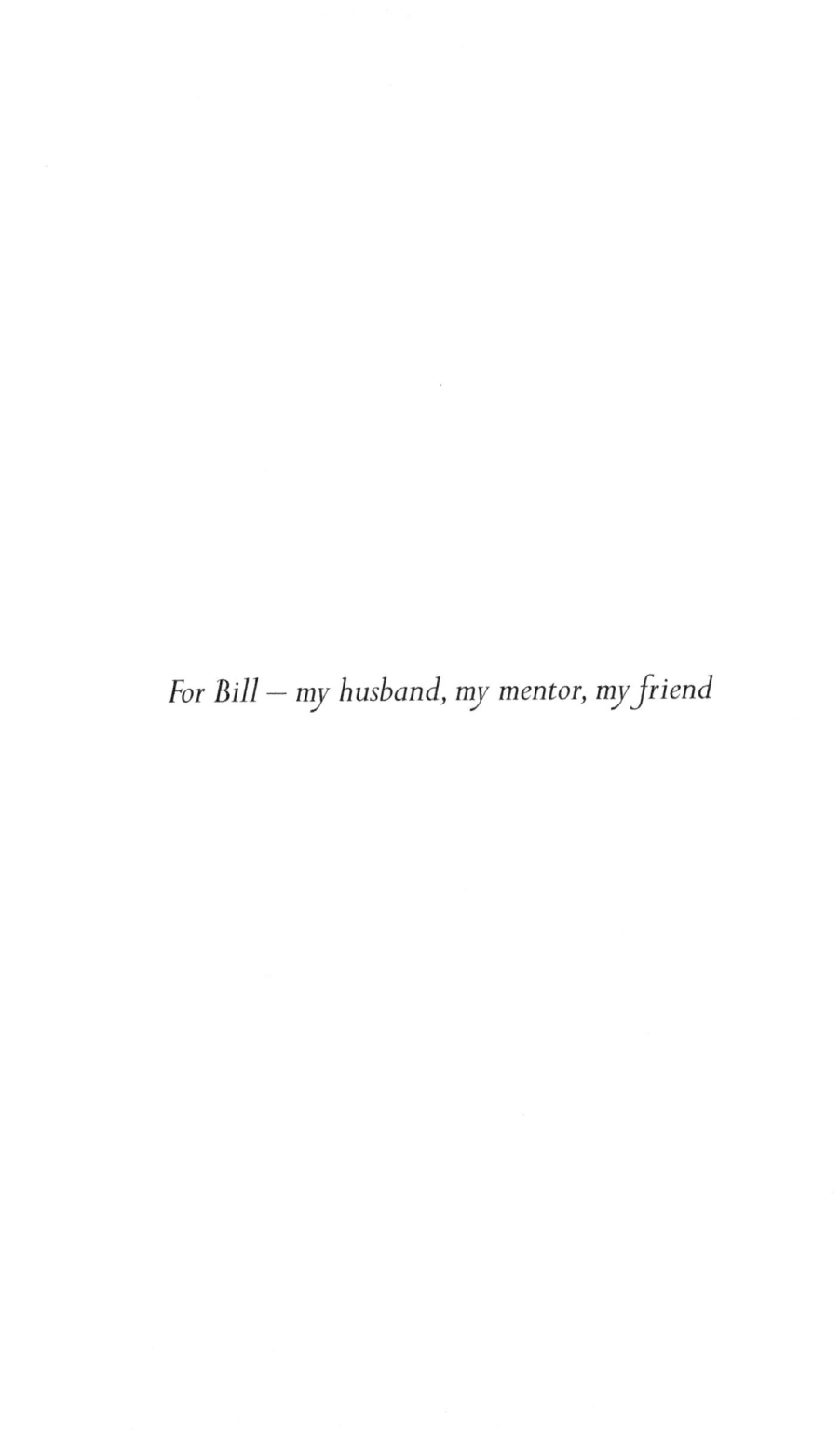

*Tho' much is taken, much abides; and though
We are not now that strength which in old days
Moved earth and heaven; that which we are, we are;
One equal temper of heroic hearts,
Made weak by time and fate, but strong in will
To strive, to seek, to find, and not to yield.*

                From Ulysses by Alfred, Lord Tennyson

Only a fool puts everything on paper.

                Ed Kuswa (my dad)

Chapter One

Karen's fingers hovered over the keyboard while she tried to remember the killer argument she'd been about to make, but the idea had faded. Not for the first time that day, she wished the hall outside her door hadn't become the official gathering place for coworkers in search of gossip and idle chit chat.

It wasn't like her to lose focus so easily. Karen couldn't afford to slow down, not now when time seemed to have accelerated, racing up behind her so fast she could feel its hot breath. No, at her age, and in this economy, a person had to run hard and keep running. She returned to the keyboard.

A rap on the doorjamb interrupted her again. "You busy?"

Karen turned to face the young man slouched in her doorway. Thank God he'd finally ditched the eyebrow ring but his slacks were still too baggy. "Hey, Ben. Sit."

Ben slumped into a chair in front of Karen's sprawling desk, his eyes bloodshot. It wasn't due to partying. The kid practically slept in his office. "Wes told me to fire Ashley."

"Seriously?"

"Yes." He rubbed his face.

"Unbelievable, even for him." Karen began scribbling notes on a pad. Sometimes she hated human resources. Like most people, she chose the career thinking she could help others. Instead, every day seemed to bring new confrontations. "He knows her husband is sick, right?"

Ben nodded. "He said we can't let that dictate business priorities. Quote unquote. I don't know what to do."

"Give me a minute. Let me think." Karen turned to the window where, ten stories below, Newport Harbor bustled with all manner of maritime traffic. Fishing boats, their outriggers bent like spider legs, chugged past the breakwater out to sea. Just past the mouth of the channel, long-nosed speedboats flew across the waves, and a biplane slowly towed a banner. Something about beer.

She spun back around. "Is Wes in?"

"You think you can change his mind?"

"I can try." Karen slipped into her suit jacket. She marched down Mahogany Row and stopped in Wes's doorway. "Do you have a minute?"

Wes looked up, his eyes narrowing. "One."

"There's a problem." Karen stood in front of his desk. "Ashley's husband has pancreatic cancer."

"Irrelevant. You know that."

"I know that, and I'm still asking you not to fire her."

He pushed a tablet across the desk at her. "So give me a name."

"What?"

"Somebody else I can fire instead." He sat back in his chair and chewed on a pen.

Karen hoped it bled into his mouth, but she forced her face into a semblance of thoughtful concentration. "I'll need a few minutes to think."

He tossed the pen on his desk. "I was just playing with you. She's already gone. I saw her outside and gave her the good news." Wes put his feet up. "So, when do you start your vacation?"

Karen folded her arms across her chest. "It's a funeral, Wes."

"Oh yeah? Who died?"

"My mother." Her voice cracked.

"Sorry."

Karen didn't answer.

"And how long are you going to be gone?"

"I'll be back in a couple of days." She turned to go.

"Hey."

Karen stopped. "Yes?"

"Keep your phone on."

At the other end of the Row, Karen pushed open a door to an office in which the air carried a hint of mothballs and the heavy perfume favored by older women when their noses stopped working. Behind the desk, Peggy frowned at the spreadsheet on her computer screen. "I'm busy."

"Who isn't?"

"I don't want to hear it." Peggy's grey suit hung on bony shoulders, and her hair was thinning in back from stress.

"Too bad."

"All right, fine, but first, help me with this. The damn thing's frozen."

Karen crossed to the old woman's desk. "Ashley and her husband need a continuance on their insurance."

"What are we up to now? Twenty, thirty families?"

"Hide it in the account Wes uses for boat repairs. He'll never know."

Peggy turned to Karen with a heavy sigh. "Somebody will. Then we'll get fired."

"We should be so lucky."

"Aren't you brave? Talk to me again when you're out of a job. Now, what does it mean when the little arrow goes like that?"

"First tell me we can cover Ashley."

Peggy looked up at the ceiling, calculating in her head. Dark red lipstick crept into the deep wrinkles around her mouth. "Six months, like the others. Now will you help me?"

Karen bent over Peggy's shoulder, checked out the screen, and pressed a key. Immediately the document unlocked.

"Oh, for God's sake." Peggy stabbed at a couple of keys. "Used to be we had people to do this. Now I have to do everything myself."

"Why don't you ask IT?"

"Screw them. They act like I'm retarded. I swear to Christ, next time I get a shot at early retirement, I'm taking it," Peggy said. "When are you leaving?"

"Tomorrow morning."

"How're you doing, kid?"

For one minute, Karen stopped running. She leaned into Peggy for a hug.

"We all have to go through it, sweetie." Peggy broke the clinch. "I don't mean to sound like our asshole boss, but don't stay away too long. Don't give them an excuse."

"I won't."

That night, Karen drove through the entrance of her gated community, exhausted. As the gate arm came down behind her, her shoulders relaxed. She turned into the driveway of the darkened house, parked in the four-car garage, and picked her way through piles of outgoing furniture and clothing. In the kitchen, she switched on a light, revealing a great-room combo that sprawled the length of the house. She never used it. Steve was the one who needed six thousand square feet of split-level, with four baths and five bedrooms and a pool and hot tub. He had lusted for a domestic showplace and paid cash for the house after one particularly good year.

Karen kicked off her heels and considered a Scotch, but it was almost midnight and she had a flight to catch in a few hours. Instead she navigated through the dark living room out to the patio where the land rolled away in a sprinkling of lights and ended at the Pacific Ocean. The view would be hers for... what? Another six months before Steve would want his return on investment? The coastal damp smelled of salt and settled on her bare arms, chilling her. She would have to think about moving, but not tonight.

She thought about Wes, and shivered. Leaving work for a couple days was a risk, but skipping the funeral would be asking too much, even of her. Even for Wes. Her work was done to the extent possible, and Stacey, her assistant, knew how to reach her. Everything was in place.

She stared off into the black distance. All future crises would have to wait until tomorrow afternoon, when she returned to her hometown on the Northern Plains.

Chapter Two

The thirty-seater bucked and lurched toward Teddy Roosevelt Regional, but Karen continued to study her computer screen, assessing the plusses and minuses of Wes' latest cost-cutting scheme. Only once did she pause, grasping the laptop to keep it from sailing to the floor, but she never stopped, even when the attendant warned the passengers to return to their seats and buckle up. Like most CEOs, Wes had been using the Great Recession as his excuse to slash staff to the bone, thereby showing positive growth on the company's balance sheets. Anybody who managed to creep up the salary ladder was fair game. Age was a target, too. The older employees were tossed onto ice floes and shoved off into the dark waters of the frigid economy.

At fifty years old and the top of the pay scale, Karen would not let that happen to her.

The plane jerked hard and a papery hand shot across the aisle to grab her arm. Karen glanced up. "Don't worry. We'll be down safe in a minute," she said, the vernacular of the Plains already reasserting itself.

The old woman peered at Karen through her trifocals. "Are you one of the Schulers?"

"No. Sorry." Karen looked out the window. Far below, her home town of Dickinson, North Dakota sat like a fat hen in the middle of a checkerboard. Crops fanned out to the horizon in every direction, divided into sections by narrow strips of road. Tomorrow, the cortege would follow one of those roads to a newly-turned grave, put her mother in the ground, and Karen would officially become an orphan. Except at her age, she had lost the right to consider herself such, and she wondered when was the cutoff. She hadn't been warned. It didn't seem fair.

She returned to her work. One more memo, one more critical task to finish. When the flight attendant tapped her on the shoulder, Karen slid the laptop into its case next to her return ticket. She would make her escape right after the funeral. Otherwise, the vast web of her extended family would ensnare her, trying to draw her back into the fold. It happened every time she visited, although she'd returned less and less in the past few years.

For a moment the plane leveled off and floated above the runway in that sickening pocket of silence before the wheels hit. It landed hard, bounced once, and braked. As it slowed, she opened her eyes to see the old woman smiling at her. Karen smiled back. "See? We made it. Enjoy your visit."

"Oh, I'm not visiting," the woman said as the plane jerked to a stop. "I'm home." She stood, her back crooked with age, her thin sweater rucked halfway to her shoulders. Karen reached over and gently pulled it down.

Outside, a man in a reflective vest and ear protectors wheeled a metal stairway across the tarmac to the door of the plane. At the exit, the wind painted Karen's scarf across her face, blinding her.

She followed the small group to the terminal, where she spotted her cousin, Lorraine, and wrapped her in a hug. For a moment, Karen was lost in Lorraine's perfume, reminiscent of summers when they piled into station wagons headed for Patterson Lake, baked their taut brown skin under a sheen of cocoa butter, and impressed the boys with graceful dives from the floating swim dock.

"Where's Steve?"

Karen blinked, lost in her memories. "He's not here. He couldn't come."

Lorraine reached for a suitcase. "Is everything okay?"

Karen stopped what she was doing and looked Lorraine in the eye. Around them, the terminal cleared as North Dakotans headed for town. "I think we're getting divorced."

"Oh, no. I'm so sorry." Lorraine hugged her. "I don't know what to say."

Karen shrugged and got in the car. What else could Lorraine say? They hadn't seen each other but a couple of days in the past thirty years. "Thanks."

Lorraine placed the suitcase in the back seat and sat watching her cousin. "How long has it been since you decided to separate?"

"He moved out a few months ago."

"That's so sad." Lorraine stared through the windshield a moment before starting the car. "It's weird. The same thing happened to two of my friends just in the last six months. Both of them had been married for like, thirty years. It's like an epidemic among old people."

"Steve's just having a midlife crisis. Not too original," said Karen.

"Well anyway, you still have us. And I have no doubt you'll be fine. You've always been the strong one." Lorraine reached across and squeezed Karen's arm. "Are you ready for tomorrow?"

"Ready as I can be." As much as Karen dreaded the thought of the funeral, almost more foreboding was the thought of her childhood home filling with mourners. She would play hostess for the bereaved, wearing her game face for the family and friends, but only until it was time to leave. "Can you do me a favor and bring me back here after the wake?"

"You just got here. What's the big hurry?"

"Work." Karen snuck a look at her phone. One hundred fifty-seven new emails since she boarded the plane this morning. She wished she could shut the stupid thing off. Once she had even tried, right after a wellness seminar on keeping your life in balance, but learned her lesson after seeing the resulting load of messages in her inbox. Wellness would have to wait.

Lorraine turned onto the highway. Thanks to the oil boom, new subdivisions sprouted on the outside of town, new banks and restaurants within. Karen saw what looked like car dealerships, but the showrooms were filled with shiny green tractors and farm implements. North Dakota had sailed through the Great Recession with full employment and was enjoying a wave of reverse migration, with young professionals swarming in from the godless coasts to rear their children in the bosom of the heartland. Or what was left of it, with all the fracking.

"There's the new rec center." Lorraine pointed at a two-story structure occupying an entire block, and the parking lot was packed. They passed a strip mall where a new rib joint offered local beers. Next-door stood a yoga studio where you could burn it off.

Lorraine slowed for the bridge over the Heart River. Placid and golden in the afternoon sun, it seemed not to have changed since Karen was a kid. Cattails waved on both banks, the tough shoots decorated with red-winged blackbirds.

The highway narrowed as they approached the old part of town, where tattered businesses marked the passage of time since her birth. She saw a brick two-story, where a friend—what was her name? Marla? No, Marlene—had lived above a furniture store with her parents and brother. Karen wondered whatever happened to Marlene and the rest of the kids from the neighborhood. Had they left the state too?

A boarded-up gas station sat in the middle of a stretch of blacktop, where weeds and sunflowers grew up through the cracks and a giant elm threatened to settle onto the building. The neighborhood seemed smaller and shabbier than she remembered, and the loss weighed on her. Everything was diminished, but she had been warned. *The past is a fantasy*, her father used to say. *Memory gets distorted over time, and pretty soon it's no longer true*. Karen didn't want to believe it. If you couldn't count on your memories to tell you who you were, where did that leave you?

They turned a corner onto her old street, where shade trees formed a canopy over the road, and a wave of nostalgia washed over her. "Do you remember riding bikes? Every day, morning to night, all summer long."

"Yeah, right behind the mosquito spray truck." Lorraine turned into a grass driveway, centering the tires on two cement strips.

Karen opened the car door, and the smell of creosote and diesel hit her, roiling the deep sediment of her memory. The lawn in front of her childhood home had thinned to dirt in places. A blue fir tree, planted early in the last century, towered over the house. The cement still bore tiny imprints of her hands, the fading impressions almost half a century old. How small the porch seemed now, and how inadequate the wobbly handrail. The screen door was handmade, the mesh rolled out tight and tacked down under wooden strips.

"Hey Mom, it's us." Lorraine opened the door without knocking. Karen trailed after, struck dumb by the familiar aroma of beef stew and freshly-baked bread.

"*Lieb kind.*" Aunt Marie wore a floral shirt tucked into the elastic waistband of a pair of polyester slacks.

Karen embraced her, trying not to crush the woman who looked to have shrunk a foot since her last visit. Aunt Marie held her at arm's length. "You're thin."

Karen studied back. Her aunt still wore her gray hair braided and wrapped around her head like an elderly version of Heidi of the Alps. Her face was lined, and her frank blue gaze required no explanations.

"The calves aren't going to feed themselves. I have to go." Lorraine kissed her mother. "See you tomorrow, nine-fifteen." The screen door banged shut behind her.

Aunt Marie's knobby fingers tapped Karen's arm. "Did you eat? I made supper."

"I had a snack on the plane."

"You have to eat. You know an empty potato sack won't stand." Aunt Marie led her into the kitchen where two chairs nudged up against the old Formica table. On the table sat her mother's tin salt and pepper shakers, half a century old. A dish rack stood empty next to the sink, waiting for the next load, just as she remembered. The varnished maple cabinets shone as if Marie wiped and waxed them monthly, the same as her mother had. Karen grasped the back of a chair to steady herself.

Aunt Marie ladled stew from a Dutch oven into a yellow Pyrex bowl. "Should be good and done. I started it this morning." She clanged down the heavy cast-iron cover and set a loaf of round bread on the table next to a jar of dark purple jam.

Karen pressed the wax down on one edge and popped the round seal out of the jar. She almost couldn't resist licking it. "Chokecherry!"

"From the trees out back. Go ahead and eat before it gets cold." Aunt Marie wiped the counters, rinsed and wrung the dish cloth, and hung it over the neck of the faucet to dry.

Karen sunk a battered spoon into the stew and raised it to her mouth. At the taste, her eyes stung with unshed tears, and she choked down the warm broth. Of course her aunt would make it the same way her mother had.

Her mother's tools still decorated the kitchen walls. A wood and metal washboard hung by the back door, and a metal rug beater next to that. These weren't curios from an antique store. They were family history.

Aunt Marie set a plate of apple streudel in front of Karen. "A little sweet to help you digest."

Karen tried a taste, but found it impossible to swallow around the lump in her throat. "I'm sorry."

"You don't have to finish if you're too tired. Come. I'll help you get settled."

Karen carried her suitcase to the bedrooms at the end of the hall. In her old room, the twin bed was covered with a white chenille bedspread. A narrow chest of drawers, the one she had used as a child, stood on one side of the bed. On the other, the night stand held a glass lamp on a crocheted white doily. Across the room stood her mother's treadle-foot Singer on which Karen had learned to sew. The polished wood pedestal looked almost new, except for a missing knob on one of the drawers. Her mother had refinished the surface every ten years or so; the last time, Karen had helped, scrubbing away with steel wool until she thought her fingerprints would disappear, but she loved the machine with its determined needle and insistent foot pedal, and the free-flying hum of a long, straight seam. All during her teenaged and young adult years, she made her own clothes. She remembered how the hours passed, her mind at peace as her foot worked the treadle, her fingers easing the fabric toward the needle. She didn't sew anymore, but Karen still knew which way to press a dart, and that a dry bar of soap worked better than tailor's chalk to mark stitch lines.

A card table stood cluttered with pieces of cloth, a glue gun, and various notions. Karen picked up a piece of felt. It was cut in the shape of a rabbit. "Her crafts for the church..."

"Lena was always working on something."

"Tell me what happened."

"You're so tired. Maybe tomorrow."

"Would you mind telling me now? If it's not too hard."

Marie settled into the rocker. "I was watching TV in the living room," she said, the floor creaking as she rocked. "Lena was working on her crafts. I heard her call out. I got scared and ran in here." Marie's fingers worried the plastic pearl chain attached to her reading glasses. "She was in that chair over there by you. She said she couldn't catch her breath. I called for an ambulance, but she was gone too fast. They said it was her heart."

"I should have been here." The words scratched Karen's throat.

"There was nothing you could do."

"Still." Karen looked away from her aunt. The near wall was covered with family pictures, the tarnished gold frames picked up at yard sales, ten for a dollar. In one, her father stood beaming in his army uniform, hugging a young Lena. Another showed him standing by his work truck, his tank-like body ramrod straight, brimmed hat pushed back on his big, round head. Dakota Gas, the sign on the truck said. There was a black-and-white snapshot of the three of them, Frank and Lena in their Sunday best, holding baby Karen in her baptismal gown on the front steps of St. Joe's. "I didn't know she was sick. Whenever I asked she said she was fine. The only thing she admitted was that maybe she was a little tired."

"I don't think she knew either."

Karen walked over to the window. A single street lamp illuminated the tree on the front lawn, its branches fanning gently. The street was quiet. At seven thirty on a weeknight, all the residents were inside, finishing supper, watching TV, or maybe working on a favorite quilt.

Marie brought an extra pillow from the linen closet down the hall. "Tomorrow's going to be a long day. You should sleep."

Tired as she was, though, Karen couldn't sleep. She lay in the light of the street lamp, breathing the familiar air of her old bedroom and suffocating with guilt.

Three decades ago, she had abandoned her parents and boarded a plane to California, returning only for short visits. Even when her father died, she stayed only two days and then hurried back to the west coast, worried about her job.

After a period of mourning, though, her mom had done fine. Lena wasn't one to slow down, not even for grief. Right after the funeral she invited Marie to move in, and the two sisters went about the business of widows, making themselves useful to church and community. Karen tried to be a good daughter from afar, calling often and remembering birthdays and holidays, but her gifts and phone calls were a poor substitute for her actual presence, and she and her mother had aged separately, half a country apart.

Now she pounded her pillow into different shapes, none helping to bring sleep. She wished tomorrow was over, and felt bad for the thought, but how does a girl get through a funeral Mass for her own mother? She would try to remain stoic in the German tradition, but like everyone in her family, she had overactive tear ducts. And after all, it was her mother. No one would judge her if she collapsed, wailing, on the church floor.

And oh God, the Mass, with its choreographed standing, kneeling and verbal responses—rituals familiar only to the regulars. Karen would be outed as someone who no longer attended. She would embarrass Aunt Marie and Lorraine, and sully the name of her poor mother, burdened even in death with that selfish daughter from California.

She remembered her dad's funeral, and the grief that had overwhelmed her. Tomorrow, strangers would surround her, crying and hugging her and saying how much they missed Lena. To bear the pain alone was hard enough, but to see other folks trouping into church—to see them grieving for Lena—would slay her. It would be too much. Karen rolled over, mopping at the sudden deluge of tears with the edge of the scratchy, line-dried sheet. She wished she could have stayed in California, dealing with the pain in her own way, buried in work, caffeinated and stress-driven. At least there she would function normally, familiar in her routine, running hard to keep her job, ignoring all the evidence of her poor excuse for a life.

She punched the pillows, trying to get comfortable. Outside the window, an owl hooted softly.

Chapter Three

*K*aren stared at the full-length mirror in the corner of her old bedroom, and the mirror stared back, thankfully without laughing. Clearly, she had forgotten how to dress for prairie funerals. With its gold buttons and white piping along the edges, the expensive pantsuit seemed gaudy.

Aunt Marie stuck her head in. "You look nice."

"Is it too much?"

"You're from California, so people understand. And you never know what the weather will do. It might be sunny, or you can get a thunderstorm. Last summer when we buried Amos, it snowed."

Karen hung the jacket back on the hanger. "How long do we have?"

Marie glanced at her watch, a big, round black-and-white job with a fake leather strap. "Lorraine should be here in a half hour."

At the kitchen table, Karen opened her computer to the memo she had tinkered with on the plane. Reading the words made her mad all over again. Wes wanted more cuts, but her staff were so burned out it was affecting their home lives. As the director of human resources, Karen had listened to many closed-door tales of crumbling marriages, kids doing drugs, and employees barely holding off nervous breakdowns. She had become so adept at finding good treatment and counseling services for her staff that she felt like a social worker. At least she was able to help. That part made her feel good.

But it wasn't just her staff that was burning out.

"You work too hard," people told her. "You worry too much." Those people were stupid. Karen was running hard, both figuratively and literally, because the company she worked for had been sold four times in the last dozen years, and she needed to be even sharper than usual. She got up before dawn each day to run on her home treadmill, and after a ten-hour-day and a microwave dinner at the office, she often stopped by the gym.

Driven by fear of a metaphorical Katrina, Karen worried if she failed to stay in shape, both physically and mentally, change would hurl her life around and drown her in deep, dirty water. She envied people who lacked that primal fear. They were probably more at peace than she was, popping pills like candy to quell the acid in her stomach. Some nights, when she pushed the seated leg press, her glutes and quads screaming, she remembered the videos of helpless, three-hundred pound women being lifted into lifeboats.

In the living room, the sounds of the morning crop report intruded from the TV. Corn was looking good, but soybeans were too early to tell. How many mornings she had heard that same report while she dressed for school, cleaned her room, and waited for permission to leave. Before she walked out the door, her father required her to summarize her studies from the night before, and her mother checked her room, sometimes handing her the dust rag or requiring the bed be remade over a minor wrinkle. The penalty was weekend restriction.

Karen stared at the computer screen, trying to refocus on the memo. Lately she was more easily distracted, especially by noise. She would reread the same paragraphs, absorbing little, her mind dancing from subject to subject. It may have been the relentless pressure at work, but work had always been rough. No, she suspected it was her age. One had only to look at one's face to know the truth. Now the skin near her eyes creased into a starburst of fine lines when she smiled, and parentheses bracketed her mouth. Her young staff would be horrified if they knew she had been around when pantyhose were invented, and her first computer was an Apple IIe with five-inch floppies. Now, having a phone plugged into the wall in your house was considered so archaic they resurrected a word from World War II to describe them—*land lines*—although people didn't use the phone to communicate anymore, and even email was almost passé in favor of texting. To remain relevant, you had to belong to a half-dozen social networks to alert your friends when you were about to brush your teeth.

Karen was on top of all of it. She wasn't going to be steamrollered by the passage of time and changing conventions. Even though it took a lot of energy and constant vigilance to compete, she didn't intend to lose her job to some kid. Over the years she had developed a thick mental playbook for managing young employees confused by W-4s and the need to hide their belly-button rings. She nurtured them, but not too much; used humor, but only to a point. Hovered discretely and disappeared. So far it had worked, and she planned to continue that strategy until she retired.

She shut the laptop. There would be time enough after the funeral to save the world.

At the church, a white hearse stood vigil at the curb and a long line of cars snaked out of the parking lot and into the street.

Half of Dickinson seemed to have turned out to pay their respects. Mourners surged across the parking lot in waves, dressed in modest dark clothing and low-heeled shoes. Karen didn't see "Juicy" written across a single butt, bellies were covered, and bra straps stayed tucked inside blouses. Small town life had its compensations.

A man stood at the parking lot entrance, wearing the black suit and cape of the Knights of Columbus. Waving toward the Lexus, he removed his feathered chapeau and bowed. Then he lifted a traffic cone out of their way and signaled them forward into the spot behind the hearse. As they passed, Aunt Marie turned toward the window. "God bless you, Robert." She gestured toward the back seat. "Do you remember Lena's girl?"

"So sorry about your mama," the man said, reaching for Karen's hand. She felt the sting of tears, and they weren't even inside the church yet. At the base of the stairs, she was surrounded by well-wishers. Aunt Marie ran interference, calling out the names of long-forgotten friends and neighbors as they approached, saving Karen from the embarrassment of not remembering. She greeted stoic relatives and tearful friends who either nodded to her or hugged her desperately depending on their degree of anguish, but when the driver stepped to the rear of the hearse, every voice fell silent. Karen heard the clasp release as the driver turned the door handle. Strong young pallbearers, standing in for Lena's elderly friends, eased the burnished oak casket out of the vehicle. A truck driver, approaching on the narrow street, stopped his rig and shut down the motor. The smell of creosote wafted across the field from the rail yard.

Flanked by deacons and altar boys, Father Engel waited at the door of the church. The pallbearers placed her mother's casket on a rolling carriage and wheeled it into the foyer, where it was encircled by Karen's family. When quiet fell again, Father began to speak, his voice magnified by the microphone on his collar.

"We welcome Lena, here in the narthex," he said, "the part of our church where the sacrament of Baptism is performed. In this way we symbolize the cycle of life and death. We celebrate the end where we celebrated the beginning, as all life is everlasting."

Karen swallowed hard as the priest sprinkled droplets of holy water onto the casket while murmuring a benediction. He handed the dispenser back to an altar boy and placed his hands on the wood, eyes closed in prayer. Then he stepped back, and the men eased the carriage through the double doors and up the center aisle. Karen and Marie, arms linked, trailed after to the strains of a violin from somewhere near the altar. At the front of the church, they genuflected and entered the first pew. Lorraine, her husband Jim and their children and grandchildren followed, filling the next two rows. She heard her nieces and nephews sniffling, but Karen herself had no children to mourn the death of their grandmother. Even if she had, Lena would have been a stranger to them, a little old lady from far away who sent them greeting cards on birthdays, with perhaps a few dollar bills folded neatly inside.

At the altar, Father Engel waited until all were seated. When the music stopped, he made the Sign of the Cross. "The grace of God our Father be with you."

"And also with you." The parishioners sat down with a great whoosh, and Karen followed their lead. She no longer knew the rituals, having become what her mother called an Easter-egg Catholic.

The choir began a hymn, one she remembered from the early years, when she was required to attend Mass every Sunday and on all Holy Days. "You don't want to die with a mortal sin on your soul," Lena would say, as determined to save her daughter from Hell as from getting run over by a car. Even if they were on vacation, camping in some distant mountain range, Lena would find out the time and location of Sunday Mass, and for the rest of the week remind Frank and Karen to save one pair of jeans so they'd have something clean to wear to the campground service.

The rich harmonies of a Latin choir still had the power to bring her to tears. Their voices swelled along with the fragrance of burning incense as the censer clanged against its chain. Karen groped in her pocket for tissues.

When the priest strode across the marble floor of the sanctuary to the podium, the music ceased. "We are gathered here today," he began, "to celebrate the life of Lena Hess Weiler, and her ascendance into heaven to join our Heavenly Father in everlasting joy."

He glanced down.

"A reading from Paul to the Romans."

Karen bowed her head, mindful of those who still believed. Father's voice faded as her eyes wandered across the altar, and the marble floor made of sand-colored squares alternating with white, to the back of the church, the sanctuary, with its high altar holding the Tabernacle. On the floor at the base of the podium stood a clear vase filled with golden spears of wheat. Dickinson, community of farmers, revered the grain, the basis of life in biblical terms. An abundant harvest was a sign of divine favor.

"'For you did not escape slavery to fall back into fear...'"

Karen rolled the words around in her mind, thinking of their applicability to her own life. She had felt so proud to have earned the title of executive, when to have stayed in Dickinson might have sentenced her to a lifetime of minimum wage jobs. Yet what had she accomplished? In reality, she was little more than a slave herself; a slave to Wes, a slave to the employees whose welfare caused her to lose sleep, a slave to the fantasy of self-sufficiency. How independent was she, really?

Aunt Marie nudged her. "Are you going to take Communion?"

"I'm not prepared," she said, grateful for the phrase that excused one, without explanation, from parading up the center aisle to receive the body and blood of Christ. That lack of preparation could result from failing to make time for Confession the day before to robbing a bank and committing murder on your way out the door.

"At least come up for a blessing."

"I don't understand."

"Come."

Feeling foolish, Karen followed her aunt to the altar, where she mimicked the example of others by crossing her arms over her chest in the shape of an X, fingers touching shoulders. Instead of stepping back in revulsion, Father Engel placed his hand on her forehead and prayed, the warmth of his skin as reassuring as a parent's embrace. Karen's plan to grieve privately began to crumble. When she returned to her seat, she fumbled for a new package of tissues.

As the swelling voices of the choir ended the Mass, the pallbearers returned the casket to the hearse, and the church emptied into the parking lot. Led by a police escort, the cortege rolled through the industrial district and over train tracks, past dealerships and storage units, and on into farmland, where early hay lay drying in windrows. The narrow road carved a path through fields intersected by streambeds and cutbanks. They passed a crumbling set of cement steps standing alone in the middle of knee-high grasses, and Karen recognized the remains of her mother's one-room schoolhouse. A dirt lane ran past the school and over a rise, beyond which lay a valley and the farm where Lena had been born. Like most of its contemporaries, the farm had had no running water and no electricity. Survival was subject to the whims of weather and the price of commodities. In one good year, the wheat harvest overflowed the granaries, depressing prices in the teeth of the Great Depression. Lena had spoken of the Dust Bowl when great dark clouds loomed over their farm. Her family ran for the house, but grit coated their teeth and settled in their lungs and across their fields. The wind brought dust and locusts but, in the "dirty Thirties," little rain.

The family endured as the earth cracked and the harvests withered. Lena and her sisters wore dresses made of feed sacks, but when the feed ran out for the last time, the starving horses and cattle were sold. Until the families could move to town, they accepted commodities from St. Elizabeth's church. In her adult years, Lena would become nauseous at the sight of raisins.

Karen felt goose bumps at the memory. Having escaped to California, her life seemed safer than that of the farmers, but only because she cultivated her career with the same desperate eye to the weather. She felt that she lived on a razor's edge between success and disaster. The keen appreciation for catastrophic change that loomed over the horizon lingered in her genetic memory, whether wrought by tornado or grassfire, economic downturn or the caprice of an overfed CEO.

She may have failed to apply that same care to her marriage, but at least she still had a job.

A short white sign poked up through the grass on the shoulder of the highway to announce the remnants of the village of Lefor, and here the hearse slowed and turned. No more than a dozen houses remained to mark the town, and these were ramshackle and hidden under the ancient, spreading limbs of elm and cottonwood trees. Broken-down cars and rusting farm equipment nudged up against the homes, and weeds dominated the yards. The hearse followed the narrow road until the pavement ended, then bumped down the lane and through the wrought-iron gates at the entrance to St. Elizabeth's Catholic cemetery.

Karen stepped out. The sound of car doors slamming and muted voices, the occasional chuckle or a baby crying displaced the quiet of late morning. Lena's family and friends followed the pallbearers up the gentle slope, weaving carefully through the headstones and monuments. Adjacent to the graveyard stood St. Elizabeth's Church, a banner proclaiming "Queen of the Prairie" unfurled in the breeze. Originally built of sod and then of stone, St. Elizabeth's was rebuilt one final time, in 1929, of cement and rebar, and finished with bricks. She had sheltered the farmers from dust storms, tornadoes, and blizzards. Her steeple soared over the shrinking parish, having presided over the birth and death of a culture.

The mourners pooled around the open grave, some of them finding chairs under a shade awning. As Karen took a seat nearest her mother's casket, a blacktail deer burst from cover and trotted along the fence line, ambushing a covey of pheasant.

"Lena would have loved that," said Aunt Marie, watching the deer bound over barbed wire fences until it faded to a beige speck against green fields. The cemetery seemed even more remote than when Karen attended her dad's funeral, but Lena had liked the idea of being laid to rest in the middle of nature, surrounded by family. She said it would be like an everlasting picnic.

Father Engel took his place at the head of the casket. When the group quieted, he opened his Missal and began the prayers. Karen bowed her head. Her mother's body lay almost within touching distance, yet forever out of reach. The cicadas droned along with the priest, and Karen's attention wandered as her mind returned to matters of corporate survival. Had she filed that last report on time? Did she remember to update everybody about the new terms of the collective bargaining agreement? Was that sexual harassment suit going anywhere? She itched with anxiety, covertly checking her watch.

Gesturing for the congregation to stand, Father moved toward the gravesite, where he sprinkled droplets of holy water on the open grave, consecrating the ground where her mother and father would spend the next million years. "Let us pray. 'Our Father,'" he began, leading the beloved communal prayer. Karen chanted along, her throat tight, the familiar words returning. When the prayer ended, silence enveloped the crowd. She heard a bit of rustling behind her and then the simple notes of "Amazing Grace," from Uncle Rudy's accordion. The family sang along, right through two entire verses.

They must have had a lot of practice to know the words, Karen thought, wiping away tears.

The song ended, and silence fell again. Father Engel stood with his hands clasped in front of him, allowing for a moment of meditation. A light breeze rippled his vestments. Overhead, a meadowlark rode a telephone wire and sang complex melodies.

It is peaceful here, Karen thought. She closed her eyes and inhaled the aroma of grassland and freshly turned earth. *I wish you weren't going to be so far away, but this is where you wanted to be. I'm happy you found peace.*

The cemetery workers repositioned bouquets of flowers, clearing a path to the casket. They wore solemn gray slacks and work shirts, and moved about their duties quietly and without haste. The wind whispered through the trees, and wispy clouds drifted overhead.

"Hang in there, sweetie." Lorraine's arm crept around Karen's shoulders. "It's almost over."

The priest touched the casket as he prayed, and the workers stood ready to operate the mechanism that would lower her mother into the community of the dead. When Father Engel paused, the funeral director walked over to Karen and held out a basket of roses. For a moment she failed to comprehend, but then reached forward and selected a small red bud. The congregation passed the basket around until everyone held a rose. When the director turned and walked back toward the casket, the family stood and followed him. Each one rested a hand or touched a forehead to the burnished surface.

As the line filed past, most wiped away tears, and Karen choked back her own. These folks seemed to care so much for her mother— these bent-back women with their thinning hair and blocky figures, the men frail and withered. Soon these shuffling old children of immigrants would die with their memories of near-starvation, or of a neighbor trampled by a team of horses, or a child suffocating during a dust storm. Their own parents, already gone, were the only ones who remembered saying goodbye on a German dock to come to America and live in a hole in the ground until they could build a house from sod. They bore children and cultivated the prairie, alone under the sun, the only sound that of the plow blade ripping through the astonished grasses.

Karen closed her eyes. Her mother had known her to her very bones, knowing without asking what her daughter was feeling and what she needed, whether reassurance on a windy morning or fifteen hundred miles of distance from a difficult father. Karen had always thought her gratitude was enough, but now she tasted the acrid bitterness of doubt.

Father Engel reached the end of the last prayer and closed the book. He gestured to Karen to come forward. With Aunt Marie and Lorraine clutching her arms on either side, she approached the casket, her legs wobbly. The breeze freshened, snapping the canvas tent cover, and the trees rustled and bent in the wind.

As a child, Karen had been terrified of the weather, and especially of the wind and dark storms that formed funnel clouds. While her parents slept, she would lie awake in the early hours of a morning, listening to the branches of the trees beat against her window. She worried that a tornado might whirl through town, pick up their house, and kill them. Torn between hiding her head under a pillow and remaining on guard to warn her parents at the first sign of danger, Karen would thrash, alone with her burden, until she heard her mother's voice calling softly from down the hall.

"It's just the wind, honey. There's nothing to be afraid of."

Chapter Four

*B*ack at the house, cars lined the street up and down the block, and the walls of the house practically bulged with people. Inside, Karen found a feast that expanded by one dish per every new arrival. Meatloaf, fried chicken, mashed potatoes, and green bean casserole crowded the kitchen counters. Shivery Jell-O molds in red and green with bits of fruit suspended within, potato salad dusted with paprika, *fleischkuecle,* and sliced ham were followed by coffee cake, brownies, and rhubarb pie.

As soon as decency allowed, she slipped into her bedroom, closed the door, and called Peggy. "You need to get back here PDQ," said the older woman.

"What's going on?"

"Wes is on a rampage. He's been firing people all day. Calls them into his office in little groups."

Karen heard Peggy inhale. "Are you smoking?"

"What the hell are they going to do to me? Just a sec." Karen heard Peggy stabbing out the cigarette. "Manuel the security guard had to walk so many people out of the building he started hyperventilating. We had to call 9-1-1. Are you still there?"

Karen sat on the bed, head in hand. "Manuel? He's a rock."

"Not today. Sorry to be telling you this on top of everything. How are you holding up?"

"The house is full of people. I'm hiding in the bedroom."

"Get out there and get some hugs, like on your way out the door. I'm not kidding. You and me are all that's left."

"I'll be there at the crack of dawn, day after tomorrow."

"No sooner?"

"Peggy, I can't astral-travel." Karen hung up, pained by the stress in her buddy's voice. She considered her a friend, even though they never saw each other outside of work, and there was an age gap. But they'd worked together ten years, and they'd had each other's backs since the beginning.

She stuffed the phone back in her purse. As soon as she got in the air, away from all the grieving and politicking, she would think of something. She always came up with something. By the time the wheels touched down at John Wayne in Newport, she would have a strategy for reining in Wes.

Her flight left in two hours. In the meantime, she needed to get out there and show the flag. Closing the bedroom door behind her, Karen dove into the crowd and moved from group to group, accepting condolences and making small talk, working her way from the front sidewalk to the back porch. By the time she got through the rope line, she was exhausted.

In the living room, Father Engel nibbled a brownie and listened to a woman's earnest tale. A crowd of women, all about Karen's age, stood in the center of the room discussing something with great animation. A tall woman with short gray hair spotted Karen and stepped away from the group. "Hey, you. I'm Glenda. I was a grade ahead of you at St. Joseph's."

"I thought you looked familiar," Karen said.

"I knew your mom from the convalescent hospital. We volunteered together. I'm a nurse." Glenda maneuvered Karen toward the group of women. "Recognize any of these characters?"

Karen's mouth fell open. "Marlene. I remember you from—"

"Yes, sixth grade." A zaftig brunette hugged Karen. "We fought over a boy."

"Paul something. How embarrassing that you remember."

"I not only remember. I married him. Look over there." Marlene pointed.

Karen recognized the man, rounder now, his curly dark hair a distant memory, but when he smiled shyly and waved, she saw the boy again. She waved back.

A tiny blonde with a camera pushed forward. "And I'm Denise."

"I don't believe it," said Karen, embracing the woman. "You took pictures at all the high school football games."

Denise nodded. "It was a great way to meet boys. Now I'm a photographer for the historical society. What about you? You always talked about seeing the world."

"I got as far as California."

"You make it sound like nothing much, but your mom was very proud of you," said Glenda.

"When did you see her last?"

"A few days ago." Glenda frowned. "She didn't seem like her usual self, almost as if she'd lost some of her spark."

"I thought so too, last time I talked to her," Karen said, "but she said she was fine. I should have dropped everything and come back here."

"Don't beat yourself up." Glenda had a funny, wry smile that seemed to say nothing much rattled her. "It wouldn't have made any difference. That last afternoon, I have to be honest with you, she told me she was tired and she missed Frank."

"When you hear that—" Denise shook her head, not finishing the thought.

Karen turned to Glenda. "When you saw her last, did she still seem clearheaded?"

"For the most part. She was a bit more distracted. It's not that uncommon in elders. People think they're going to live forever, but we get to a point where we really do wear out."

"Lena will be sorely missed," said a woman who joined the group. Karen didn't recognize her. "She was so good, even to strangers."

"She helped me serve hot meals at the homeless shelter," said another woman. "I don't know who got more out of it, her or the needy folks."

"She started after Frank died. She said she needed to feel useful," said Glenda.

While the women offered their memories of Lena, Karen felt a burning sensation in her gut. Maybe if she had stayed in North Dakota, her mother would have been happier. She wouldn't have had to adopt strangers in order to feel needed.

"Lena jumped right in after Frank died. Got to work and stayed busy, almost like nothing had happened."

Karen drifted inward. *It's called duty,* she thought. *Weiler women are good at that.*

"She worked so hard. Never slowed down."

"She worked tirelessly for others."

Aunt Marie, joining the circle, put her arm around Karen. "You look pale. Come and eat." She took Karen into the kitchen and loaded a dish with North Dakota grief relief. Karen sat down at the table, picked up a fork, and studied the mound of food.

"Eat until you feel stronger." Aunt Marie stood by the edge of the table, waiting for Karen to respond.

"I'm fine. Go and visit." Karen took a big bite, releasing her aunt. The kitchen was crowded with women. They stood at the sink, hip to hip, washing, drying, and putting away. With their reddened hands and faded aprons, they kept the production line going, a sort of old-fashioned ministry. As they worked, they talked and laughed, elbowed each other playfully, dismissing the occasional tear with the swipe of an arm.

"Lena was such a tiny thing," said one. "I remember when she came to St. Joe's, she wore clothes from the poor box. I always had to roll up her sleeves because they were too long."

Another woman nodded. "I wore a lot of those charity clothes too, and I was happy to have them. We all were. Those were hard times."

Karen took a bite of hot potato salad, tangy with cider vinegar and dill. She remembered her mother talking of losing the family farm in the Great Depression. Lena had been sent to live with a relative in town who worked her as a maid in exchange for room and board. She was eight years old.

"She may have been tiny but she was a spitfire," said another. "I remember she played the drums in the high school band, which was unusual for a girl at the time."

"Lena was independent. She never let anybody boss her."

Until she got married, Karen thought.

An old auntie approached, cradled Karen's face in her warm hands, and said something in German. Smelling the familiar gardenia perfume, Karen mumbled an excuse and escaped to the back porch where she sat down on the chipped cement steps. In the distance a tractor chugged across a field, its blades releasing the rich aroma of freshly turned earth.

Karen rested her head on her arms. She was exhausted and her back hurt. The warmth of her family comforted her, but she needed to get back to California. In all the years since fleeing North Dakota, she had found only one place she felt safe, and that was work. Within the structure of a career she had matured and developed an identity, and that identity sustained her. Even if it seemed at times too narrowly drawn, those were the contours of her life, and if she didn't get back to it as soon as possible, she felt that something bad would happen. It was a superstition, but one that had served her well.

The screen door squeaked and Lorraine sat down next to her. "I thought I'd find you out here. They can get to be too much."

"They mean well." Karen leaned toward the greenery, broke off a piece of dill from a leggy plant, and inhaled the tangy fragrance. She performed this ritual whenever she found fresh dill, and it always brought her back to this garden, this yard.

But this time, I'm really here, she thought, inhaling deeply, her eyes closed. *I've been gone so long, and I don't know when I'll be back.*

"Aunt Lena was a hero in this town," said Lorraine.

"I've heard nothing else for the last hour. It's horrible she's gone, but at least I got to hear how much everybody loved her. She was happy at the end, and I'm proud of her." Karen stood and stretched. Her bones were aching from sitting on the hard cement.

"You're really going to leave?"

"I'm sorry, Cuz. I wish I could stay."

"I saw you talking with your old friends. You looked like you were having a good time."

"It was great to see them again. They're wonderful people." Karen was surprised at the sudden ache of longing in her chest, but she had meant the comment as a simple platitude and brushed the emotions away.

"Denise is planning a picnic out in the country next week. Why don't you stay a few more days and hang out with us? It would be good for you. For us, too."

"No, really. I can't. But I promise I'll try to visit more often."

Lorraine stood up and faced Karen. "Mom misses you. She's told me a hundred times how much you remind her of Lena. If you run off, she'll have that much more to grieve. And how many years do you think she has left in her?"

Karen lifted her chin, trying to pretend she wasn't drowning in guilt. "I really will come back around the holidays."

"That's months from now. What difference would a couple days make?"

"With my job? It's life and death. I mean, I hire doctors and nurses."

"You're so dramatic." Lorraine grasped Karen's arm. "Every time you visit, you run right home, but this time it has to be different. Now that your mom's gone, I know we'll never see you again."

"That's not true."

"It is. Once you leave, you'll never come back. This is the time, Karen. Don't have regrets."

Karen shrugged off Lorraine's hand. "I need to get back. I really do. I'm sorry." Head down, she walked to the bedroom and closed the door, leaning against it in relief at the relative privacy. Did Lorraine think she had no feelings? Karen was grieving, too, but she had to stay the course. Real life offered no alternative. Lorraine's talk of Aunt Marie and Lena and the old relatives didn't change reality. All her load of guilt produced was another knife-twist in Karen's heart. Just being here in this house was tearing her up, so little had it changed since she was a kid. The afternoon light had mellowed, gilding the furnishings in the small room. How was it possible that this room, and in fact the whole house, still felt the same, even smelled the same, as when Karen grew up here? On top of the dresser, her mom and dad grinned at her in black and white. Between them they held up a big watermelon from the garden. She remembered that picture. She had taken it, on a day when her teenage friends called to her from an old Chevy station wagon, waiting at the curb for Karen to finish humiliating herself. Like most teenagers, she disliked her father most of the time and ignored her mother as much as possible, just to make a point. She knew it was nature's way, but at the moment the memory seemed unbearably cruel.

God, so many years lost. What would she give now to be able to hug either one of them?

Her suitcase yawned open from its spot on the floor, waiting for last-minute items, like her toothbrush and toiletries, and a pair of shoes in the closet. She hung her jacket over a chair and sat on the bed, sighing. The thought of the long flight home practically made her nauseous. First a puddle jumper would take several hours to crab its way out of North Dakota to Denver. After a two-hour layover followed by almost three hours on the California leg, she would collect her luggage, find her car, and drive home. The house would be empty and silent.

Her back ached from hours of standing, and she felt lethargic. How good it would feel to take a power nap, just a half hour–long enough to get her energy back?

Just to be safe, she set the dual alarm on the nightstand clock. Her shoes fell off as she lay back, sighing into the pillow. In spite of the pain of losing her mom, the service had been cathartic. Father Engel had done a good job. The readings were personalized to Lena's life, something that would only be possible if he knew and cared about her. Karen made a mental note to send a donation to the church as soon as she got home.

Chapter Five

*B*ut the next morning, she was still in North Dakota.

In the bright light of mid-morning, two boxcars thundered together down at the freight yard, dragging her back from her dreams. In that middle place between awake and asleep, Karen sensed she was wrapped in her designer pantsuit and covered with a quilt.

She writhed out of the shroud and reached for the clock, but its face was dark. The plug had fallen out of the outlet. A bad fit, an unreliable alarm, and disaster in Newport. She could feel it.

She found her watch. It was barely seven in California. Maybe she could still do damage control. In a few minutes, she would call.

The small house was so quiet she could hear the faucet dripping in the bathroom. Karen hung the pantsuit in the closet and put on her mother's robe. She padded down the hall, looking for her aunt. In the kitchen, Felix the Clock hung over the stove, swinging his metronome tail and laughing silently at her. How soundly she had slept, setting a new record of fourteen hours. Her back and neck felt stiff. On the chipped grey laminate table, Aunt Marie had left a note, a scrap of paper propped against the salt shaker. "Cereal above sink," it read. "Dinner at noon." Nothing on the note about why she had let Karen sleep through yesterday's flight.

She found her phone and dialed the airline, only to find that Great Lakes had no flights out of Dickinson today. The next flight out wasn't until Tuesday, unless she caught a cab to Bismarck, one hundred miles east.

And leave a note for Aunt Marie? Something along the lines of *Sorry, had to run! See you in a year!*

She glanced at the date on her phone. Wes wouldn't come in today. On Fridays he sailed out past the jetty and into open waters, a fact Karen knew from his bragging about it every flippin' Monday morning, how he'd moored at Catalina or headed north toward Santa Barbara. Karen had never taken him up on his offers to skip work and sail with him, and he'd long ago stopped asking.

Maybe Stacey would be in. Karen dialed her assistant, who answered on the first ring and immediately offered to rearrange Karen's appointments. "Your family needs you and you need them. Take a few extra days," she said.

"It's just today and the weekend. I'll be home Monday."

"That's what I'd do." Stacey yawned. "I hate this place. Last night I went home and told Jason we weren't eating unless he took me out. We went to Bayside. It was awesome. I'm a little hung over."

"How's Peggy?"

"She's unhappy, same as everybody." Stacey lowered her voice. "I could be wrong, but I really think I smelled alcohol on her breath this morning."

"Can you transfer me to her office? I need to talk to her." Karen examined her nails while listening to Wes' latest brainstorm, canned commercials for health insurance, while she waited on hold. And then she had an idea.

Peggy picked up. "Why aren't you here?"

"I missed my flight last night. But listen, isn't Wes going to be in Chicago all next week?" Karen waited while Peggy flipped a page on her calendar.

"You know what? You're right."

"That marketing group, right?"

"Right. He'll be gone all week. Hallelujah, cue the dancing boys."

Karen grinned. This might just work. She had her laptop. She could work from anywhere. "I'll be back a week from Monday."

"Monday's a holiday. Fourth of July, remember?"

Karen had forgotten. Holidays didn't mean that much to her. Usually she worked, but this would give her an extra day. "Okay then. Tuesday."

"You deserve a break, honey. It'll be good for your mental health. If I need you I'll call. See you July 5."

"What about you?"

"Hell with it. I built this place and I'm going to see it through. They want to get rid of me, they're going to have to haul me feet first." Peggy took a drag on a cigarette. "You, though. When you get back, you should look for another job. I'm serious, I don't care how bad it is out there. Life is too short. Go be happy."

Karen glanced up at Felix, who laughed at her. "Maybe in a few years."

"Listen, it gets harder, the older you are. Don't wait until you're my age."

The bathroom floor was covered in gray-and-white hexagonal tile. The stark white sink, its pipes in full view, had a separate faucet for hot and cold. She chose cold, rinsed the sleep out of her eyes and dried her face with a white towel, scratchy and sweet-smelling from yesterday's clothesline. The bathroom had no shower so she took a bath. Weird to sit in a tub in the morning, a luxury usually reserved for that rare evening when she got home from work early, determined to have a life.

She dried off and found a pair of shorts and a top in her mother's dresser. In the kitchen, she filled a bowl with cereal and milk and went outside. It was already after ten and she could smell the garden in the warming air. Sitting on the back steps munching corn flakes, Karen watched a jet cut a trail across the deep-blue sky.

She contemplated the garden at her feet, a study in Midwestern Zen. Long wooden planks, their edges rounded from weather and footfall, served as paths between rows. A wider set of boards, lying two by two, formed a walkway from the porch to the alley. Forty years ago, Karen and her friends raced up and down the planks, playing hide-and-seek behind the tomato plants. They picked peas and ate them right off the vines, winced at tart chokecherries, and spit seeds at one another.

Her mother taught her how deep to bury seedlings, how much water they needed, and how to thin the growing plants so the strongest thrived. Every inch of the back yard was planted in rows of vegetables and herbs. By the end of the summer, their neighbors avoided eye contact so as not to receive yet another box of zucchini. Before she finished sixth grade, Karen knew how to can vegetables and preserves.

The warming earth, well rested from a winter under snow and ice, pushed up bachelor buttons and morning glories. The tomato plants were covered with yellow flowers, and the squash and cucumbers already threatened to take over. The yard ended at a wire fence on the other side of which ran a lane, unpaved in her youth but now blacktopped.

A lawn mower started up in the distance, recalling memories of playing outside in the summer, charging barefoot across a wet lawn and through the cold water arching from the chattering sprinkler. When she was older, she spent most of every day hanging out at the community pool with her girlfriends, flirting with boys, and showing off the cute new swimsuits she made herself. Life was so simple then.

She took the empty bowl inside, rinsed it in the sink, and wandered around the house. In the living room, the front left window still stuck, and the floorboards in the hall creaked in exactly the same place they had when, as a child, she tried to watch TV instead of going to bed. The house seemed tiny now, almost more like a cottage, with two small bedrooms, one bathroom, and a root cellar.

She ran her fingertips over a painted white wall, the plaster finish cool to the touch. One hundred years ago, her great-grandfather packed dirt into the gap between the interior and exterior walls. The primitive construction made for good insulation through winters severe enough to make her ancestors wish they had chosen Siberia, and how many summer tornadoes had threatened this poor structure? Yet in the start of the twenty-first century it still stood, defiant.

Old homes–older than this one–lined the block. Instead of knocking them down and rebuilding, as was the practice in Southern California, owners here simply remodeled a bit on the inside, or kicked a wall out into the yard if they needed space. North Dakotans had a reputation for repurposing objects longer than anyone else in the country. A leaky hose became a garden drip line, an old tire became a planter, a glass insulator a doorstop. How well she remembered her parents admonishing her for tossing out a pair of ripped sneakers. "They can use these at the poorhouse," her mother explained while fishing the shoes out of the trash can.

Karen flopped on the sofa. Aunt Marie's selection of reading material ranged from TV Guide to Readers Digest. The TV offered only game shows and the crop report. The house closed in on her. She jumped up, her chest constricting.

Leaving the back door of the house unlocked, she went through the wire gate into the alley. At the end of the street she turned right and found the old path that ran next to the railroad. As a child, Karen and her little buddies rode their bikes along this path, darting like mosquitoes around the ruts and rocks and broken bottles left by hoboes. Yelling though the underpass, their voices echoing powerfully, the girls zipped up to Villard Street, intent on the five-and-dime with its rows of nickel candy. If they were short of coinage, they'd peer through the back door of the café until the cook noticed and slipped them freshly-cooked donuts.

Following the map in her memory, Karen hiked eight blocks east through neighborhoods that seemed to have shrunk in the past thirty years. Clapboard homes stood alongside small bungalows, some dilapidated, others fiercely meticulous. The century-old sidewalk was cracked and buckled, turning back into aggregate in places. Except for an old woman sitting on her porch, the streets were deserted, the residents having left for work.

She found the community park, abandoned in favor of the new recreation center. A chain link fence surrounded the swimming pool, now drained and peeling. The playground equipment stood rusted, the monkey bars a mottled red-brown. Swing sets lacked swings, grass grew in the sand boxes, and weeds carpeted the tetherball court. When she climbed on the merry-go-round and pushed, it screeched in complaint but turned, rough and slow at first and then faster, as if remembering how. Once she had it going she lay on her back, hands under her head, feet braced against a crossbar. The clouds whirled in circles overhead.

A hundred yards to the south, the Heart River flowed silently past, the wind rattling the cat tails. Karen inhaled the new-oxygen smell, like putting her nose in a freshly-opened bag of potting soil. She and her friends played in and around the river, over the years graduating from making mud pies to sneaking smokes and kisses in the tall grasses along the banks. After school they skulked along the river, scuffing their Catholic saddle shoes in the dirt, their uniforms riddled with foxtails.

Nothing stayed the same. This abandoned lot started out as prairie, but with the oil boom, contractors would soon scrape it off to build a new condominium or strip mall. Karen whirled around under the blue and white sky. The merry-go-round creaked and groaned. The funeral was a cloud with a thin silver lining. Instead of racing home, Karen could visit with long-lost relatives and old friends, fill her lungs with clean air, and rejuvenate. She could use the next few days in Dickinson as a retreat, meditating and resting. Having lost mother, father, and marriage, some downtime might be helpful. Wes would never know. By the time she saw him again, she would have a new attitude, her spirit renewed. Everything would be all right.

Chapter Six

Aunt Marie stood at the edge of the garden, watering seedlings with a faded green hose. She turned off the faucet when she saw Karen. "Come, I have something to show you." Pulling a key from her apron pocket, she unlocked the creaking double doors of the wooden garage.

The sweet, musty smell of old wood and yard equipment, baked in summer and frozen in winter, enveloped Karen. She had played in this garage, hidden in it, swept and cleaned it, and shared endless hours working on projects within it. There on the far side stood the workbench where she made a wooden table for her Barbie doll. Toward the back wall, the overhead shelf still bore tacks from the sheets she and her girlfriends hung as curtains for the plays they produced. An ink-stained wooden desk bore a hand-written note. "Saved when they tore down school," said Lena's graceful cursive.

Atop the desk stood the wooden poppy seed grinder, handmade by a distant relative. Karen blew on it, launching dust into the dry air. As a kid she had watched her mother crank the silver handle until the ground seeds, as fine as black sand, fell through the blades into a petite wooden drawer. Then Lena would empty the drawer into a bowl and mix the seeds with sugar and melted butter. She troweled the mixture onto a rolled-out sheet of pastry and rolled it up, a black swirl decorating the side of the roll. After brushing the top with melted butter and sugar, she baked it. Karen would always associate the sweet, earthy taste of the seeds with this place, with North Dakota and her simple beginnings. "Do you still have her recipe?"

"I'm sure somewhere," Marie said. She opened a folding chair and sat down. "You can have the Singer, too. I never use the thing. I like things electrical. The old days are good to remember from time to time, but I don't miss them."

Karen picked up a box of Ball jars and set it aside for the Goodwill. She did not see herself canning vegetables in California. A plastic tarp covered a mound in the center of the floor. Pulling it back, Karen found handmade quilts passed down from long-dead aunts and grannies, albums of black-and-white photos anchored on each corner with black chevrons, sewing patterns from her 4-H class in high school, and a collection of ceramic trinkets .

"Hey, look at this. Grandma's old phone." A wooden telephone, twice the size of a shoebox, leaned against the back wall of the garage. A black metal microphone protruded from the front of the box, a hand crank attached to the right side. The phone lacked a dial, as the concept of personal phone numbers hadn't then existed. Grandma had told of winding the crank on the side of the phone to summon the operator at the switchboard in town, who then connected the caller to the other party. Later, when technology improved, customers could dial numbers for themselves, but everyone in the neighborhood shared the same line. No conversation was private, at least not in the view of the adolescent Karen and her girlfriends. They would eavesdrop on other people—until the victim caught on—and hang up screaming with laughter.

"I love this phone," she said. "I can see it on my wall at home."

"Only one problem," said a voice from the doorway. "How are you planning to get it there?"

Karen turned. A woman stood framed in the door of the garage, her thin hair sitting like a gossamer nest atop her head. Her grey polyester pants draped around stick legs, and she leaned on a metal cane, favoring one side.

Aunt Marie stood. "Karen, this is Frieda Richter. She lives over on the next street."

"I would've come to the funeral but I was in the hospital. Just got out."

"Nice to meet you," said Karen.

"Nothing important. A little shortness of breath. Thanks for asking." Frieda aimed her chin at the pile of heirlooms. "Lena was a packrat."

"Would you like to sit down?" Karen stood, brushed the dust from her hands, and opened a folding chair. Without comment, Frieda shuffled across the dusty concrete to the empty chair and eased into it, her arms as thin and sharp as bird bones.

Karen turned back to the pile and reached for a potato ricer. She remembered squeezing the metal arms together, forcing a boiled potato through the holes in the metal basket to create what looked like small, steaming grains of rice.

"Lena was lucky."

"How so?" Karen looked up.

"She's dead and I'm stuck in North Dakota." Frieda focused rheumy blue eyes on Karen. "Did you ever wish you could die?"

"*Acht*, here we go," said Aunt Marie.

Karen stared at the woman. "Pardon?"

Frieda pushed her glasses up on her nose and looked out the door of the garage. "The yard has gone downhill. You should hire someone."

Aunt Marie sighed and reached for a bread box.

"That's kind of blunt," said Karen.

Frieda nodded. "You will be too, you get to be my age."

The woman was obviously demented. Karen decided to follow Aunt Marie's lead and focus on the work. She opened a cardboard box and gasped at the folds of delicate embroidery.

"Now that's worth saving." Frieda leaned forward on her cane to get a better look. "Your mother was known all over North Dakota for her needlework. She used to win awards at county fairs."

"I didn't know that."

"Probably a lot you don't know. For example, I have a new great-granddaughter. They're calling her Sunshine. Don't know why they didn't give her a regular name."

"Congratulations." Karen went back to sorting. She remembered when her mother picked up needlework, but she never thought of it as anything more than a hobby. These doilies and tablecloths were the work of an artist.

Frieda nodded, or maybe it was palsy. Her head seemed unsteady on its neck. "She was born a couple weeks ago."

"That's nice."

"Not really, because I'll never get to see her. Lena promised to take me to Denver but now that she's dead, I don't have anybody to drive me."

Karen fingered a table runner with delicate pastel threads.

"You're going to need a way to get all of this back to California." The old woman gazed at the assortment of antiques, her mouth working silently, as if still involved in the process of speaking. "Have you thought of that?"

"Not yet."

"Course not." Frieda stared at Karen. "You're young. You've got time. I'm ninety years old and I need a ride to Denver."

"Can't Sandy come and get you?" asked Aunt Marie.

"Sandy. Now there's a laugh. No, she won't drive this far and Richard works."

Karen's knees were beginning to hurt from scrunching around on the floor, and her empty stomach rumbled. She stood, hoping Frieda would get the hint. "Well, good luck. I hope you can find a ride."

"I didn't say I didn't have a ride. I have a vehicle but I can't drive it anymore. Maybe you'd be interested."

"Actually, I have to be home in a week. Sorry."

"It's a Roadtrek 190, a small RV. You pull into a campground and you're good for the night. I need somebody to drive it. That somebody could be you."

Karen chuckled. "Not me, Frieda. I am not your camping type."

"Well, you might do yourself a favor and rethink that. Being in the Roadtrek isn't like camping at all. It's very comfortable, and it is one hundred percent self-contained. If you need a bathroom, it's right there. Kitchen, too. Beds, all of it. And it's easy to drive, I used to myself until I had the stroke."

Aunt Marie got up from her chair. "She has to go back to California, to her work."

"At her age she should be able to go on vacation when she feels like it."

"That's between her and her employer," said Aunt Marie.

"She ought to stick up for herself. A person can't go through life letting other people dictate what you're going to do. Anyway it wouldn't take that long. We could be in Denver in two days if you're in that big of a hurry. Then a couple more to get to California. That's all." The speech seemed to exhaust her. She sat back, breathing hard.

Karen wasn't thinking about Denver. She was calculating how much of the loot she could take home in a cheap new suitcase from Walmart, and how much she would need to ship if she called a moving company. The cost would be significant, but she still had access to the household account. At some point she and Steve would have to discuss how to divide it, but so far he'd left it alone.

Frieda pointed at the pile with her cane. "In the Roadtrek, there's room for some of this junk, if you pack it right. After you drop me in Denver you go on the rest of the way by yourself, if you're not afraid. Sell it after you get home and send me the money. If it was me, I'd be thrilled to go somewhere by myself, but since I'm old, I'm resigned to company."

"She can leave these things here as long as she wants to," said Aunt Marie. "In fact, Karen, maybe next summer you could fly back out here, rent a truck, and drive it home."

"By next summer we could get hit by a tornado." Frieda worked her thin hips to the edge of her chair and, using the cane, levered herself upright. She shuffled past Karen, the top of her head barely reaching Karen's chin. "Let me know when you make up your mind."

"I already have. I'd love to help you, but I just don't have the time."

Frieda turned. "Young lady, you have nothing but." She walked slowly down the street, the tip of her cane tapping on the sidewalk.

Chapter Seven

On Saturday morning, Karen stopped at Dickinson Moving and Storage to arrange shipping. At the counter, she angled the phone so the clerk could see the picture on the tiny screen.

"Sure, we can handle all that. If you want, we'll wrap and pack it, too. The woman consulted her charts, wrote down a figure, and pushed the paper across the counter. "That should do it. We charge half to get started and the rest on delivery."

"Yikes." For that price, she could buy seats in first class and fly it all home with her. The woman took back the paper. "You could leave behind some of the bigger pieces, like the desk and that sewing machine."

"That's my favorite piece."

"Then really, your only other option would be to see if you could borrow a truck from a friend. Drive it back yourself."

"Let's do the bigger items. The Singer, and the desk. A couple of the boxes." Karen handed over her card. "How soon can you get started?"

Back at Aunt Marie's, Karen bootlegged an unsecured internet connection from a neighbor and checked her email. She saw nothing but messages of support from her coworkers, so after sending appreciative responses, she shut the computer down.

The screen door squeaked as her aunt shoved it open with one hip and carried a wooden box into the kitchen. "It's getting too hot for lettuce, so Mary Jane cleaned out her garden." Aunt Marie dumped the box on the counter. "Just look at all this."

Karen saw a ladybug trying to escape and put it outside. "What can I do?"

"Get the stewpot and fill it with cold water." Standing at the sink, the two of them rinsed, chopped, and bagged the greens while Aunt Marie caught her up on the news of the neighborhood. "I thought fried chicken for dinner?"

"I'll help."

"And tomorrow after Mass, I invited the relatives to come over so they can visit with you before you leave." She shook the water off a head of lettuce and set it on a clean towel. "How long will you stay?"

Karen dried her hands and leaned against the counter. "I'm going to take a chance and stay the week."

Aunt Marie looked out the window. The wind was picking up ahead of a late-afternoon monsoon. "Are you sure?"

"I work hard. I don't take vacations, and I've got about a year's worth of sick leave saved up. I am never away from that stinking office and I'm tired of it."

"It's all right, dear. I just asked."

"Let me explain something." Karen felt reckless, as if admitting the narrowness of her existence now compelled the telling of more secrets. "I feel bad about ignoring Mom. I know you say there's no need, but I feel guilty. I should have come to see her more often and I didn't, and now I'd like to make amends. Even though she's gone, I can at least spend time with the family, and with friends. I'd like to think Mom will somehow be aware I'm hanging around, and if she is, it will make her happy. So that's my decision, and I don't care if I get fired. Well, I do, but I don't think I will, because I have too much history with the place and they'd be insane—well, anyway, my boss is out of town and he'll never know."

Aunt Marie nodded. "I understand, but it's too bad."

"What is?"

"That you work for such a *dumpfbacke*."

Cousin Joan dropped a corn fritter into the caldron of hot oil and stepped back as the batter bubbled. "You know Frieda's crazy, don't you?"

"It doesn't matter. I told her no. She'll have to find another way to Denver." Karen swiped a strand of hair out of her eyes. The kitchen was hot from all the baking and cooking, and the proximity of relatives. She hardly remembered some of them. Aunt Lizzie was so old and thin, you could practically see through her, and Joan used a cane. There was more than one wheelchair parked out on the back porch.

"Pound the steak real good." Aunt Marie watched over Karen's shoulder as she wielded the meat tenderizer tool. "That way you can get away with a cheaper cut."

With flour up to her elbows, Karen rolled the cutlets around chunks of onion, wrapped a strip of bacon around the roll-up and anchored it with a toothpick. After browning the rollups in a frying pan, she transferred them to a casserole dish, drowned them in tomato bisque soup, and set the oven timer for forty-five minutes.

"Perfect," said Aunt Marie. "You'll be a chef in no time."

"Joan's right about Frieda." Lorraine pulled a chair from the kitchen table and sat down. "She had a yard sale about a month ago. Practically gave all her stuff away. Nobody can figure out why."

"I can," said Joan. "She's goin' to Denver to die. I would say good riddance but I don't want God mad at me. Got enough problems."

Marie's eyes crinkled with mirth. "Don't mind Joan. She's still unhappy about that baking contest. What's it been, thirty years?"

"Frieda cheated. And it wasn't that long ago." Joan ladled hot fritters from the kettle.

"It surely was," said Aunt Lizzie, her voice a raspy whisper. "I believe the peanut farmer was president."

After dinner, Karen carried plates of cake and ice cream into the living room where the men were fooling around with musical instruments. Uncle Roger tested the keys on the piano while Lorraine's husband Jim plucked at a guitar. Uncle Rudy opened a black case and lifted out a long, skinny accordion. The bellows were hexagonal and edged with mother-of-pearl. Rudy slipped his hands into the straps at both ends, looking up at Karen from under bushy white eyebrows. "It's a concertina, almost a hundred years old," he said, fanning the bellows. "My father brought it with him from the Banat, in Austria-Hungary."

"I'd like to hear it."

"We should be done warming up about the time everybody's through with dessert. Go on and get some for yourself."

Karen went back to the kitchen. Without a break in the gossip, the women scooted their chairs aside to let her into the circle. Joan was showing off her new wood-burning kit. "This angled thingy here? You use it for edging," she said. "Say you've got a picture frame you wanted to gussy up, you can personalize it with designs or lettering or what-have-you. There's even a tip for calligraphy. See here?"

"You guys are all so creative," said Karen. "I'm in awe."

"I crochet," said Aunt Lizzie. She wore a faded blue shirtwaist and knee-highs that were rolled down to her ankles. "My specialty is baptismal sets."

"Some of the ladies around here have gotten real good at quilting," said Lorraine. "They were even featured on TV recently. On the Today show."

"They're famous," said Aunt Lizzie.

"Famous is relative," said Joan as she packed up her woodworking tools. "Remember we are talking North Dakota."

"I wish I had time to be creative," said Karen.

Joan shrugged. "It's no big thing. Gals around here are used to working hard, and when the kids grow up and move away, they don't know how to stop. So they find other things to do."

"The men, too," said Lizzie. "My Earl used to like to garden."

"As long as they're digging around in the dirt or playing with knives, they're happy."

"Many of them paint or do wood carving."

"You have to do something, especially in the winter. Otherwise you go crazy with boredom."

"Only if you're retired," said Lorraine. "Some of us don't have time to get bored."

"Quit complaining. You'll get your turn."

"I doubt it, the way the country's going. I'll be working until I drop."

"Who wants more cake?"

Karen held out her plate for another guilty slice. Her aunts and cousins might not wear the latest styles nor do Pilates four times a week, but they knew how to keep their families healthy during a North Dakota winter. They were expert cooks, even if they still prepared food as if their families worked all day in the fields. They could decorate their homes with what they made by hand, and clothe their children with a few yards of cheap cotton from the fabric store. Did the world still appreciate that kind of strength?

The first jubilant notes of a polka called to them from the living room, and the women pushed back from the table. Karen dug her camera out of her purse.

The older women scrunched together on the couch, while the younger ones sat on the carpet. Karen found herself singing along with her elderly relatives to a familiar beer-hall polka, and felt both dorky and sad. Aunt Marie, always seeming to sense her moods, squeezed her shoulder. Rudy pressed the accordion's buttons and moved the square bellows in and out, the mother-of-pearl embellishments twinkling in the lamplight. The women clapped, keeping time, and Karen remembered seeing her parents whirling around the floor of the banquet hall at St. Joseph's. As a child she had learned to dance with her father, but he was impatient and she, self-conscious. The best dancing she ever did was with her mother, when the bandleader summoned the children onto the dance floor for a twirl with their parents.

The music brought back another form of nostalgia, reminding Karen of her neighborhood back home in Newport where it wasn't unusual to hear polka music coming from a passing car or truck. In California they called it *banda* music, the familiar polka beat having migrated into Mexico in the eighteen hundreds from German settlements in Texas.

Rudy's work-worn fingers moved quickly across the keys, and he opened and closed the bellows as he had for the last seventy years, as his father had taught him before leaving European soil. A blanket of melancholy threatened Karen. When the notes finally faded, Lorraine nudged her. "I think I heard your phone."

Karen checked the display and called voicemail. Steve sounded upset, so she slipped into the back bedroom and called him at work.

"We need to list the house," he said without preamble.

"I'm fine, thanks, and you?"

"Sorry. I've been trying to call you for the past day and you haven't answered."

"And now that I have, I find you're calling to kick me out of our house." She felt her pulse accelerate, readying for battle.

"Look," he said, his tone softer, "I know you're pissed, and I've told you a million times that I'm sorry. But let's be practical. Sell it to me and we can skip the realtors and save ourselves a bundle."

Her fingernails gouged half-moons into her palms as she pictured his new family in her house. The cul-de-sac, the multiple bedrooms, the pool–it would be a perfect nest. Just not for her.

"The upkeep is a bitch," he said. "You don't like the house anyway. This is your big chance to buy something more to your liking, and I can make you a generous offer."

"You've been planning this for a while, haven't you?"

"What difference does it make?"

"None, but I want to know." She could picture him, head bent, fingers pinching the skin between his eyebrows.

"Drama doesn't help."

"Tell me," she said. "When did you decide to go out and get a new life, Steve? When did you decide to get rid of your old wife and impregnate some kid?"

"She's not a kid. She's thirty-two."

"Oh, fuck. You could be her father."

"Come on, Karen."

"So I just want to know, when exactly did you decide to obliterate our marriage?" She was shouting at him in a frantic whisper, pride gone, futility no object. "I want to know when, because I want to try to remember what I was doing when you were fooling around with Miss Thirty-Two. Or did you decide before that, with the red head? Or the brunette?"

"You're hysterical."

"Are you all right?" Lorraine stood in the bedroom doorway.

"Fine."

Lorraine leaned into the phone. "Tell the asshole I said hi."

"Very nice, Karen. Way to make your whole family hate me."

"You deserve it." Karen hung up. She reached a hand out to Lorraine, who pulled Karen to her feet.

"You'll be fine, Cuz."

Karen wiped the tears away with both hands. "I know."

"Want me to tell them you don't feel good?"

"No, I'll be out in a minute."

Lorraine closed the door, and Karen closed her eyes. She'd known about Steve's women, but they were biennial blips that faded away, whereas she and Steve had hung together through miscarriages and parental deaths and that breast cancer scare a few years ago. Their marriage endured even as they grew apart, and Karen had taken this to mean that, while the gloss was gone, the foundation was strong. That's what she saw with her mom and dad's marriage, and she assumed that was how it would be for hers.

She noticed the distance between them, but figured adults grew apart as they matured. There was nothing wrong with pursuing your own interests. Both of them were workaholics—that's what attracted them to each other in the first place. If Karen had to work late yet again, she knew Steve was self-sufficient. No matter what happened, she and Steve would be together until death. They would make the best of things.

But then, about a year ago, she noticed he was on the computer long after she went to bed. He told her it was work, and got irritated when she pressed. Then one day he packed his things and left. Said he wasn't sure anymore. He needed time to think.

At first, she argued, then railed, then bargained. It didn't matter. Steve left with a trunk full of suitcases. Said he'd be back to get the rest of his things, and that Karen could have the house.

She raged through the house, dragging his things out to the garage and the trash. When she wore herself out, she drank prodigious amounts of wine and missed work for the first time in years. Peggy covered for her until she was able to function normally again, and as weeks and then months passed, Karen accepted Steve wasn't coming back. What she hadn't figured out was what was supposed to happen next, so she worked long hours and deferred the question. They hadn't spoken since her birthday, when he called to ask if she still had his golf clubs.

Chapter Eight

On Monday morning, Karen stood in front of her mother's closet, sifting through for something to wear. Lena had been about the same size but a foot shorter. Luckily it was summer, so the length wouldn't matter. Karen set out a pair of Capri's and a tee shirt and went to start a bath.

Marie tapped on the bathroom door.

"I help at the food bank on Mondays. You want to come with me? We can use another hand."

"I'm going with Lorraine out to the country today." Karen opened the door. "Some kind of historical field trip with Denise. And a picnic."

Aunt Marie nodded. "Say hello to the farm for me."

"Here you can see what's left of the house." Denise pointed at the bare remains of a stone foundation. "Down the slope over there, that little bit of rock marks the footprint of the barn. Let's go look." Karen lagged behind as her new friends tromped down the slope, flushing pheasant from cover. The birds' metallic-green and copper necks flashed in the sun as they angled low toward a patch of wetland, intent on the reeds that thrived in runoff from the farms.

Lorraine slipped past her. "You okay?"

"I'll be fine." Karen listened to the women's voices fade. Behind her, a meadowlark trilled and the grasses waved across dormant fields. She'd seen the same wind patterns moving across the waters at Newport Bay, and the comparison between ocean and prairie didn't escape her. Both were endless and, in the wrong season, unforgiving. To think her mother had lived here as a child, played and worked and suffered the winters here in a barely-insulated farmhouse, almost defied imagination. It was a side of her mother Karen almost couldn't imagine.

The warming air carried the essence of clover and bog. She inhaled deeply, drunk on the fragrance of the land and the absence of sound. All around her, the remnants of her family's history spoke in whispers, calling to her, but the landscape had changed.

In the decades since Karen last saw them, the ramshackle buildings had fallen or been knocked down, the materials salvaged or trashed, and farmland restored. The breeze picked up and she closed her eyes, turning her head one way and another to adjust the degree of quiet, until she heard distant voices shouting at her to catch up.

"Watch where you walk," said Glenda. "Somewhere around here is the pit for the outhouse, and you can still fall into one of those holes and get seriously hurt."

"On the plus side," said Denise, aiming her lens at them, "if you look carefully once you're in there, you might find an artifact or two. People tended to drop things."

The women picked their way through the grass, watching for snakes and alert for treasure. "I like to think of Lena's family living here," Marlene said. "I can see kids playing under the trees, and chickens scratching around by the house, and laundry flapping on the line, and maybe even a team of horses plowing up and down that field over there."

"That's how she described it to me," said Karen.

Denise capped her lens. "I'd like to go to the cemetery next. I want to get some of the old headstones, but it can wait if you're not cool with it."

"I'm good," said Karen. The women piled back into the trucks and headed south, passing the beaten sign that marked the town of Lefor, or what remained of it. "It's kind of pathetic," said Lorraine. "Little old sign whipping around in the wind for nothing."

"But people still live here. Look, there's laundry on that clothesline." Karen imagined herself stepping outside with a basketful of wet laundry on a balmy spring day.

"I think it's depressing. I never come out here."

"I would," said Karen. "It's peaceful."

"We've got peaceful right in town. You don't have to go anywhere to get it." Lorraine followed the cars ahead as they turned off the highway and rumbled up a dirt road, dust coating the fence posts as they passed. The yards were overgrown and the homes looked tired. Lefor was a museum piece, a colonial village that seemed almost to exist solely to demonstrate how life worked in the olden days. The disparity between her perspective and that of Lorraine's made Karen feel like an outsider. She felt the pull of homesickness for California, while at the same time knowing she'd feel as disoriented if she were back home. With her parents gone and her marriage kaput, nothing felt like home anymore. She and Lorraine fell silent.

"There's the old bank," said Lorraine. "Somebody burned it down in the twenties, but by that time, Lefor was deteriorating, so they never rebuilt." She drove slowly past the rock-walled structure, no bigger than a one-room jail.

Karen studied the old building. About the time Butch and Sundance committed their first robbery, the first Model-T chugged out of Henry Ford's factory, and San Francisco shook and burned to the ground, forty-two German families fled Europe for the Great Plains. They arrived here, sometimes living in dugouts scooped from the earth until their fortunes improved sufficiently to allow the building of sod houses. Later, if they were especially prosperous, they built homes from the abundant rocks dredged from the farm fields.

The caravan stopped in front of St. Elizabeth's, and the women piled out and climbed the two flights of cement steps to the unlocked entrance. Inside, the aroma of old incense and candle wax reawakened Karen's memory of daily Mass, and she felt lightheaded. The wooden pews were cool and smooth to the touch, and the hardwood floor was so old it dipped in places. Along the wall and under the stained glass windows, the Stations of the Cross were inscribed in German, barely understandable and yet deeply familiar. Denise snapped discrete photos as the rest of the women moved quietly to the door, where Karen touched her fingertips to the bowl of Holy Water, made the Sign of the Cross and went back outside.

Following her friends up the path towards the cemetery, she wondered how often the early settlers walked over this specific stretch of packed earth? How many of her relatives had preceded her toward the burial grounds, their eyes focused resolutely above the graves, their grief assuaged by a firm belief in a glorious future?

In order to feel more at home after leaving Europe, the immigrants chose homestead parcels in the same configuration as in the old country, so one's neighbor to the south in the Banat occupied the same placement in the new town. They built a church and named it after the one they'd left behind. They fenced off a cemetery, and unlike the original church, the burial ground endured, welcoming generations of settlers and their children and grandchildren.

At first Lefor had thrived, with a post office, a mercantile exchange, and even a primitive bowling alley. There was talk of a railroad, and funds were raised, but World War I interfered, and the town began to decline. Over the years the younger generation, continuing the original migration, moved away from the farms to cities, and to other states. Now the spire of St. Elizabeth's rose above a cemetery whose occupants far outnumbered the residents of the town.

Drying vegetation crunched under her feet as she made her way across the slope, reading the names on the primitive stones. The rest of the women stopped here and there to visit the graves of relatives while Denise took pictures of the oldest headstones, some imported from Germany and others, more simple ones, made of local stone. Some of the graves held the remains of immigrants who were buried eighty, ninety years ago. Karen stood before one that bore a familiar surname, her mother's. Katerina and Johann, *geboren* and *gestorben*. Born and died. Karen felt guilty, alive under the bright sunshine, thriving in the twenty-first century, comforted by all manner of modern invention. What debt did she owe them, those plain-faced great-aunts and grannies? Done with their short, hard enlistments, their bodies worn out from bearing children and tilling the soil, they lay waiting for her to make their efforts worthwhile.

Stopping at her parents' graves, Karen crouched down and touched the letters of her mother's name, carved into the headstone and adorned with twin sheaves of wheat. Lena and Frank had ordered them years ago when they bought the plots of land for their final resting place. Gruesome, Karen had thought at the time, but now she understood her mother would be reassured to know where she would lie at the end.

"How are you doing?" Lorraine grasped Karen's shoulder.

Karen, wiping her eyes, backed away from the newly-turned earth. "Sometimes it's too much."

"Let's rest." They meandered toward a shaded bench and sat. Already the grass was yellowing at the tips, and soon the afternoons would turn steamy, brewing up thunderstorms and the occasional tornado. Southwestern North Dakota wasn't an easy place. Unlike the dark, rich farmland in the eastern part of the state, here on the highlands the land was dry and windswept on its westward climb toward the Rocky Mountains.

Lorraine pulled off her big floppy sun hat and shook out her hair. "You're processing a lot right now. Take it easy. Breathe."

"So much is changing, I feel disoriented."

"Then slow down and take it all in. You have a lot of years ahead of you."

Karen chuckled. "You're younger than me. How come you sound so smart?"

"I'm not so smart, but Mom always told me it's my life and I should be the one to make the big decisions. So don't let us or anybody else pressure you."

"'*Man plans, and God laughs.*' Or something like that." Karen picked up a rock and tried to scrape off the tiny cactus sticking to the side of her sneakers. Only a fool would wear sandals to this cemetery.

They watched Denise work, angling this way and that for the perfect shot of the old headstones.

"I can't believe this is so close to your house," Karen said. "You drive a half hour and you're standing right on top of the original homesteads. You can see a tree still growing that was planted by the first relatives to set foot in America, and you can sit by their graves, if you want."

"Not like we ever do," said Lorraine. "I know they're here and that comforts me, but I don't come out here. We go to work, come home, eat dinner, do chores, go to bed, and on the weekends, we run errands."

Karen gazed across the open landscape. "In California, everybody is from another place, and nobody stays put. They move in, they move out. The house next door to mine back home is only fifteen years old and it's had three owners already. By contrast, this,"– she opened her arms to take in the whole of the countryside,– "seems so permanent."

The two women fell silent as Denise folded up her tripod. Then they drove back across the highway and down another dirt road, this one heading east. The Jeep turned in at an abandoned homestead and parked beside a rusting tractor. "This farm is still in Glenda's family," Lorraine said. "We're going to have lunch here."

Glenda gathered the group around her. "There's a creek down here behind the barn, and a nice shady place to eat. Follow me." The women followed, carrying chairs, food, and picnic supplies. Their sneakers mashed down the overgrown grass as they trod, single file, through a grove of whispering cottonwoods to a lush clearing.

"Who wants wine?" Marlene opened a bottle of chilled Riesling and passed it around, followed by a plate of ham and cheese sandwiches. Someone brought potato chips; another, grapes; a third, brownies.

"So, what did you think about your mom's old place?" asked Denise. "Was it how you remembered it?"

Karen shook her head. "There's nothing left of what I remember."

"It's all going. We're at that age," said Glenda.

"Speak for yourself." Denise finished her sandwich and began fitting a new lens to her camera. "Did you know most of the farmers lived in *soddies* all their lives? They whitewashed the walls and sealed the dirt floors with a mixture of water and cow manure, which hardened into a smooth surface. Tough people. Kind of an inspiration."

"Mom never mentioned cow poop floors."

"Denise is our historian," said Glenda.

"You can't do photo-documentaries without getting caught up in the research," said Denise. "Who wants to look for shells?"

Marlene and Denise rolled up their pant legs and waded out into the creek while the others lolled around like overfed pups. Karen unbuttoned her waistband for the small relief it gave her. Usually she was much more careful about portions, but ever since she arrived, she'd eaten like a horse.

The sound of splashing and shrieking brought her back. Glenda laughed at the women in the creek. "They're like a couple of kids."

Karen reached upward, stretching and yawning, more relaxed than she'd been in months. Denise trudged up the bank and held out a handful of dripping shells. "Look what we found. They're *Lampsilis radiata* shells. The Native Americans made them into tools. See? It's the tip of a knife."

Marlene trailed behind her. "Like fossils," she said, wiping her hands on her shorts.

"Native Americans lived here for four thousand years before us," said Denise. "These were their ancestral hunting grounds. When the government opened it up for homesteading, the native people were so pissed off they started murdering everybody."

"That's what I would have done." Lorraine held out her glass and Karen emptied the rest of the wine into it. Overhead in the rustling cottonwoods, songbirds tried to drown out each other's territorial claims. Dappled shade splashed patterns across the remains of their picnic. Eyes closed, Lorraine rested her head against the chair back. Denise had flopped down on a blanket, and Marlene's head was dipping. The brook rippled across small stones, and cicadas began buzzing overhead. Karen tried to imagine up a similar space in Orange County where she could find the same respite. The Back Bay at Newport came to mind, but that was often busy with cyclists and other nature lovers. Here, though, in the farmlands around Dickinson, solitude was abundant.

I could live here, she thought.

"Nothing stopping you," said Glenda.

Karen opened one eye. "Did I say that?"

"You mumbled something about living here and so I say, move. Nothing stopping you now."

Karen stared at Lorraine, who grinned. "There's no such thing as a secret in Dickinson," she said.

"Don't let it throw you," said Denise. "I've been single almost a year now. It gets easier. Good time for introspection. You can find your authentic self."

"Authentic self, my butt. Just get the biggest settlement you can." Marlene tossed the empty wine bottle in the trash bag.

Glenda folded up her chair and slung it over her shoulder. "Ladies, I'm out of here. I have to drop by the clinic and sign some checks. Karen, you've seen big-city health care. Want to see how the other half lives?"

Chapter Nine

Glenda turned onto the two-lane highway away from town and headed deeper into farm country. Rows of evergreen trees ran from north to south, protecting the farm fields from wind and reminding Karen of the Christmas tree farms back in California. In the middle of a yellow canola field stood a herd of deer, antlers still covered in velvet.

Twenty miles south they drove into the remote community of Regent, which consisted of a sleepy main street and a few dozen houses. Glenda parked in front of an old feed store bearing the name Farmers Health Collective. Inside the clinic, crayon drawings by school children were taped up on the walls and soft music wafted from an iPod player at the receptionist's window. Two women thumbed through magazines while a child played in the corner with alphabet blocks.

Glenda waved to the receptionist. "Is Annie around?"

"She's giving a tetanus shot. Should be done any time."

"Would you ask her to see me? I'll be in my office."

Karen followed Glenda down the hall and into a cramped room. On the desk, a multicolored array of case folders was stacked next to medical textbooks. A teddy bear, clad in surgical scrubs, grinned at them from the top of the books.

Karen spotted the nameplate on the door. "You're the boss?"

Glenda reached in the drawer and pulled out a jar of candy. "Unofficially. There's a chief physician in Grand Forks who's technically responsible for the whole network, but I only see him a couple times a year. Otherwise, we do video conferencing, email, and phone calls. Want a peppermint?"

Karen unwrapped a candy and popped it in her mouth. "I'm guessing you're the main health care in the area?"

"Yup." Glenda leaned back in her chair, put her feet up, and rolled a peppermint around in her mouth. "The only. We serve the whole south end of the county. If they need more, they go to Bismarck or Dickinson."

"You're pretty far away from things. Is it hard to find staff?"

Glenda nodded. She gestured toward the door and lowered her voice. "I'm worried about my assistant, Annie. She's burning out. She doesn't complain, but I can tell. There isn't much more I can do to make things easier. The work is what it is."

"How's the pay?"

"About two-thirds of what they can earn in Grand Forks or Bismarck, but the cost of living is proportionate, and it's a lot quieter out here at night. Lots of stars."

"Hard to hire people based on that."

"Tell me about it."

Karen rolled the candy wrapper between her fingers until it was shaped like a ball. Laughter resonated from down the hall, and a copier hummed outside the door. Hand-made mobiles of colored foil dangled in front of the windows, reflecting the late afternoon sun. The pen scratched across paper as Glenda signed checks. The clinic had that peaceful, Friday afternoon feeling she missed.

When a shriek knifed through the air, Glenda was out the door before Karen had managed to stand up. They reached the waiting room just as a young woman lost her hold on her husband. He slipped to the floor, leaving streaks of blood on his wife's chest. Glenda knelt at his side while the receptionist tucked a jacket under his head. One of the other patients braced herself against the far wall, hands covering her mouth.

"Easy, easy, Johnny, we're here." Glenda tucked a stethoscope under his shirt and cocked her head. The man's blond hair was dark with sweat, and a blood-soaked towel was wrapped around his right hand. His wife clutched the other. "He was working on the thresher," she said, "and the wheel turned when he wasn't expecting. The blade fell on his arm. I saw it out the kitchen window."

A woman knelt beside Glenda with a satchel of medical instruments. "Annie. Thank God you're here." Annie filled a syringe and handed it over.

Karen stood back, her nostrils flaring at the metallic tang of blood. The young wife stared at her husband, who moaned as the soothing molecules of morphine began circulating through his system. Glenda and Annie prepared to transfer the man to a gurney.

The receptionist touched the wife on the shoulder. "Lanie, you can ride in the ambulance."

"How can I? I got cows, and the kids're about due home from school." The woman, looking at her husband, began to tremble. "What am I gonna do? I told him to be careful. He thinks he's a gosh-darn hero all the time."

"Most men do." Karen stifled her urge to bolt out the door and instead knelt down next to Lanie. Working in the administrative offices of an HMO was very different from doing actual medicine. Lanie smelled of sweat and blood.

"I thought we'd never get here. The darned truck died every time I slowed down. I thought he was gonna bleed to death."

"When did it happen?" asked Glenda.

"'Bout fifteen minutes ago."

Karen checked the clock on the wall. It was almost three.

"The kids'll be getting home from school, and I always pick them up at the bus stop. If I'm not there they'll worry. And the cows need milked. We got two of 'em." Lanie wiped snot and tears against the back of her hand.

"Do you have a neighbor?" asked Karen. "Somebody you can call?"

"John's folks can meet me at the farm but they're gonna want to head to Bismarck right away. I'm shakin' so bad, I don't think I can drive. Can you help me?"

Karen hesitated. After so many years in the big city, she was leery of getting pulled into the drama of strangers. If she could hand this duty off to someone else—but there was no one. Glenda, Annie, and the receptionist had their hands full.

She picked up Lanie's purse. "Let's go."

"Are they going to move him pretty soon?"

Glenda nodded.

"We'll hurry." Karen held the door open. They ran to Lanie's truck, a rusting green hulk with a horse blanket across the front seat. Karen got behind the wheel and stopped cold when she saw the three-speed shifter on the steering column. She glanced over at Lanie, who seemed about to pass out. Running quickly through memories from her teen years, Karen took a deep breath, pushed in the clutch, turned the key, and gassed it slightly. She eased the gearshift into what she hoped was reverse. Clenching her jaw, she let the clutch out slowly, and the truck started backward. She covered the brake pedal with her right foot until the truck had rolled back enough, wiggling the shifter around until it slipped into first gear. Just as the old Chevy began to stutter forward, Lanie yanked her door open and threw up.

A half hour later, Karen was perched on a three-legged stool with her forehead nudged up against the warm flank of a cow. Pigeons cooed from the rafters overhead. Karen tugged gently on the cow's teat. Nothing in her city-girl adult life prepared her for this. The cow snorted.

"It's the opposite of what your hand is used to." Lanie, milking the cow next to her, had calmed with the routine of chores. Her own bucket was already half-full. "Get your hand up by the top, right against the bag, then tighten your grip from the index fingers down, that will squeeze the milk from top to bottom so it comes down through the teat. Alternate your hands and get a rhythm. Remember, it's not pulling, she won't appreciate that. You get kicked and I'll be taking you to the doc's, too."

A giggle escaped the little girl who leaned against her mother's shoulder. "Mommy, she don't know how."

Karen got in a good squeeze, and the milk squirted out.

"Hush. She's getting it now." Lanie grinned at Karen. "You keep at it, miss. You're doing' fine."

A truck pulled up out front, its front tires biting hard into the gravel.

"Grandpa's here! Grandpa's here!" shouted the little girl.

"Go in the house and tell Buddy we're leaving in two minutes." Lanie took the bucket from Karen and poured it into her own. "You can drive yourself back in the truck. Just leave the keys in it." Lanie quick-walked out of the barn, milk sloshing from the bucket.

Chapter Ten

The rest of the week passed quietly. Every morning, Karen let the sun awaken her, ate a hearty breakfast and read the Dickinson Press. Using the internet signal from a router somewhere in the neighborhood, she handled as much work as was possible, with help from Peggy and Stacey. Wes checked in periodically but seemed oblivious to the game.

Every few days she went to Mass with Aunt Marie, for no better reason than she had the time and she wanted to be a good houseguest. It turned out to be a pretty good form of meditation, forcing her to slow down and relearn the rituals.

Karen wasn't geared for sitting around doing nothing though, so she helped with housework and laundry, weeded the garden, and shopped for groceries. Aunt Marie taught her a few simple recipes, meals that had strengthened the backbone of the Midwest for the better part of a century: Swiss steak smothered in brown gravy with a hint of barbeque sauce; scalloped potatoes from scratch; and pork chops, mashed potatoes, and green beans, all baked together in a Pyrex bowl. And although the calories and fat content nagged at her, Karen found herself sleeping better than she had in years.

On Friday they went for lunch at a downtown diner. The waitress, led them to a booth at the front of the diner where they could watch the action on Villard Street. A few minutes later, Lorraine slid into the booth wearing stylish trousers, heels, and a blazer. As her mother gave her an update, Lorraine unwrapped a straw, laughing. "You're not getting that much rest, Cuz."

"I'm relaxing. It's nice." Karen glanced at the lunch menu. It looked like a choice between fried and fried. She chose a Reuben, figuring she'd burn it off doing chores.

Lorraine ordered soup. "I can't stay long. Everything's crazy at the office."

"What's going on?" Karen asked.

"It's like a 'be careful what you wish for' story. A couple months ago I had this idea and it worked so well the partners made me the marketing director. So now I'm doing that, on top of my old job of office manager." Lorraine's phone buzzed. "Gosh darn it; not again." She read a new text, tapped a quick reply, and stuck it in her purse. "I hate being a supervisor."

Karen felt her pulse quicken. "What's the problem? Maybe I can help."

"You can't help."

"Try me."

"Okay. There are these two legal secretaries in my office, and they're in a competition to see who can do the least work. So nothing gets done, the attorneys get mad, and I get blamed."

"And you're the supervisor?"

"In name only." Lorraine paused as the waitress brought their entrées. She placed a steaming Reuben sandwich in front of Karen.

Sauce dripped out the sides and the aroma of hot pastrami made her weak with longing. She bit into the sandwich. The rich tang of warm Thousand Island dressing nearly brought tears to her eyes.

Lorraine took a couple of quick tastes of soup and set the spoon down. "The three of us used to be friends, but then I got promoted so that got messed up."

"But you're the boss now," said Karen.

"I'm a glorified paralegal. I know zip about supervision and don't have time to learn. It's hopeless."

Karen stirred artificial sweetener into her drink. "Law offices are all about billable hours, right? So why not have the women keep work logs, and have them do a weekly review with the managing partner. Tell them it's a new policy to make sure the office bills enough. That way they'll be forced to show how much work they do, but it won't look punitive."

"They'd hate that." Lorraine cocked her head to the side. "You know what? That is actually a brilliant suggestion. Thanks."

"Welcome." Karen took another hearty bite of the sandwich. The sauce alone was to die for. She licked a finger.

"So are you going to hang around for a while? Glenda and the rest of the girls want to hang out. We could drink too much and complain about work."

"She can probably use a day off," said Aunt Marie. "I've worked her pretty hard."

"It depends on how things are going back at the office." Karen set the sandwich down. With the help of Skype and email, and the excellent camouflage provided by Peggy and Stacey, she had managed easily. "As long as I get back by Tuesday morning, I'm good."

"What about Steve?" asked Aunt Marie.

Lorraine stirred her soup. Karen took a gulp of iced tea, which gave her brain-freeze and bought her a few agonized moments to figure out how to break the news.

"Is anything wrong?"

With Aunt Marie, it was best to be honest. She'd figure it out anyway. "We're separated. He moved out a couple months ago."

"I am sorry," said Aunt Marie, "but I'm not surprised."

"You're not?" Karen and Lorraine spoke in unison.

"No. Lena saw it coming. She told me she was worried about you two. Then, when he didn't show up here, I thought something must have happened."

"How could Mom have known? I never said anything."

"She's your mother." Aunt Marie reached over and grasped Karen's hand. "Every Sunday after you called, Lena and I would talk, and we agreed there were signs. For example, you rarely mentioned him."

"But why didn't she ask me?"

"She didn't want to pry. She figured she'd wait until you said something."

Karen thought she had done a pretty good job of hiding the truth from her mother, couching any marital updates in vague terms. Now she felt sick. "I made her worry, and she knew I was lying."

"She knew you were unhappy, but she said her prayers and hoped it would work out."

"I tried," said Karen, her eyes settling on an indeterminate point in front of her. "We both did. We've been struggling for years. It goes all the way back to when I was trying to get pregnant."

"Lena thought you were going to separate back then," said Aunt Marie.

"We almost did. It was hard for both of us, but for Steve—I don't know. People thought he was a workaholic but I knew why he stayed so busy." They were a perfectly matched pair, hiding in their work. She couldn't remember the last time they had dinner together, let alone sex. Karen had tried to tell herself it was about middle age. Given their work schedules, he'd taken to sleeping in the guest bedroom, and she didn't resist, although some nights she missed the simple comfort of his body next to hers.

"Every couple finds their own way of coping." Aunt Marie turned to Karen. "Is there any chance you two might be able to work things out? Have you tried counseling?"

"He had an affair, and now his girlfriend is pregnant."

Aunt Marie looked down at her plate, but Lorraine was not so subtle. "What an unbelievable bastard."

"I can't imagine him having children at his age, dear."

"Nevertheless." Karen signed the bill, aware that her hand was shaking, and put the pen back on the plastic tray. The three of them sat in silence.

"Well, this is depressing." Lorraine moved to stand. "I don't want to seem heartless, but I have to get back to work. You guys doing anything fun this afternoon?"

Aunt Marie nodded. "We have an appointment with Patrick at the mortuary."

Chapter Eleven

*A*t Stevenson's, they almost ran into Patrick on his way out the door. "Oh my gosh, I apologize, but I have to leave right away. Our bookkeeper can help you. Let me show you to her office." He led them down a deeply carpeted hallway, past the chapel and into a bright, well-organized room. "This is Jennie. She'll take real good care of you."

Jennie smirked when she saw him. "Aren't you going to be late for your meeting with Dr. Green?" She pantomimed a golf swing.

Patrick blushed. "Again, ladies, I apologize."

"Where are you playing?" asked Karen.

"The Bully Pulpit, in Medora. Do you golf?"

"Not for a while."

"Why don't you join us?"

"I don't have clubs or the proper clothes." Karen indicated her new Walmart ensemble.

"You're fine," said Patrick. "They rent clubs, and I don't think you're going to violate the North Dakota dress code. Why don't you come?"

Karen knew the Bully Pulpit was challenging, and her game was rusty. On the other hand, it would be good to get outside, and she could use the exercise. She looked at her aunt, who made a gesture like *get outta here!*

"Are you sure you don't need me?"

"No, you kids go on. Have fun."

The Bully Pulpit clubhouse sat on a bluff overlooking the Little Missouri River. Down below, the fairways wove in and out of a miniature Grand Canyon, with extreme elevation changes between tee box and green. Karen hoped she wouldn't embarrass herself.

At the pro shop, she bought a logo shirt, glove, and visor. Outside, Patrick was high-fiving a man who looked vaguely familiar. When they came through the door she extended her hand in wonder. "Curt Hoffman."

"All I get is a handshake? Come here." He swept her into a hug, and then held her at arms' length. Karen studied him back. His dark hair was now short and dusted with gray, and his eyebrows perched full and straight over deep-set brown eyes. He wore beige linen slacks that nipped his waist and flowed to the cuff. The boy who at seventeen seemed a toothpick with shoulders had evened out nicely.

Patrick ambled over, pulling on a glove. "You two know each other?"

"Earth science. Eleventh grade. I helped him with a term paper," Karen said.

"Remember those sparkly pink sneakers you used to wear?"

"I still have them." What else did he remember? The way she and her best friend watched him like two sad-eyed puppies?

The man behind the cash register pointed out the window. "Folks, you're up."

Curt held the door, and as she passed, she glanced sideways at him, curious to examine his middle-aged face and body, but he caught her looking. They both laughed, and she looked away, blushing. At the carts, she saw he had placed her bag next to his. Patrick was left to drive solo. They drove through the crowd of golfers waiting their turn to play.

At the championship tees, the young man whipped his club through the air with blinding speed sending his ball beyond their ability to follow it, yet the lanky Curt outdrove him. Both of their shots landed far down the fairway, in the middle of the short grass. The gallery applauded.

Now it was Karen's turn. She felt nervous at the prospect of hitting the ball for the first time in months. In fact, the last time she played was over a year ago at Pelican Hill in Newport, and she had been rusty then.

She pulled the rented driver from the bag. Golf was hard enough when you were familiar with your clubs. Playing with a strange set increased the challenge, and here she stood with a dozen men watching.

Waiting for her to fail.

Oh, she knew she shouldn't think that way, and tried to force positive thoughts. She would not worry about her score. It was a beautiful day and she was here to enjoy the exercise and the company of her partners. The course was beautiful. The Bully Pulpit was laid out in the middle of the North Dakota outback. The steep bluffs and buttes of the Badlands shaped the course. Cottonwoods, willows, and elm trees lined the fairways.

She approached the tee box, trying to ignore the players who awaited their turn to start, but it was a challenge. Karen still felt awkward under the scrutiny of older male players. Things were changing, but Karen had been born into a transitional generation and still remembered the feeling of being unwelcome. She had learned to play in her late thirties, and only because she was tired of being left at the office while the men escaped for an afternoon of corporate golf. At first she held her own with good sportsmanship if not expertise. Later, as her skills improved, she began to enjoy the game for its own sake. Every time she played, she vowed to get out on the course more often, for fun rather than work. Somehow, that never happened.

Now she bent over and stuck a tee in the ground, knowing the men were watching her. If she hit the ball poorly, it would reaffirm their belief that women shouldn't be taking up space on a golf course. Today the men's chattering reinforced her insecurity. Where they had been appropriately quiet for Curt and Patrick, they now joked loudly among themselves, ignoring the first rule of golf etiquette. She took a practice swing and tried to focus on the beauty of the day, the birds singing sweetly, and the light breeze riffling the nearby trees.

It didn't work.

She couldn't shut out the noise. Were she to hit the ball now, she might shank it, justifying their low expectations. Yet with their distracting noise, they would be the cause. The whole scenario was beginning to seriously piss her off.

Karen turned to face the men. With one hand on her driver and the other on her hip, she struck a pose and waited, staring pointedly. The first one to notice shushed another, and one by one, they fell silent. Touching her visor in mock salute, she took a practice swing, lined up her target, and swung.

Crack! She tagged it right on the screws, her spine loose and balance perfect. The ball sailed into the air, drawing left a bit and then arcing back to the right. The men burst into applause and she waved, grinning.

"Beautiful shot," Curt said as she climbed into the cart. "That went about two-ten."

"What a relief." Karen hit her next shot straight down the fairway, and all three of them finished up with a par.

"I thought you said you were rusty," said Patrick. "Hate to see you when you're not."

They bantered easily, returning to the carts. When Curt steered around a corner and slowed to a stop, she drew in a breath. At her feet, the path dropped away to a valley where deep green fairways, mowed in a crisscross pattern, unfurled in front of them. The valley was surrounded by soaring pink and grey rock formations, cut by layers and rising at odd angles. "It's beautiful," she said.

Curt pointed at the eroded buttes edging the canyon. "That used to be swampland. We've found fossils of palm trees and crocodiles in the rocks."

"We?"

"Me and my students at U.N.D. About twice a month we haul our equipment and sack lunches and go looking for stuff. It's a lot of fun."

"I'll bet." They sat quietly, the only sound was that of sagebrush rattling in the breeze.

After a moment he pressed the pedal to the floor. Karen grabbed the safety grips and held on, the two of them laughing as they sped down the slope toward the second hole. Patrick raced after them.

The next tee box was located on a hilltop outcropping from where they could see all the way to the blue-gray buttes on the western boundary of the state. The men pulled drivers out of their bags and walked toward the championship tees, heads together, talking. Karen stayed behind, enjoying the view and the sensation of the wind rocking the small cart. She was mesmerized by the silence, and the miles of open land in front of her. How different this was from home, with the contiguous cities and suburbs there.

Her mother had understood this need to get out and away from everything, to simply listen to the silence. She must have known what Karen was giving up when she moved west, but never tried to change her daughter's mind.

When Curt returned, he put one arm on the wheel, the other on the seat behind her. "Patrick told me you just lost your mom. I'm sorry. Do you want to talk about it?"

She shook her head. "No, but thanks."

He released the brake and rolled forward toward her tee box. "I met Pat when my parents died. That was about six years ago."

"Both of them at once?"

"Mom passed, and Dad declined shortly after that. We had two funerals in six months. Pat and his family sort of adopted me."

"Do you have siblings?"

"I have a sister who lives near in San Francisco."

"How did you get through it?"

Curt stopped at the forward tees. "The pain doesn't go away completely, but it diminishes. Every now and then it hits me hard, but as time passes, it happens less often."

"Thanks." She climbed out and pulled her club from the bag. In spite of her blurred vision, she managed to hit a nice long shot right up the middle.

They drove in silence to their shots. Curt climbed out, selected a club, and then leaned back in, one eyebrow raised.

"I'm fine. Thanks." She watched him turn and walk toward his shot. He moved easily, his back straight, laughing over some silly-ass joke with Patrick, and she realized she was holding her shoulders up somewhere around her ears. She let go and took a deep breath, watching him follow through with his swing, pivoting at the waist, his shoulders achingly broad.

When it was her turn she grabbed her own club and walked across the thick grass, wondering if grief built up as a person aged, like calcium deposits in a faucet, eventually clogging your pipes and weighing you down until you couldn't function anymore. Maybe that's what we die of, she thought. It's not old age; it's the accumulation of suffering.

Karen shook off the gloom. Today's round had been a great distraction. When she smacked her ball and watched it sail through the sky against the backdrop of the Badlands, her heart lifted a little. The physical exercise helped, and she felt pleased at how quickly her game had returned. The men were great company, too. They enjoyed having an audience for their good-natured ribbing, deriding each other's shots and making fun. When Patrick got a call from his fiancée, Curt teased him about being on a short leash.

"I met Rachel at the university," Patrick said. "She was Curt's research assistant."

"Do you teach?"

"Mostly geology," said Curt, "and some life science, and I also do environmental consulting for a couple of oil companies." He handed her a card.

"Environment and oil companies? Isn't that a contradiction?"

Curt stepped on the gas. "Well, at Hoffman Environmental—"

"Very clever."

"It looks good for the oil companies. They're doing a lot of damage right now in Williston, for example. I can't undo it, but I try to work with both the farmers and the oil guys. I have better luck with the farmers." Curt steered the cart down a steep, curving path.

"How do you manage time to teach and do consulting?"

"Rachel teaches a lot of my classes, and between semesters I can get away. I sometimes travel on assignment during the winter. Go someplace warm."

"Do you travel alone?"

He grinned and bumped her playfully with his shoulder. "Yep. I'm divorced. You?"

She shrugged, but her face burned.

"I saw the ring," he said.

"It's a fossil. From the Paleocene."

Curt smiled at her until she couldn't help but smile back. What was the harm? It felt good to flirt, even if she was seriously out of practice and felt like a total dork.

For the rest of the round, they found plenty of excuses to nudge and touch each other. When he accelerated along the curving path, forcing their bodies together, they laughed like teenagers. Halfway through the course, he parked the cart, his arm on the back of her seat as they waited for Patrick to hit his ball out of the rough.

When Curt looked away, Karen studied him. She liked watching his expressions, his concentration when sizing up a shot, or the way his eyes crinkled when he laughed. She thought she saw darkness behind his eyes when the laughter stopped, but it was probably her own need that made him look that way.

Hunger. As in lust. What a lovely, unfamiliar feeling. Yes, she wore a ring, but now she wondered why she bothered.

As she climbed a knoll toward the tee box, she bent down to stick the tee in the ground, aware of the fit of her clothing and the appeal of her long shapely legs. She knew that Curt was looking, and she liked it. She straightened up, took a practice swing and landed the ball right in the middle of the fairway, just as she had all day long.

"Boring," Patrick said, faking a yawn.

Curt made some calculations on the scorecard and stuck it back on the wheel with an exaggerated sigh. "She's beating us."

At the last green, Karen watched him line up his putt. In a few minutes they would finish the round, return to their cars and go their separate ways, a prospect that made her feel lonely and old, but she didn't have the guts to ask for his phone number. Technically, she was married, and besides, she was supposed to be grieving, not stalking a man.

His ball dropped into the cup. "Your turn," he said, brushing past her.

Karen shook herself out of a hormonal fog, picked up her marker and lined up her shot. When her putt went in, the round ended. As was the custom, the three of them shook hands, Curt's grasp lingering as he pulled her forward and kissed her on the cheek. They returned the carts to the garage and walked slowly across the nearly-deserted parking lot.

Karen knew she had to make a move, but she hadn't asked a guy on a date since college. What was the protocol nowadays? What if he acted surprised, or worse, not interested?

It wasn't like she wanted to marry him. She wanted to–what? Talk to him? Have dinner? None of the above, she thought as she watched him lift his heavy golf bag into the truck.

I want him naked.

The thought made her smile, but then the logistics struck her. Only Steve and her doctor had seen her naked in the last thirty years.

God, if it's going to happen, it had better be dark.

You can't do this. You're married.

I'm separated. And anyway, that didn't stop Steve.

What if he says no?

If I don't ask, it's like he already did.

Curt straightened up, closed the door, and turned to her.

"Some of my friends are coming by for a barbeque tomorrow night," she lied. "Why don't you join us?"

Curt leaned against the bed of his truck, studying her a moment before answering. "Thanks, but I have another commitment."

"Okay, maybe another time." She reached for the door of Pat's car, sensing her future stretching out as empty as the North Dakota freeway, and cursed herself for taking a chance. Of course he would turn her down. He worked at a college surrounded by nubile young things, while she was a half a century old. Women her age didn't date. They owned cats and went to the movies with girlfriends.

"Hey." She felt his hand on her arm and the deep rumble of his voice in her ear. He was right next to her, their bodies touching; she could feel his heat through her blouse. She turned, wanting to touch the dark stubble of his beard and suck up his lips with her own.

He smiled down at her. "Did you happen to bring a dress?"

Chapter Twelve

*C*urt's hand warmed the small of her back as they joined the throng swarming up the granite steps of March Hall. As a student, Karen had dashed up these steps hundreds of times, rushing from one class to another, always with the thought that graduation would open the door to leaving. Now she was back on campus at the University of North Dakota.

A line of vehicles advanced towards the grand portico where valets dashed from car to car. Doors flew open and divas-for-the-night emerged, taking the arms of their tuxedoed gentlemen. Last night at Lorraine's, the girls had sipped wine and pawed through a collection of party dresses until they found an icy blue number that draped Karen's body like melting silk. Now she danced along on a pair of stilettos, barely aware of the earth under her feet. Overhead, a gentle breeze lofted banners announcing the city's first ever Northern Plains Art Festival.

Inside, the crowd flowed toward the ballroom where silver and gold bunting spilled from ceiling to floor. Karen saw Marlene, who did a double take and waved them over to the VIP table. She hugged Karen and kissed Curt on the cheek. "I can't believe you. She barely gets into town and already you two are an item."

"Yes, we are." Curt said, lifting two champagne flutes from a passing tray and handing one to Karen. She took a sip, blushing, the bubbles tickling down her throat and warming her empty stomach. "You look beautiful," he murmured in her ear, and she felt it. Her pheromones must be flooding the room, so powerfully sexual did she feel in this dress and these shoes. Yet another part of her mind felt awkward, embarrassed at the fact that this was her first date in decades, and she was still married.

But it was just dinner and dancing. She smiled back. Did he have any idea how good he looked in that tux? As the room filled, they found opportunities to stand closer, and his fingers grasped hers and kept them.

Marlene linked arms with Karen. "Curt, the guys are out on the terrace. We'll see you later." The two women promenaded through the crowd, most of them in fancy new tuxedoes and cocktail gowns. An older woman in a floral pantsuit stuck close by her husband, who wore cowboy boots and a polyester suit.

"New oil. They still don't know quite how to spend the money." Marlene led Karen through an arched hallway into the east wing, which had been transformed into a gallery. A knot of people stood at the foot of a tall metal sculpture, a windblown cowboy on a scrap metal horse. "There's Glenda. Her husband is the artist."

Glenda, statuesque in a classic Grecian gown, stood near the sculpture.

"It's haunting," said Karen.

"Dave was born a century too late," said Glenda. "He sculpts scenes from the late eighteen-hundreds. By the way, you two look amazing."

"We're more than amazing. We're hot," said Denise, appearing in a vintage cocktail dress, sky-high heels, and a camera around her neck. "The guys are outside trying to regain their composure."

"The works are all by local artists." Glenda led the women to a watercolor depicting a sunshine-yellow canola field bounded by rolling green hills. One of the hills was topped by a rusting combine.

"I had forgotten about these," said Karen. "When I was a little girl they reminded me of big metal insects."

"I used to think it was kind of a sin, environmentally," said Denise, "but now I see it as folk art. And what else are you going to do with them?" She squinted at the signature. "I know this guy. He was a security guard and started painting when he retired. That other one is his, too."

Karen studied the remains of an old barn and windmill. "I can't get over how artistic the people are around here."

"There isn't much else to do during our long, cold winters," said Denise.

"Not true," said Curt, coming up behind Karen. He grasped her bare shoulders, and his touch left her skin burning. "Come on. We're being seated."

Karen's spot was in front of a place card that said, "Dr. Hoffman Guest." She reached for a brochure which read, *Like Oil and Water? The Future of Commerce and Ecology on the High Plains.* "Very impressive, Dr. Hoffman."

He kissed her fingertips, smiling. "The balloon guy cancelled."

At dinner they feasted on herb-stuffed tenderloin in a chardonnay sauce. Karen had expected rubber chicken, mashed potatoes, and something greenish. When the empty plates were replaced by tiramisu and coffee, the MC stepped up to the podium. He thanked the organizers, told a good joke, and then introduced Curt.

"Save my seat." Curt folded his napkin and strode to the podium, tall and handsome in formal attire. He spoke of the difficulty of reconciling energy and conservation, and the creative solutions that were emerging. She saw people scribbling notes on the backs of programs. When he returned to his seat, she applauded not just for him but for the festival and her new friends. They were smart, curious, and ambitious, exactly the kind of people with whom she would surround herself if possible.

But as the applause faded, so did her good mood. Home was California, and as appealing as the new Dickinson appeared, she didn't fit in anymore. Life was different on the West Coast. Although it was in some ways harsher, she had learned to thrive there and no longer questioned its requirements.

On the dais, the MC had given the podium over to the governor of North Dakota. A compact man, he stood before them, his eyes piercing behind wire-rimmed glasses. When the crowd fell silent, he gestured toward the exhibits in the far wing.

"Ladies and gentlemen, who knew that right here in our midst we have such a rich diversity of artists? Such talented and heartfelt people–doesn't it make you proud?" He held up a sheaf of papers. "I brought some notes about the economy and such, but after I walked through the east wing, it didn't seem relevant.

"Tonight, as I was getting ready to come here, I raced out the door, my mind on work. You all know how that is, don't you? We rush through our days, and sometimes we forget the important things." He gazed over the heads of his listeners. "We forget who we really are, and where we come from. But tonight, I'm remembering, and I owe that to the artists."

Karen thought of the paintings she had seen before dinner, especially that of the broken-down windmill and barn, and she imagined the wind tearing through the abandoned structure. Now that things were hopping in Dickinson again, how would the artist deal with his or her memories? What did he see when he stood at the edge of his old farm?

The governor's voice cut through her thoughts. "… they worked from dawn to dusk farming rocks. It was their life plan. The Germans who immigrated here from the Banat region in Europe had a saying: 'To the first generation is death; to the second, hardship; to the third, success.' May we justify their sacrifice and fulfill their dreams."

Karen saw she was not the only one at the table who was moved. "I wish I could meet him," she said.

"Follow me." Curt led the way to the front of the room, pushing through a throng of admirers. The governor turned. "Dr. H."

"I'd like you to meet Karen Grace. She's a Weiler, from Dickinson, although lately of California."

"Welcome back." The governor took her hand. "I hope the professor is extending plenty of North Dakota hospitality."

"He definitely is. In fact, we played a round of golf yesterday at the Bully Pulpit."

"Beautiful place. I wish I had more time for that." He guided them to a semi-private corner. "What brings you back home, Karen?"

"I'm visiting family."

"The best of reasons." He signaled the photographer. "Let's get a picture of the three of us. Give me your email address and I'll have a copy sent to you."

Karen handed her card to the governor.

"Human Resources? My goodness, the eighth circle of hell."

She laughed. "It can be."

"I'll tell you, Karen, I have this assistant who's driving us all crazy. I mean, he is talented but moody, and if he's having a bad day, it's all over with for the rest of us—wait a second. I'm sorry. We shouldn't be working."

She took the card back and scribbled her cell number on it. "I'll be here for a few more days if you want to talk."

"Just a few? Too bad for North Dakota." The governor's aide pulled him away and Karen followed Curt out to the terrace. The early June evening had already turned cool and he placed his jacket over her shoulders.

She leaned against him and they watched the red of sunset fade to purple dusk. The terraced grounds sloped downhill and away from the great hall, which loomed over the campus commons. In the distance, the carillon tower chimed eight o'clock.

Curt turned her around to face him. With his fingertips, he traced the line of her jaw from her earlobe to her chin, and Karen felt shocked, and then her resolve slipped. She lifted her chin and their lips touched, gently at first, then with more urgency. Her nerve endings tingled all along her spine as she tasted him, exploring the softness of his lips, drawing his tongue into her mouth. When she released him, she heard him exhale and felt his strong arms pull her close.

"You don't have to go back," he said.

"But I do." They kissed again, longer this time, pressing the length of their bodies together, breathing together.

The ballroom door flew open and Denise laughed. "Oh, my goodness. Well, too late now. Hey, you two, the band's starting."

They went inside where music made conversation impossible. It didn't matter. He pulled her onto the crowded dance floor and they swayed together, alone inside the swirling, noisy crowd. She moved with him, her eyes half-closed, feeling the longing in his touch. Being wanted was the ultimate aphrodisiac, and she imagined his bare skin against her own from lip to ankle.

She leaned back, rocking in his arms. He looked up at the ceiling, then back at her. Then he took her by the hand.

"What are you doing?" she asked.

"Hell with this. I'm taking you home."

Chapter Thirteen

They writhed and tore at the sheets until the candles guttered out and the old farmhouse groaned with exhaustion. When they slowed to catch their breath, they heard the yip and howl of coyotes hard at a meal and went at each other again, until her skin was raw and his was scratched. And still they feasted.

In the morning, a meadowlark sang Karen awake from its perch just outside the second-story window. Clothing was scattered across the braided rug and flung over a ladderback chair. Careful, not wanting to wake him, she rolled over and studied his face, pure in sleep. A small white scar, now almost hidden by stubble, cut across his jaw. She longed to trace the lines between his charcoal-grey eyebrows and kiss the crinkles at the corners of his eyes.

A breeze drifted across the room, in one window and out another, and Curt sighed. In the light of the morning she remembered everything they had done to and for each other, and smiled to think how beautifully her body had performed. Last night was madness—fabulous, soft, hot, wet insanity.

When his eyes opened she gasped in surprise and laughed, and he pulled her toward him, back to front. They lay like spoons, his voice deep against her ear. "You stayed."

"Should I have played hard to get?" she teased, but when the silence stretched, she felt stupid for asking.

"I'd have no defense," he said sleepily, and tightened his arms around her.

An hour later, she awoke to his warm hand sliding up her thigh and across her belly, and she tensed, remembering all those Midwestern meals she'd enjoyed of late. But when his fingers cupped her breast as if holding a baby bird and gently squeezed her nipple, she stopped thinking.

In the shower he soaped her up and down, made her sudsy and sleek and then leaned her against the warm tile and kissed her so deeply she couldn't feel her legs. When she opened her eyes, he turned her around and rinsed her off in the multiple jets, and she stood still and let him.

When the hot water started to run out, they dried each other off. He handed her a terrycloth robe from his closet and pulled on a pair of jeans and a U.N.D. tee shirt.

"Breakfast?"

"Starved."

Downstairs, she detoured into his office to check her email. While the computer booted, she studied her surroundings, trying to get a sense of him.

The room was furnished in Early Cattle Baron, with chocolate leather wingchairs and a pelt of some kind draped across the back of the sofa. A lariat hung on the wall next to a painting of two elk challenging each other in an evening meadow. A dented red lantern, its chimney cracked, perched on the edge of a book case. Yet in spite of his penchant for rustic and rugged, the room hummed with electronics, some of them so new Karen felt jealous. On a shelf above the desk stood a framed picture of a young girl on a horse. Her dark eyes and straight brows left no doubt as to who her daddy was.

When the website came up, Karen entered her login name and employee password and waited. The computer beeped, the login failing twice, but she felt only mild frustration. Wes often scheduled maintenance for the weekends. Next, she called her corporate voicemail, but there were no new messages. No news was good news. Karen stretched, reaching for the ceiling in a delightful shiver. Later in the day she would call Peggy at home. Right now, though, she was hungry.

The aroma of bacon lured her into the kitchen, where Curt whistled an off-key tune while scrambling eggs. "Find anything interesting in there?"

"Your daughter's picture."

"That's Erin. She just finished her first semester at Florida State."

Karen sat in a chair by the window. Outside, a weeping willow draped the front lawn and red climbing roses laced a fence along the driveway. "Is she coming home for the summer?"

"Nope. She told me she wanted to stick around for the summer session, but I think it's more about a boy with a boat."

"And her mother?"

Curt turned off the flame. "She got tired of Dickinson a long time ago. I raised Erin."

"That's rough."

He piled eggs and hash browns onto their plates. "It was a privilege."

When they finished, Curt took Karen out to the barn to see the baby. "She's three weeks old," he said, letting the foal nibble his fingertips. "Her mom needs a break. Do you ride? My neighbor's got a nice old gelding we can borrow."

Karen petted the mare's soft neck. "I used to, but I got thrown, and right afterwards I read a horse isn't much smarter than a chicken, so I never got back on."

"I'll get you back on." He grasped her by the robe's belt and kissed her.

"I believe you," she said when she could breathe again.

"When are you going back?"

"Day after tomorrow." She touched the foal's nose, a perfect velvet miniature of his mother's.

"What a drag." Curt left the horses and crossed the barn to the far wall. He sat down on a hay bale and patted the spot next to him. "Come tell me about your life there. Where you live, and about your work."

She clomped over in his big flip-flops, sat down and told him about it, how human resources had started out as something beautiful and promising and then turned into triage, but still she loved it. She talked of the energy and diversity of California, of desert and farmland and coastline and rainforest, of art and music and commerce.

When she paused for a breath, she remembered the time and grabbed his wrist. "I was supposed to go to church with Aunt Marie. She's probably called the police by now."

"Not a chance. Everybody knows where you spent the night."

"What is she going to think?"

"That you jumped the fence, and you ain't apologizin'?"

"Christ!" Karen hurried back to the house and changed into her cocktail dress and heels. When Curt saw her he started laughing.

"No sneaking in with this on, is there?" She looked forlorn.

He took her hand. "Come on. Let's get you home."

They rode in silence through the brightness of midmorning, through the fields sprawling away from his farmhouse to the leafy green streets of her neighborhood. In front of the house, Karen leaned back in his window and kissed him lightly. She wanted more, but felt eyes watching her from behind every lace curtain within one hundred yards.

When she straightened up, he sighed. "Not even a couple extra days? Are you sure?"

"I have no choice."

"There's always a choice."

She pecked him on the lips and went in the house, dashing into her bedroom and changing before Aunt Marie could see her in last-night's dress. Although Karen was flattered by Curt's attention, his attitude about her job irritated her. Nice that he'd carved out a sweet niche for himself, but that didn't mean everybody could swing the same deal. Especially now, in this economy, and at her age.

She checked her messages, and called Peggy. "There's something different in your voice," the older woman said.

"No, I'm just relaxing. This trip has been really good for me."

"Well, I'm about worn out. I'll be glad to see you back here."

"Day after tomorrow," said Karen. "It's been fun but I'm ready."

"See you then."

Aunt Marie was working in the garden, so Karen went outside to help. As she pulled weeds and tied up raucous young beans and peas, her fingers moved automatically in old, familiar patterns, freeing her brain to analyze every delicious detail of last night. Who knew her body would work so well? Turns out maybe she wasn't so old after all. She looked up and caught her aunt smiling.

Karen sat back on her heels. Aunt Marie's fingers, knobby with age and arthritis, were half-buried in the fragrant earth as she pulled weeds from around the base of a coriander plant. She hummed softly, looking up in surprise as Karen leaned down to hug her.

That evening she finished packing, checking and rechecking her tickets for tomorrow's flight. Finally, all that remained was to check her messages one last time. The last one was from Wes. He'd left it an hour ago, early evening in California, and he wanted her to call him right away. He answered on the first ring.

"Hey, North Dakota girl," Wes said. "You're up late."

"It's only nine. How was the conference?"

"It was helpful."

She waited, but he was silent. "I was just checking my messages and you wanted me to call."

"Yeah. I'm going through your files—"

"My files?"

"Yep. Got 'em here at home with me."

She heard ice clinking in a glass as he took a sip of his drink. "Did you have a question?"

"Thing is, Karen, I can't find your notes about contract negotiations with the lab workers, and I'm going to need them."

"The reason you can't find them is because I have the file with me here."

"I need it back."

"Sure. I'll bring it in Tuesday, bright and early."

The ice clinked again. "Why don't you go ahead and overnight that file to me, and anything else you have relating to these negotiations?"

Karen hesitated. "None of it will reach you before I get back there."

"While you're at it, why don't you send me anything else you've got?"

"Wes? Did I not mention I'm coming back Tuesday? Anything I have will be on your desk in a little more than a day."

"How about instead you overnight me those files, and then you can stay back there in the country for as long as you like?"

"That's nice of you, but I'm all packed. I have my tickets and I'm flying home tomorrow."

"Payroll's drawing up your last check, and I told them to throw in any of your unused sick leave."

"Pardon?"

"Well, you earned it, and I want to be fair."

She felt her legs wobble and flopped into a chair. "That isn't necessary. Not at all. I can be home by tomorrow afternoon."

"No need."

She took a steadying breath. "If I read you correctly, you're unhappy I took a week off, but I'd like you to understand. My mother died. I needed to take care of her affairs."

"That's a personal issue. You know I don't take those into account."

Karen gripped the phone so hard she accidently pressed a button and it beeped. "Right. But what you should take into account is my value to the company, and the difficulty and expense of replacing an employee at my level. I understand you may be annoyed that I was gone, but you have a lot on your plate right now. Let me just come back, pick up where I left off a week ago, and keep things rolling at the office."

"Thanks for your concern, but I can handle it just fine."

She finally cracked. "It's not a firing offense, for God's sake."

"Good-bye, Karen."

Her mouth opened, then closed. Air wasn't moving. Karen lowered the phone from her ear and stared at the thing as if expecting it to explain what just happened. Wes was insane. She'd only been gone a few days. She hadn't taken time off in years. She worked sixty, seventy, eighty hours a week on salary. The man was a fucking maniac.

Did he just fire me?

Aunt Marie walked over, dishtowel in hand. "Is something wrong?"

"Um, no. Nope. Not at all. Everything's cool," she babbled. "You know what? I think I'll go for a walk."

"It's dark, honey."

"I'll be careful."

She sprang from the porch like a puma and hit the pavement in a sprint. Turned left at the sidewalk, but the sidewalk couldn't contain her, and then she was in the street, her footsteps landing hard.

Fucking bastard fucking bastard fucking bastard.

Her mind raced as fast as her pulse.

Fired? He was out of his mind. She was so busy, she had so much going on, that he was a fool to fire her; too stupid to even know it. He would learn it eventually, but by then the damage would have been done.

And who the hell was he to fire her? San Francisco corporate loved her. Lou, the CEO, had told her so many times that he appreciated her dedication, her expertise, her institutional memory. They don't make 'em like you anymore, he said. He couldn't have approved this.

A car honked and she swerved back toward the curb, wild eyed and winded from the unaccustomed effort. She needed to call Lou immediately. Wes had no right. Karen had proven herself over the years. She was loyal, effective, and reliable. They couldn't be letting her go. She was too important; she had done too good a job. The people at corporate knew her, knew how long and hard she had worked. Nobody knew the job like she did.

Her pace slowed. What if Wes really did have the blessing of Lou and the higher-ups in San Francisco?

Could they be that stupid?

She sat on the curb, breathing in huge gasps. Karen knew the answer to that. Even in spite of her distaste, she had worked hard to form bonds with the porcine executives who treated Global Health as their personal bank, and she had no illusions. She kept her mouth shut and did her job, playing it safe while working behind the scenes to protect the company. As a result of her efforts, the guys at the top were printing money. Apparently it wasn't enough. They wanted her salary, too.

Overhead, a pair of bats circled the street light.

It did not make sense. If the top guys at corporate knew all the projects she was working on, and that she was in the middle of a dozen high-profile operations, they would never have let her go, if only to save themselves money and effort. A ton of work remained on her desk, critical work no one else could do. Who would finish recruiting a dozen new nurses for the city hospital? Who would interview the physicians for neonatal intensive care? What about the contract negotiations with the electricians? They'd threatened to walk, except Karen had won a temporary reprieve while she reworked management's offer. Who would handle that now? What would happen to the office?

What would happen to her? Finding another job would be impossible. Prospective employers would take one look at her resumé and know she was expensive. Even if age discrimination weren't in play, she'd probably have to take a giant pay cut to land a job. The idea of competing with some young thing fresh out of graduate school slayed her. Going on interviews would be like sitting in a bar trying to convince a guy that your clever, witty self should compensate for your wrinkles.

This is what my life has come to. I come back for my mother's funeral and I lose my fucking job. They can't fire me. I'm too valuable. They need me. People know me.

What am I going to do? Twenty-five years, my whole career, gone in one little phone call? Karen took a deep breath. She would call Lou Cullen at corporate. Lou would overrule Wes. He had to.

She turned back toward the house.

Chapter Fourteen

After a sleepless night, Karen waited until nine and then punched in the number of the executive secretary to the CEO. Even though the office was closed, she knew Janice would answer. Janice was never away from her phone. She worked even harder than Karen.

She waited while the call connected. Louis Cullen would fix this. Their friendship, or at least their professional acquaintance, spanned two decades. Over the years, she'd kept Lou up to date on the challenges and victories at Newport, and he had been appreciative, sending her encouraging messages in return. Every Christmas he tucked a complimentary, hand-written note into her bonus envelope. It didn't seem possible he would agree to her firing.

The phone rang and rang, seconds ticking away, until the executive assistant picked up. "Karen, I heard. I'm so sorry."

"You heard already? Does Lou know?"

"He would have to."

"Where can I reach him?"

"You can't. I'm serious. He left Friday for a month-long trip to Africa."

Holy shit. Karen sagged against her aunt's table. "Who else can I talk to? What about Freeman or Esperanza?"

"It's a holiday. Everybody's gone."

Karen lay on the sofa, fifteen hundred miles from home, jobless, and on the verge of divorce. Her delusions of security had vanished. Everything she knew seemed abnormal; everything she knew seemed to have changed. In middle age she was discovering it was true: a person could do her best at a job for years and still be out on the street because some fat-assed CEO bought himself an island and needed the money.

Aunt Marie stood in the doorway. "I'm fixing lunch. Are you hungry?"

"No, thanks." Karen moved her legs so Aunt Marie could sit down next to her. "I lost my job."

"Oh, dear. Just now?"

"Last night." Karen stared across the room, unblinking. "It's like I'm trash. Like I'm nothing."

"Can they do that? After all the years you worked there?"

"They can do whatever the hell they want. Sorry."

"You should talk to Lorraine's lawyers. Maybe they can help you."

"It's not illegal," Karen said. "I'm old. If they can hire somebody younger and cheaper, they can and do. Why not? It's business."

"Used to be, people would work for one company all their lives," said Aunt Marie. "Your father did. So did my Henry. They were loyal, and Dakota Gas took care of them."

"Yeah, well, those days are gone forever."

Aunt Marie brightened. "Maybe now you don't have to rush home."

"I still need to work. I need to go back and find another job."

"There are plenty of good jobs in Dickinson, what with all the oil. Maybe you could look here."

"I can't think about it right now."

"Maybe in a few days. You're in shock right now, but once you leave, you don't know when you'll ever get back. Think how happy it would make Lena, to know you're living here and safe."

Right now all Karen wanted to do was escape. She'd done her best and where did it get her? All that duty and obligation hadn't protected her from anything. She wiped her eyes and leaned into the warmth of her aunt's embrace.

"Change is hard," said Aunt Marie. "But in the long run, maybe this is better." She gave Karen a squeeze. "I don't want to add any pressure on you, but if you decided to stay, you could have this house back. Free and clear."

Karen pushed away. "This is your house."

"It's still in Lena's name. Let me finish," she said when Karen began to protest. "Years ago, Lorraine and Jim asked me to move in with them. They even remodeled their place so there's a mother-in-law's cottage at the east end of the property now."

"I'm not moving back, and even if I were, I wouldn't kick you out."

"You wouldn't be kicking me out. It would be a blessing. Listen to me, dear. I'm eighty-six and living alone is getting harder. We knew this day would come. So you can have your house back."

"I'll deed it over to you."

"Do what you like. I'll still move in with the kids."

Karen wanted to escape, to go somewhere where nothing mattered, nobody knew her, and she was entirely free. For the moment, though, she was stuck in North Dakota. "Can I borrow the car?"

Dakota Blues

She hit I-94, a strip of solitary asphalt stretching across the state. Propelled by a sense of claustrophobia, she motored through seemingly endless farmland, racing westward toward the Badlands. The rush of the wind coming in all four windows stung her eyes, but the tears never showed up. A half-hour later, she turned off the freeway at Teddy Roosevelt National Park, passed the visitors' center, and followed the narrow road along the Little Missouri until, at the end of a tree-shrouded lane, she arrived at a campground. She cut the motor and sat quietly, listening to the shriek of a redtail hawk and the rustle of the cottonwoods.

What am I going to do?

No answer.

Locking the car, she trotted down a willow-edged dirt path until reaching a clearing, past a deep depression in the soft sand, still wet from the bison that had rolled in it after crossing the shallow waters. The wallow was large enough to accommodate a car. Beyond the wallow, the path disappeared over a berm. The herd could be right there, just out of eyesight.

You're insane, she thought as she marched up the berm.

I don't give a shit, her inner brain responded.

"Hey!" She yelled, topping the berm. Lucky for the bison, the herd had moved upriver and now grazed along the banks of the Little Missouri, safely out of range. Karen stood glaring at the dozen animals, muttering to herself and thinking she was losing her mind.

Get it together. You're not twenty-two anymore.

Back in the car, she cruised slowly through the park, gathering herself and feeling calmer. She played tourist, stopping at turnouts and viewpoints, using her phone to snap pictures of the red scoria buttes and cap rock pillars. Near the western overlook, a small band of wild mares and foals clattered across the road in front of her, their iron-gray stallion bringing up the rear. He stopped in the middle of the road, nostrils flaring, tossing his head imperiously and pawing the ground. Way too soon, the horse wheeled and charged after the mares. Karen didn't move, awed by the sight.

Thank you, she whispered, the breeze stealing her words.

That night she sat out on the porch with Aunt Marie. The two of them watched fireworks streaking overhead through the dark sky, her very own independence day.

Chapter Fifteen

Karen knocked on the door and waited. She heard shuffling, and then Frieda appeared through the dusty screen. "I thought you'd come by eventually." She unhooked the door and walked away, leaving Karen to let herself in.

Inside, the air was thick with the smell of new paint and cleaning products. The living room was bare and the carpet bore tracks from a vacuum cleaner.

"Spring cleaning," said Frieda, hobbling into the kitchen. "I got some of the kids from down at the college to help me."

"Where did the furniture go?"

"Want some coffee? I can make fresh."

"No, thank you."

"I'll get you water, then." Frieda took a glass from the cupboard and held it in the general direction of the dispenser in the refrigerator door, splashing most of it on the floor. She backed away, the glass still mostly empty. "I hate this stupid thing. I told Sandy I didn't want it. Get me a plain old icebox, I said to her. I said I don't need anything fancy. But no. Girl's got more money than brains."

Karen tore a couple of paper towels off a roll and wiped up the floor, then washed her hands, filled two glasses with ice water, and set them on the table near the window. While she worked, Frieda stuck a knife into the center of the pie and sawed crooked lines toward the edges until she had managed to carve out two uneven slices. "Get some plates from that cupboard there. The whipped cream's in the Frigidaire."

Karen sat down and took a bite of the pie. Either processed food was improving or her standards were slipping. It was delicious.

"Have some whipped cream."

"I shouldn't." Karen took the can from Frieda.

"Stop worrying. You can do with a few more pounds."

"I'm glad you think so, because ever since I got here I've been eating." Looking around, Karen noticed the kitchen counters were bare. The walls held no pictures or knick-knacks of any kind. Even the window over the sink lacked curtains, although she could see nail holes in the upper corners.

Frieda nodded out the window. "There's the Roadtrek. When we're done I'll show it to you."

The RV, parked under an aluminum canopy, resembled a large passenger van whose top and back end had been extended. The roof sloped upwards behind the driver, giving the inside an extra foot and a half of headroom and allowing for a bank of skylights along the front. The tires were shaded by big square pieces of plywood, and the windshield was covered by a heavy vinyl drape. The light-blue paint gleamed.

Frieda juggled a ringful of keys until she managed to unlock the double doors on the passenger side of the van. "Take a look here."

Karen opened both doors wide and stepped inside, half-expecting to see an overheated, dusty cavern sprinkled with mouse turds. Instead, the interior looked almost new. She helped Frieda up the step.

"You see how nice it still is? Russell kept everything looking good." Frieda's fingers moved slowly over the blue velour, coaxing memories from the fabric. Then she pointed at the glove box. "In there's the manual. You can read it while I get some air in here." She moved toward the back, cranking open windows.

Karen slipped into the driver's seat and began thumbing the pages. The van was called a Roadtrek 190 Versatile because of all the ways the interior could be rearranged to suit the traveler's needs. In the rear, for example, a dining table stood between two bench seats. At night, the table could be stowed and the benches made into a bed. In the van's midsection, a person could shower in the walkway between the galley and bathroom by closing expandable folding doors on both ends and letting the water run out through a drain in the floor. Toward the front, the driver and passenger seats swiveled around backward so the campers could eat at a small, removable table. If needed, the shotgun seat and the one behind it could be connected to make another bed, and that area partitioned off from the rest of the van for privacy. It even had an awning outside that would shade the entire passenger side of the vehicle, creating a porch over the double doors. "It looks like it's never been used."

"We used it plenty, but Russell kept it up. He even built the carport so it would be out of the weather."

Karen felt around the base of the seat until she found the lever that released it to swivel around. Facing backwards into the van, she noted that the galley was equipped with a sink, stove, microwave, convection oven, and a small refrigerator. A television hung from an overhead cabinet, easily visible from the pivoting captain's chairs in the front of the van. A control panel behind the driver contained LCD displays for power, water, lighting, and temperature.

If a person wanted to take a nice slow trip across the country, the Roadtrek would do the job.

"Even though I don't drive it anymore, I have Nate come by twice a year and look it over, so it's in good shape," Frieda said. "What do you think of my chariot, young lady?"

"I think you could get a pretty good price for it."

"You're dodging me." Frieda shook a finger at Karen. "You know what I'm asking. Now that you've seen it, doesn't it make you want to go?"

"Camping would be hard on my back."

"I can get any drugs you need. One of the benefits of old age." Frieda sat at the dinette. "So many memories. Do you remember that one year Russell and I went with your family and a bunch of other people to Yosemite?"

Karen nodded, but the memory was vague.

"You were little. But maybe–do you remember the Firefall up on the cliff? They don't do that anymore but it was something."

"I do remember that."

Frieda nodded. "But then the government put a stop to it."

"I remember us singing."

"That's right. Even though there were hundreds of people watching in the meadow, it would always get real quiet before they shoved the coals off the cliff. And everybody would sing 'America the Beautiful.'" Frieda's eyes were closed. "I always thought that should be our national anthem."

When Frieda went to stand, Karen grasped her arm, her skin cold even on this warm afternoon, and helped her step to the ground. Frieda locked the van and turned toward the house.

"Can you imagine being out under the stars at night? I hate hotels. For my money, if you've got an RV and the weather's nice like it is now, why, you open out the awning and eat outside. You listen to the birds and or you wave to the neighbors as they walk by. You can make all your meals in your own little kitchen. You save money, you don't have to dress up, you eat when and what you want."

Karen heard ravens squawking and looked up. High overhead, a pair cavorted in the warming breezes, climbing up and diving together, over and over again. Suddenly one flipped over and glided upside down for several seconds before righting itself. She blinked with surprise. "Did you see that?"

"They do that all the time around here."

"I've never seen anything like it."

"Probably lot of things you haven't seen." Frieda started up the porch steps. "You're missing out on life, girl. You need to get out on the road."

"I have obligations."

"You might be passing up an opportunity. Lots of people say they do their best thinking on the road. Something about the whatchamacallit—the lizard part of your brain—working while the thinking part runs free. Maybe it would help you figure things out. Anyway, when was your last vacation?"

Karen didn't answer.

"You can't remember, can you? You need some time off, but you're afraid to take it. You think if you keep your nose to the grindstone, nothing bad'll happen, but you have to learn there's no guarantees. Lord, I have to catch my breath."

Frieda sat down on the porch swing and gestured for Karen to join her. "I don't know if you remember but I worked at the city office. Lena brought you there to see me a couple times. Then you got older and you'd be with your friends, hanging out at the dime store next to where I worked. Sometimes I'd go in there to pick something up and I'd see you."

Karen smiled. "I liked the soda fountain. The root beer floats were the best."

"You were always quiet. Seemed like the smart one. Unlike those gals you hung around with. You never got in any trouble. Lena was proud of you. I thought you seemed old for your age."

Karen had in fact felt as if she were an old person from a very young age, getting good grades, earning her own money babysitting, and working as a Candy Striper at the local hospital. She hung around with girls who offered superficial friendship in a world defined by adolescent superficiality, but it was the only available hedge against loneliness.

"If I were you, I wouldn't be in such a hurry to get back."

"I'm not sure what I'm going to do."

"And now you're sparking with that boy Curtis. You know he's never going to marry again, but he'd be good company."

"I'm not sparking with anybody. I'm married."

"You didn't let that stop you, from what I heard."

Karen started to get up. "Aunt Marie has a bunch of relatives coming over tonight."

"Let me tell you something." Frieda stared off across the yard, past the Roadtrek and the fence, to the open fields beyond, where a man drove a tractor up and down rows. Her head bobbed on her crepey neck, and her hands shook. "I feel bad about all you've been through, but it was lucky for me when you came into town. The minute I saw you, I got a feeling we were going to make this trip. Lena knew my ways. Now she's gone. You're all I've got."

Karen noticed the scent of lilac, and saw the vines overhead were dripping with the delicate blue clusters. She stood and plucked a blossom, holding it close to her nose.

"But I'm not in the best health and in case you didn't notice, I'm old. You should think about that while you're deciding what to do. I'm ninety-one years old this October, if I make it. I've had a good life. I miss Russell but I don't stop living."

Karen didn't answer.

"Who knows why things happen? Life is funny. So when you showed up, I tell myself, 'If I can get her to take me on the road, it'll be good for her and I'll be able to see my great-grandbaby.' Anyway, I don't know who else can take me there. If they're young, they're working. If they're old, they can't drive any better than me. You're right in the middle. You're perfect." Frieda paused, her bird-like chest heaving with the effort of her speech.

I'm perfect. Karen smiled.

"It's hard when you're my age, is all I'm saying. I don't get around so good. Don't hear so good either. I want to see the baby and after that, I don't care." Together they watched the man on the tractor work the field. "That's Albert," Frieda said. "He still likes to farm that little piece of dirt. He doesn't get around that good any more, and before long that tractor'll be more than he can handle. Come to think of it–" she squinted at the small figure,–"that might not be Albert. His son, maybe. Albert used to put in canola. It was real pretty when it bloomed, yellow as mustard all the way across."

The five-o-clock whistle blew down at the freight yards. "I do believe it's happy hour," said Frieda. "Help me up." Inside, she turned on the kitchen light, hooked her cane over the back of a chair, and hobbled over to the cabinet next to the sink where she filled a glass with water and lined up an array of pills. "Bottoms up." She tilted her head back and swallowed down the tap water, popping pills until they were all gone.

"You're probably wondering why I bother." Frieda sat down at the table. "At my age, even if I get a stroke or heart attack, whatever happens, it won't be a problem for long."

Any reassurances on the tip of Karen's tongue died from sheer banality. What could one say to a frail ninety-year-old? For that matter, what did Frieda tell herself at night when she was alone with her large-print Readers' Digest, or the television squawking about a humongous used-car blowout over on Villard Street?

"I used to be a ball of fire, like you. Now I feel tired all the time, ever since a year ago when I lost my breath and it never came back. Up 'til then, I could forget about my aches and pain by staying busy, but now about all I have energy to do is sit and think. I think about Russell being dead, and Sandy and me not speaking, and the world changing so fast, and I kinda wish I had the guts to let go. But if I could just see Jessie and the great-grandbaby, I would stay alive long enough for that. If I thought you'd drive me, why, I could fall asleep easy at night thinking about getting out on the road for the first time since Russell died. What would that be like, seeing the Black Hills again–because that's what I'd like to do. See Mount Rushmore one more time, and sleep overnight in the forest. I want to smell pine and wood smoke, and eat dinner under the trees. I want to sit by the fire in the morning and have my coffee."

"You know I have to get back to California."

"That's what you've been saying."

"So I can't dilly-dally around, stopping at every tourist trap and point of interest."

"That's not a problem."

"All right then." Karen stood up. "I'll pack the van tomorrow and take it to the mechanic for one last look. Then I have a couple of other people I need to say goodbye to. Can you be ready to leave Friday morning?"

"I'm ready now."

Chapter Sixteen

Wednesday morning dawned humid, with thunderheads peeking over the horizon, and Karen turned on the air conditioner. As she approached downtown in the unfamiliar van, she appreciated the slow pace of traffic. The other drivers slowed in actual observation of the speed limit. They let each other cut in and out, not even honking when the car in front took a little longer than normal to turn into a driveway. Karen didn't mind. She waited while a car cut in front of her, confident nobody would pull out a gun and start shooting.

At St. Joseph's Catholic Church, Karen followed a sidewalk around the back of the red-brick building until she found the office, which was unoccupied. The telephone on the desk was ringing, but no one appeared to answer it. Finally the answering machine picked up. Karen sat in one of the visitor chairs and pulled her checkbook out of her purse.

When the phone started up again, she heard a distant curse followed by hurried footsteps and the clatter of beads. Father Engel barreled around the corner into the room, his face reddening when he saw Karen.

"Oh, my goodness, I'm sorry," he said. "I didn't know you were here."

He took the call, nodding and scribbling on a message pad as he promised to send a fax. He hung up and loaded a document into the machine. "Be with you in just one minute," he said to Karen. When the feeder flailed and jammed, he looked up at the ceiling, his lips moving.

She stood up. "Can I help?"

"I don't think it's fixable," he said, shaking his head. "It's been acting up but I think this time I fried it."

"Well." Karen opened the back of the machine, removed and reloaded the paper and pressed *send*. They stood together watching as the paper disappeared.

"Miraculous," he said.

"You might consider a new one." She handed him the check. "Thank you again for my mother's service. It was beautiful. You must have put a lot of thought into choosing the readings. It meant a lot to me."

"Thank you." The priest opened and closed several drawers before anchoring the check under a stapler. "I'm at sea. My secretary quit. She was the third one this year, and it's only July. I'm beginning to wonder if it's me."

The man may have been the representative of Jesus on earth, but he reminded Karen of one of her clueless young supervisors. "I'm sure it's not you."

"What else can it be? The work isn't very demanding."

"Would you like an outsider's opinion?"

The priest spread his hands in a gesture of helplessness. "Please."

"You probably don't pay a lot, and you recruit by word of mouth. You feel sorry for, and therefore hire, people who are related to your parishioners. Everybody is happy for a while, but your employee isn't very skilled and problems arise. Feelings get hurt, and you feel guilty. Then to top it off, the worker is alone here most of the time and this office is depressing. Sorry."

"Ouch," said Father Engel. "You're right. It isn't the most exciting job in town. And yes, when I have a vacancy I mention it to a few people, and there's always somebody who knows somebody who needs a job. I thought it was good for parish morale to do it that way, but the results have been disappointing." He sat down at the desk, a dejected secretary in priest's clothing.

"Maybe if you advertised you'd get a better range of choices."

"We don't have the money to advertise."

"You could do it for free online."

"Hmm." He looked skeptical.

"Okay, how about the parish newsletter? Or a flyer you distribute on Bingo night?"

"That might work."

She wrote on the back side of her business card. "Here's a website where you can download basic application forms for free. And why don't you say in the flyer that applicants should bring a certificate of competence from the state job service?"

"We have one?"

She took the card back and wrote some more. "North Dakota does job testing and training. You might want to send your flyer to the Dickinson office."

He studied the card. "You found this out in a week?"

She smiled. "It's a bad habit."

He pocketed the card. "Would you mind helping me with this?"

"I can draft the flyer and drop it by tomorrow, but I'm leaving in a couple days." She thought about it. "Tell you what. I met some businesswomen in town. Maybe they can help."

"Anything would be appreciated. Now let's talk about you and Marie. How are the two of you doing?"

Karen sighed. "I stayed longer than I should have, but I'm glad I came. It's been good for both of us." Thunder rolled in the distance.

"Looks like we're going to get our first monsoon of the summer." Both of them stood, and Father held the screen door for her. The air had grown heavy, and clouds boiled on the horizon. At the next rumble of thunder, he said, "*Der himmlische Vater zankt aus*."

"'The heavenly Father is scolding,'" said Karen. "Mom used to say that."

"A lot of the older people still prefer German. Do you remember?"

"*Ein wenig*," she said, surprised it came back. "A little. How did you learn it?"

"I grew up in Grand Forks. Everybody in my family speaks German. Here, let's sit." He gestured toward a bench near a shrine of St. Joseph. A red cardinal hopped around, pecking at the seeds that had fallen at the base of the feeder. "Do you have someone to talk to in California?"

"Oh, yeah. Tons of people." She sat down on the hard cement bench.

He pulled a pack of gum out of his pocket, offered her one, and unpeeled a strip. His hands were bulky and strong, hands that two generations earlier would have guided a plow. He crumbled up the wrapper and put it in his pocket. "Are you familiar with the stages of grief?"

"As much as anybody."

"Different schools of thought. People go through a whole range of emotions, and just when you think you're moving on, it can hit you again. We learn to live with it, but we never get over it, and I think this is a good thing, frankly. It means our relationship with our loved one continues even in death."

Karen looked down at a trail of ants discovering a crumb on the sidewalk.

"I don't think people give grief enough credit," he said. "It's essential for our development as mature human beings, but it's so painful that we try to rush through it."

"You can't blame us. Nobody wants to suffer." She stood and turned her face into the breeze, smelling the clean fragrance of rain on distant farm fields.

"What's next for you, Karen?"

She smiled down at the priest. For maybe the first time in her life she wasn't sure.

Chapter Seventeen

She dropped off the van, got a ride back to Aunt Marie's, and borrowed the car just in time to join the professor and his crew at a dig outside town. Picks rang against stone as a half-dozen college students coaxed answers from the shroud of history. Karen, protected from the sun by a big hat of Curt's, brushed at her own little mound of rock, hoping to expose tooth or bone, but they were almost done for the day and so far, all she'd found was rodent poop. She watched as he stopped by one student and then the other, offering encouragement or explaining.

"How're you doing?" He squatted next to her, his brown arms resting on muscular thighs.

She pushed back her hat and wiped her arm across her damp forehead. "Interesting but hot."

"Let's take a break." Curt called to the students, who put down their tools and drifted toward the picnic table. Early that morning, they'd constructed a shadecloth cover, and now they claimed chairs out of the midday sun. Curt reached into a cooler and handed around ice cold bottles of beer. "How else do you think I lure them out here?" he asked, smiling at Karen's look of surprise.

A young man flopped into a folding chair in the shade, beer in one hand, a bone in the other.

"I found a *Champsosaurus* last summer," said a willowy brunette. "The Smithsonian in Washington acquired it."

"What Brittany is too modest to tell you is they also offered her an internship next semester," said Curt.

"They don't pay but it's good experience."

"They'll snap you up in no time," Curt said, beaming.

When the refreshments were finished, the students returned to the dig. Karen felt the wind pick up, lifting the heat and lassitude of the afternoon. On the horizon, clouds were building in anticipation of a late afternoon sprinkle. She rested her head against the chair back, her eyes closed, as she savored an unfamiliar sense of—was that it? Contentment?

"You done with fieldwork?" Curt held his beer bottle so the condensation could drip onto the sand.

"I think I'll watch for a while. You go ahead."

"Let them. They need the experience. Want to share this?"

Karen held the cold bottle to her cheek. "What I'd do for a swimming pool."

"There's a pond not far from here. But I don't think we have that much time." He inclined his head toward the west, where anvil-shaped clouds were forming. "Another hour, max."

She handed the beer back to him. "Your students like you."

"They're happy to be outside. Beats working." He started to take a sip, but stopped. "What?"

"Watching you with them. It reminds me what I liked about my job." She leaned forward. "Josh over there reminds me of this maintenance supervisor I hired a couple years ago. He was one of my best hires. This guy was such a natural leader, he influenced people without even trying. The other department heads started asking him for advice about how to supervise, and he got invited to hospital staff meetings and everything. We had to get him an assistant. That's what I miss—the chemistry, the possibilities. In HR, if you do your job right, it's alchemy."

"You're an optimist, aren't you?"

"I do tend to see people as gems, but sometimes you have to dust them off and polish them up before they shine. But there's another thing." She stopped to watch a couple of students playing grab-ass instead of working. "It's what I know. I put in a lot of time getting to the top of my profession, and I don't want to throw that away. I just turned fifty—"

He gasped in mock horror and she laughed. "Well, I did, and I think with maturity you settle in, you feel more comfortable with what you're used to. Breaking trail is for young horses."

"Or for mature and experienced horses." He handed back the beer. "Besides, fifty is nothing. I don't count the first twenty years. What does being an infant have to do with where you are fifty years later? You're gathering data. What counts is what you do after you acquire that data."

She nodded. "I like it. That means I'm thirty. I'm in my prime."

"Exactly—you are in your prime. You're way too young to play it safe. When was the last time you did something wild? Changed anything big?'

"Saturday night."

"Oh, God, yes." He rubbed his face, stood up, and pulled on his hat. Standing with the billowing clouds behind him, he said, "There will be a time to fall back and take it easy, but right now, you're tough, smart, and full of energy. Try something new."

"When was the last time you did?"

He squinted at the distance as he considered. "A month ago. I pitched a contract to a company in Florida, doing something I've never done before."

"What's that?"

"Population counts for the local fish species." He grinned at her. "Figured if I got it, I'd get to spend the winter months in the Keys."

"I'm jealous. I remember one winter in Islamorada–" She fell silent, remembering languid tropical afternoons and sunset dinners on the beach with Steve. "Nothing. It was a long time ago."

"I understand the pull of a big city. Did you know I taught at Berkeley? Twenty minutes from San Francisco, and I loved it. Every morning, before you even put one foot on the floor, more has happened there than in a year in Dickinson."

"But you came back."

He waved the kids in, and they started collecting their gear. "I did. I prefer having my base of operations here, but I'm gone a lot. I do consulting jobs all over the country."

"What about your classes?"

"I have teaching assistants. Rachel, Patrick's fiancée, is one of them. When I'm between jobs, I come back home to teach a few classes and get my bearings." He looked down at her, his grin wicked. "Come on, Karen, do something edgy. Move to North Dakota."

She burst out laughing, but the truth was, she couldn't. A flame had ignited in her mind, still so small as to be unrecognizable, and she had to fan it, study it, and satisfy the restless hunger it had somehow created.

He asked her again later that evening as he grilled steaks in the shade of the weeping willow tree in his front yard. And again on his porch as they sipped a soft blend of amaretto and cognac and watched night come on, but her response never varied, and finally they went to bed and the subject was finished.

She awoke around two to the distant crowing of a mixed-up rooster. Careful not to make any noise, she found Curt's robe and slipped downstairs. The back door opened with only a sigh, and she padded in bare feet across the wooden patio deck, a warming breeze whispering through invisible cottonwoods. To the east, the dark landscape rolled unimpeded by light of any kind, reaching and reaching until the featureless black met the blanket of stars and she knew she was seeing the horizon.

Chapter Eighteen

Karen held the phone between her ear and shoulder as she hunted for a place to stash another photo album. "I'm working on it right now," she told Frieda. "Give me a couple of hours. By the way, do you know where the battery backups are?"

"Look at the manual. That's why I gave it to you." Frieda hung up.

The van stood in Aunt Marie's driveway, doors agape, swallowing cargo and supplies. Aunt Marie and Lorraine helped Karen load, while Frieda called repeatedly to check on their progress.

Karen chucked the phone onto the front seat with one hand, shoved the album into an overhead cabinet with the other, and reached for the user manual. She had studied the instructions on driving and parking, leveling and connecting to shore power–a term that made sense if you thought of the RV as a boat. At this point she felt she knew the vehicle as well as her own house.

Although the van was small, it was well laid-out and had lots of empty cabinets, useful for stowing heirlooms. Following the directions in the manual, Karen removed the chair behind the driver's seat and made room for another stack of boxes. She ducked back into the shed for another load and came out holding a cylindrical lamp upon whose paper shade a winter prairie scene had been painted. The lamp had kept her company through most of her childhood, and she was happy to have it now.

The screen door slammed and Aunt Marie emerged from the house carrying the poppy seed grinder. She handed it to Karen and stepped up into the van, walking back and settling into one of the bench seats bracing the dinette table. "You know, this isn't half bad. I would have loved to have it in my camping days."

Karen lifted a hinged section of counter-top. "Check this out. There's a range, and underneath here, an oven."

Lorraine dropped a sleeping bag on the floor of the van. "Don't leave Frieda alone with the stove."

"Look over here. There's a complete bathroom. We even have a shower. Isn't this clever?" Karen pulled aside a section of carpet to reveal a drain. "You close the folding doors, pull the plastic curtain around you and turn on the water."

"Everything you need." Aunt Marie said without smiling.

That night after dinner, Aunt Marie pulled out her last round of artillery, the family photo albums. She sat on the sofa with a heavy album in her lap, the book's spine crackling with age. The first page held yellowing images from the family cemetery. With the magnifying glass, Karen studied a double headstone into which a black-and-white portrait had been set. "George and Elizabeth. Were they my great-aunt and uncle? Died in nineteen-eighteen. Look at this. They were teenagers."

"They were your great-greats. Or would have been. They were only married three months when the flu pandemic hit. He died first, but they didn't want to tell Elizabeth because they thought the news would kill her. Then she died, too."

"So sad," said Karen, turning the page.

Aunt Marie tapped a finger on the photo of a hardscrabble farm. "There were some good years after that, but then they had the Dust Bowl and the Depression. The drought turned everything upside down. You'd just about get a little crop and then here come the locusts, three, four times a year. They'd even eat the paint off the tool handles."

"I wonder if the farmers were ever sorry they came over here." Karen paid close attention, understanding that the sharing of family history was important to her aunt.

"The Germans had no other choice." Aunt Marie turned the page. "They had to escape the military back home or they'd get sent to the front lines to fight the Turks. They were nothing more than cannon fodder. So when word got out that you could get a hundred and sixty acres of free land in America, you better believe they got on the ships and came."

She pointed at a photo showing a line of children standing in front of a clapboard house. A woman on one end held an infant, and on the other, a man stood next to his grown son. The children, ten in all, ranged in age from the youngest to the eldest. "That's us. Mother and Dad didn't know what they were getting into. Winters like nothing they'd ever seen before. Lot of the settlers died, either from farm accidents and no doctors, or from childbirth. Think of your grandma doing all the cooking, mending, and farm chores, and all that time she's either pregnant or breastfeeding. They had babies every two years. Some of these families had fifteen, sixteen kids."

A picture showed a young woman standing in a buckboard wagon, holding the reins of a team. "Was it true when Aunt Frances was a teenager, she had to drive the wagon to town for coal? Mom said she was embarrassed in front of the men."

"That was a man's job, but Dad was dead, and she was the oldest. In town, they would look at her." A smile creased Aunt Marie's face. "When we ran out of coal, Mother had the little ones pick up cow patties in a gunny sack. Lena almost had to be whipped to do that, because when the weather turned warm and you picked up a patty, there'd be maggots underneath."

Karen, grimacing, turned the page.

"All us kids had to walk up and down the rows of crops pulling weeds from the mustard plants," said Aunt Marie. "I had to dip a sage branch into poison and put it all over inside the chicken coop to kill the lice."

Aunt Marie looked up from the pages. The light from the kitchen caught the deepening crags in her skin. "Mother and Dad worked like animals to feed and clothe all of us. It was the Depression, and nobody had proper shoes and the winters were so bad. We kids had to haul water from the windmill. When it froze, we broke it with an ax."

"Little kids! You worked like adults."

"We had to. In town they called us 'farmers' and said we were stupid, but farm kids grew up fast. One winter, when your Uncle Carl was a little boy, he went out in a blizzard to feed the cattle and almost couldn't find his way back. That was after Dad died. Mother got scared. Right after that, she tied a rope from the house to the barn so if it ever happened again, a person wouldn't get lost and freeze to death."

Karen sat quietly as Aunt Marie fingered the pages. What would it feel like to be one of only about three people left in your family that had shared such a life; the only ones who remembered the scrape and crunch of poor shoes breaking through snow to feed bawling cattle? What happened to the memories when you died, but more than that, what happened to the lessons learned, the maturation a person gained from living through such hard times?

"We had fun, too," said her aunt. "It wasn't all work. We'd get an old box and slide down the hill for hours." She chuckled. "Your mama was the youngest, so it was her job to make toilet paper. You take a page from the catalogue and do this." She pantomimed the scrubbing motion of tenderizing a piece of paper. "We liked the Sears catalogue. It was the softest."

Karen came to the last page and closed the book. "That was nice. Thank you."

Aunt Marie nodded sadly, but she rallied when Karen hugged her.

"I'll expect you back here next summer at the latest. Don't make me wait till I'm so old I don't recognize you anymore."

"I promise." The vow came easily, a poor gift to the woman who had offered to give up her house if only her niece would stick around.

Chapter Nineteen

On Friday morning, Karen drove the camper van down the street to Frieda's. It moved heavily now that it was fully laden with luggage, heirlooms, and groceries. The mirrors stuck out from the sides like giant dinner plates, a fact for which Karen was grateful since the RV was a couple feet wider on either side than any car in her experience. It was also longer. And taller. She maneuvered it slowly to Frieda's curb and set the brake.

At her knock, Frieda shuffled down the hall, peering up through thick lenses on oversized glasses. She wore a lavender velour track suit and a scarf tied over her hair. "Would you go on around the back and check the cellar door, make sure the padlock's on?"

"I did. It's locked."

"All right then. I got in the beans and squash over the last few days, gave them to the neighbors. They tried to hide but I found 'em. Come winter, they'll be glad to have them. Now what else?"

"I'll get your bags." Karen loaded the one small suitcase and toiletry bag. Then she stood in the kitchen, arms folded, leaning against the warped laminate counter as Frieda checked and rechecked that the appliances were unplugged, shades drawn, and windows locked, then started all over again. After a few minutes Karen went back outside to wait on the front porch. She perched on the warm cement steps, the smell of diesel and creosote wafting down from the rail yards. The grandfather clock in the parlor chimed ten o'clock before Frieda finally locked up the house for good.

Now they were leaving Dickinson, heading south on eighty-five. With the excitement of the open road and a belly full of caffeine, Frieda could not stop talking.

"I've been cooped up way too long," she said as they headed through farm country. "It feels darned good to be out."

Karen nodded and pretended to listen while getting acquainted with the demands of the Roadtrek 190. When a crawling green tractor suddenly appeared over the rise in front of them, she learned how to slow the van quickly without spilling its contents. When an oncoming eighteen-wheeler passed them on the narrow road, Karen figured out how to battle the wash from the rig along with the ever-present prairie wind. The fully packed RV cornered wider now and was slower to respond, but it ran smoothly.

Frieda was too excited to notice Karen fumbling around. "There's the sign for White Butte." She gazed at the sign as if it pointed toward heaven. "The Butte is the highest place in North Dakota. Wagon trains took it as a landmark on their way west. You need that, otherwise the prairie will swallow you up. Look, here's Amidon already."

The town consisted of twenty-three residents, a derelict gas station, and a run-down market, in front of which was parked a police car from the nineteen-fifties. Someone had dressed a mannequin in a policeman's uniform and placed it in the front seat to deter speeders. Several bullet-holes pierced the driver's door.

"Not much of a town," said Karen.

"It's big enough. You're used to the big city, but to people in North Dakota this is normal. Your friend Glenda has folks here. Their farm is out there to the west. Amidon is the county seat. They're very proud of that."

They passed the courthouse, as sleepy as the boarded-up collection of shops and falling-down homes on the other side of the road. "I couldn't imagine living here," said Karen. "Where do they go if they get sick?"

"There's a clinic a couple towns over, and they've got phones. They can call for help if you have an emergency. Nothing wrong with living in a quiet little place. Folks here are self-sufficient, and they take no guff from anybody."

Karen drove by a paint-peeled bar and grill. A crooked sign saying "Bernie's" swung in the breeze, and a station wagon sat rusting out front.

"A cousin of mine was in there having dinner some time ago," said Frieda, "when these two gents drove up in fancy business suits. They go sit at the bar and wait for the bartender. Pretty soon old Bernadette comes outta the back room and asks what they're having. They say they want some kind of fussy cocktails, and Bernie leans over the bar at 'em and bellers, 'Where d'ya think you are, Dickinson?'"

A stray dog tucked tail and scooted across the road in front of them. "Lots of people live around here on ranches or farms, but they're not close in," said Frieda. "You wouldn't even know they're there unless you followed one of those dirt roads." She pointed at a distant hill. "They're out a few miles, and they keep to themselves, but if they need supplies, this is where they come. Other than that, all they have is family."

Karen wondered about children raised in such isolation. A day at the country schoolhouse would seem a welcome dip into civilization, with the rest of their time revolving around family, chores, and farm life. People would be alone so much, they'd get used to the sound of their own minds. Characters formed in such a hardscrabble Petri dish would either develop iron in their spines or a desperate hunger for escape.

Frieda jabbered on, identifying every point of interest, and not letting Karen pass a single one without stopping. As soon as the van quit rolling, Frieda would haul her old body off the seat, expecting Karen to get out and share the magic, which she did with fake enthusiasm. Although she appreciated sampling the history of the area, they were behind schedule. She had planned on four hours to reach today's destination in the Black Hills of South Dakota, but at this rate it would be dark before they reached the mountains.

Frieda bent to examine a concrete-and-brass marker consecrating the memory of yet another dirt road, its ruts cut deep a century ago by prairie schooners. Karen kept telling herself to be patient. Soon enough they'd be in Denver, and she could drop the old woman and be on her way, alone at last. She hungered for some quiet time, and the chance to think and chart a path for the rest of her life.

They watched a herd of pronghorn antelope wheeling away from the road, their white rumps flashing as they sped away. "Lord, they are beautiful. I always appreciated the years Russell and I were able to travel. Sandy enjoyed it too, at least until she got to be a teenager."

They stopped for lunch in the agricultural Mecca of Bowman. Frieda argued for getting into the van's larder and making sandwiches for a roadside picnic, but Karen, imagining a mess in the galley, talked her out of it. Instead they found a sandwich shop where they sat at a table and watched the ranch folk come and go.

A few minutes after they got rolling again, Frieda's head dipped and she began to snore. Karen took a belly breath, her body relaxing as she realized until this point, she had been holding herself rigid. In front of her, the road spun southward without end. The wild fields on both sides of the road revealed an astonishing palette of light yellow, orange, pink, blue, and three colors of green: pea, mint, and forest. They were crossing the Great Plains, the ancient seabed that had drained in the Cretaceous, its primordial shells and fishy skeletons now layered under foot. South Dakota, though treeless, was not flat. Rather it was cut by red rock gullies and dotted with fertile wetlands, ponds surrounded by cat tails, and small conical rock formations that rose from verdant fields. Although fenced with barbed wire, the land was uncultivated. Knee-high green grasses were edged with rusty gold seed heads, and when the wind blew, the grass undulated in waves. Among the miles of hillocks and swales, the occasional roof or windmill or crumbling rock chimney bore witness for long-ago families.

A burned-out homestead disappeared in the rear-view mirror, the structure abandoned as if the land had no potential and no value. To Karen, long used to the wall-to-wall crowding of cities, this abandonment defied logic, until one looked around at the vast expanse of grassland. Going about her days back home, she had assumed America would soon be filled with houses, airports, and shopping malls but today's travel along the western edge of South Dakota dispelled that notion. This land would never be developed. There was simply too much of it.

It was no wonder these uninhabited acres had called out to oppressed Europeans in the last century. They crossed the Atlantic in steerage, landed in New York, and packed aboard trains that chugged farther and farther away from the cities to remote train stations, little more than wood platforms in the middle of the prairie. From there, they continued by covered wagon until an axle broke, the oxen dropped, or winter caught up with them. Then they drove their stakes and made the best of it.

Karen felt privileged to be rolling along solid blacktop in her gasoline-powered, self-contained schooner. Now and then she noticed a clump of scraggly trees, so rare, it was clear they were planted by someone who had tried and failed to muscle the land into submission.

Occasionally they passed boggy marshland carpeted with purple lilies and yellow mustard plants. Pronghorn grazed next to fat, sleek horses, not at all like the horses she passed in dirt lots in the more rural stretches of southern California. She wished every horse could fill its belly with wild grasses and roll around in clover.

The horizon was bounded by hills and flat-topped mesas, the land in the foreground eroded with ravines and grassy draws. It made a treacherous path for stampeding herds or the lone rider far from home or help. Once out here, a person would have no choice but to stare existential reality in the face.

Chapter Twenty

*I*n mid-afternoon, the van crested a rise beyond which lay a town, and beyond that, the Black Hills of South Dakota where their evening campsite waited.

Frieda awoke when she felt the van slow. "Is this Belle Fourche already?" She pronounced it 'bell foosh.'

"Almost." The highway brought them into town past a wrought-iron cemetery, over train tracks, past a granary, and over the river. A once-critical frontier outpost of sheep and cattle yards at the confluence of three rivers, Belle Fourche stood at the dead center of the contiguous U.S.

They merged with a procession of rumbling, hissing eighteen-wheelers and ranch trucks, their big duelies caked with mud. The road broadened to four lanes and carried them at shopping speed past the Dairy Queen, a package liquor store, and Black Hills Tractor. Outside a Pizza Hut, a couple of cowboys wore spurs on their boots and numbers pinned on the backs of their shirts, identifying them as rodeo riders. City hall, a humble one-story, stood on a lawn surrounded by gnarled oaks and cottonwood trees. Their cotton-fluff drifted onto the windshield like snow.

Outside town, the highway began to climb toward the Black Hills. The van handled the grade easily, and within the hour, Karen was inhaling the crisp fragrance of pine. The forested mountains, a novelty after the flatness of North Dakota, sheltered the old frontier town of Deadwood. The van crawled along Main Street with the flood of summer tourists, past the Holiday Inn and McDonalds lurking behind faux-eighteenth-century facades.

She turned into the parking lot of a small market next to a casino. "We should get some milk and something for dinner. How about burgers?"

"We'll need more than that. You don't want to go hungry out on the road." In the store, Frieda grasped at the handle of a shopping cart and pointed it down an aisle, throwing in boxes of Hamburger Helper and cans of soup.

"You're buying too much. We'll be in Denver by tomorrow night."

"This is how me and Russell always did it." Frieda turned around, her cheeks lightly flushed, her eyes bright. "Loosen up. We're on vacation. Hey, I'm going to stick my head in next door. Who knows? Might win a jackpot." She left Karen to take care of the bill and wobbled out the front door.

Fifteen minutes later, their larder packed to the limit, Frieda returned with a paper cup full of coins and a thumbs-up. "I got lucky. Come on, girl, we're burnin' daylight. We need to find a place to stay." She reached in the door pocket for the battered guide that had seen her and Russell though two decades of camping. "According to this, there are about a half dozen good places right around here. Let's start at Rock Ridge Resort and keep going until we find one that grabs us."

Karen put the van in gear. "I already made reservations at Sunset Pines RV Park."

"But how do you know we'll like it? It could be a dump."

"It got good ratings on the internet."

"You trust that thing?"

Karen pulled out into traffic. No sense trying to teach a ninety-year-old about the greatest tool to come along since the Model-T. A couple of miles up the tree-lined highway, she found the turnoff, a dirt road that jounced the innards of the RV no matter how hard she worked to maneuver around potholes and rocks. When the van hit a bump and one of the overloaded cabinets popped open, she pulled over to check out the mess. Two cardboard boxes had toppled over, spilling their contents all over the floor. It would have to wait.

Frieda chuckled. "That'll teach you to close 'em properly."

"I thought I had." The cabinets locked automatically to prevent this kind of problem, but Karen must have missed one of them. The sight of the mess in back made her want to open the bottle of Riesling she'd bought at the market. Up ahead, a park employee in a khaki uniform waved them toward the entry kiosk.

"One night," Karen said, handing the young man a twenty.

Frieda leaned closer. "Probably two."

They drove through the campground on a meandering lane to their campsite. A large boulder squeezed their narrow parking space.

"You better line it up perfect or you'll scrape the side," said Frieda.

"We'll be fine."

"It's going to be tight."

Karen inched the van forward, almost touching the huge rock.

"Too close." Frieda leaned forward, peering into her side mirror and blocking Karen's view. "This'll never work. You need to turn around and back it in."

"Please sit back. I can't see anything with your head in the way." The fatigue of a full day of driving began to hit her.

"I'll guide you." Frieda got out and left the door open. Karen had to unbuckle, get out of her seat, and lean way over to close it. Denver couldn't come soon enough. As soon as she got rid of Frieda, she'd find a luxury hotel for the night. She rested her head against the seat back, eyes closed. What would she give right now for valet parking? She pictured an ice cold lemon drop martini, a hot bath, quiet solitude…tomorrow night, by God.

She heard voices and opened her eyes. A man stood behind the van, speaking with Frieda, who nodded. He pointed at a path into the forest, and Frieda took off.

"What the hell?" Karen rubbed the base of her skull where a headache was blooming. The man approached her window. His heavy cologne scorched her nostrils, and his thick mustache showed white at the roots. "May I help you?"

"I need to back up without hitting that rock."

"Watch my signals." He turned and marched toward the back of the van. He wore belted grey dress slacks, and his thin hair was dyed a harsh black and combed over his bald spot. He positioned himself in her side mirror and guided her with military precision.

When Karen felt the back tires nudge up against a fallen log, she gave the man a wave and turned off the motor. From the glove box she reached for the manual, which included an arrival checklist. As she recalled, there were plugs and hoses and all kinds of things she needed to extract from their compartments. At the back of the van she found her helper waiting by the locked equipment cabinet.

He rapped one knuckle against its door. "You should have a level in here. If it isn't level, your refrigerator won't work."

"I think it's in the galley." Karen opened the double doors and stepped into the van, rustling through a couple of drawers and the cabinet over the sink, where she found the level.

The man peered into the vehicle at the mess that had spilled from the cabinets.

Karen followed his glance. Shoving aside photo albums and cutlery, plastic bowls and a scattered pile of embroidered cloth napkins, she cleared a path to the door and handed him the level.

Unsmiling, the man stepped into the galley and centered the level on a countertop, then a wall. When the bubble lined up between the two black lines, he grunted and handed it back to her. "Very good. I'll connect the electrical. I suggest you secure the freshwater intake. Be sure to bleach the spigot." At her blank look, he explained. "You don't know if a dog used it last."

She dug around under the sink and found a small bottle of bleach.

"Good. Dilute it by half and saturate the spigot, then rinse." He saw her thumbing through the user manual and frowned. "The white hose."

"Right." She lugged it out of the compartment and attached it to the clean spigot while the man attached the cord for shore power. He showed her how to lock the fresh water hose to prevent tampering and chocked the tires with rocks. "You wouldn't want your vehicle rolling downhill in the middle of the night."

"I really appreciate your help. By the way, I'm Karen."

"Wallace Franklin." His handshake was firm and icy. "Are you and your mother traveling alone?"

"She's not my mother. Thanks again for the help."

Just then Frieda limped out of the forest leading a slender, elegant woman. "Hey Karen, look who I found. This is Mae. She's from next door."

The woman smiled, her blue eyes lighting up a pale, delicate face. Her white-blond hair was swept up into a graceful chignon, and she wore light wool slacks and a silk blouse. "I see you found my husband. Frieda tells me you have no plans for dinner," said Mae.

"Please join us this evening. We would love to have your company." She glanced at Wallace. "Isn't that right, Wall?"

Wallace stared at his wife, who dropped her eyes.

"We don't want to inconvenience –" Karen began.

"Dinner sounds lovely," said Frieda. "What time?"

"We eat at six." He turned and disappeared into the trees. Mae gave a little wave and trotted after him.

"Great," Karen muttered.

"What's bugging you?" Frieda sat on the edge of the picnic table bench, her cane planted in front of her.

"I'm tired. I was looking forward to an early night."

"Don't worry about it. We'll have dinner, visit a little, and come back."

"Wallace doesn't want us there," said Karen.

"Who cares? He's the entertainment."

Karen unlocked a storage compartment and withdrew a roll of outdoor carpet and two camp chairs. She unfurled the carpet just outside the double doors of the van, arranged the chairs, and opened the awning. Then she went back inside to finish straightening.

"This is the life," said Frieda. "Smell that fresh air?"

Inside, Karen sat down on the dinette bench to take stock of the project. The van was strewn with housewares, clothing and collectibles. She'd have to figure out a better way to store everything.

"Russell and I had a rule," said Frieda. "You only bring it if you can't live without it. We limited ourselves to a few clothes, food, and a book. I don't know what he'd say if he saw your mess."

"Can I get you a book or something? Magazine?"

"I can take a hint. You go ahead and clean up. I'll watch the birds."

Karen slid a photo album into a box under the dinette and bent down to pick up her mother's wooden poppy seed grinder. Luckily it was undamaged. She rewrapped it in one of the old towels Marie had donated and tucked it into a cabinet underneath a big frying pan. As she worked she found that most of the small antiques were intact, but the counter top had been chipped by a flying potato ricer. The cups and silverware went into the sink for another cleaning. Clothes were tossed on the dinette table for further processing.

Karen straightened up, her lower back aching. The place was looking a lot better already and her mood began to improve until her stomach growled and she remembered where they'd be having dinner. At least somebody else would be doing the cooking.

While she debated her next move, her cell phone rang. Karen slid into the dinette. "Hey, Stacey, how the heck are you?"

"So are you having a mid-life crisis and never coming back?"

"I'm wandering around South Dakota with a crazy old lady. How are things in the real world? Did they fill my old job yet?"

"They're not even advertising," said Stacey.

"Who's doing the work? You and Peggy?"

"Peggy quit."

"What? What happened?" A blue jay hopped into the van through the open doors. When it saw Karen, it raised its wings in warning.

"She was in the break room when Wes came in and started being all condescending and everything. You know how he does, making you look bad in front of everybody. And Peggy flipped out. She threw her coffee at him. You should have seen it."

"Was it hot?"

"Hell yeah! I think he screamed. Then Peggy went back to her office, threw her stuff in a box, and walked out. She smiled and waved all the way out to the parking lot."

"I have to call her."

"Tell her hi from all of us. Peggy's our new hero." Stacey covered the phone to speak with a coworker, then came back, her voice lowered. "Hey, listen. Atlas over in Costa Mesa is looking for an HR person. It would be perfect for you and the money's good."

"Thanks for the tip. I'll look into it. Let's have lunch in a couple weeks." Karen hung up and dialed Peggy. "So, you're free, huh?"

"As a bird."

"You're not depressed or anything?"

"If I ever get depressed I'll call up the look on Wes' face when he saw that coffee coming at him," said Peggy. "I should have quit years ago, but I thought I was so all-fired important. What a joke. Wes and the rest of that bunch took advantage of me."

Karen heard ice clinking in a glass.

"I'm just sorry I didn't act sooner," Peggy said. "I stopped by a travel agency on the way home and picked up a shitload of cruise brochures. Did you know there's a line that goes around the world continuously? I'm getting a full suite with a balcony. Butler, evening cocktails delivered to your room, the works."

Karen sighed. "I have to say, I'm a little jealous."

"You're still young, but don't wait too long."

After they hung up, Karen called her housekeeper. Jean got right to the point. "When I got to the house this morning there was an overnight envelope on the porch. It's from a law firm."

"Would you open it?" Karen heard paper tearing, and Jean began to read. The lawyer's wording was clear. Steve wanted the divorce expedited, and the house put on the market immediately. Karen was surprised at the sudden warlike tone. Stupid of her to think it would go easily. "Set it aside. I'll be home in a couple days." She hung up, feeling light-headed. Maybe it was the altitude.

"It's getting on toward dinner time," said Frieda. "We should get going."

In the fading light, a bit of yellow-gold winked at Karen from under the driver's seat. She got down on her knees and gently extracted the rosary Father Engel had given her at the funeral. The last few rays of sunset illuminated the amber beads, lovely but pointless. She zipped the rosary into a pocket of her purse. Dickinson seemed very far away.

Chapter Twenty-One

When they stepped out of the trees, Mae jumped up from her seat by the campfire. Behind her, a motor coach occupied every inch of the lengthy driveway. A chandelier glittered within. The camp table had been set for three.

"Who's not eating?" asked Karen.

"Wall prefers his meals inside." Mae glanced at her watch. "In fact, he should be about ready. Please, make yourself comfortable. I'll be right back." She went into the coach to serve her husband.

"What a pansy," said Frieda.

"Shhh. They'll hear you," said Karen. "Mae has an accent. I wonder where she's from?"

Mae returned holding a glass casserole between two oven mitts.

"You set a nice table." Frieda tapped a finger on the china plate in front of her. "Is this Royal Doulton?"

"It's an old set we use for camping."

"Mine are more like leftovers from the Chisholm Trail."

Mae placed the casserole in the middle of the table, lifted the lid, and stood back proudly as the aroma of hot stew wafted on the breeze. "*Coq au vin.*"

Frieda glanced at Karen. "Bet you're glad now."

Mae began to ladle the steaming casserole onto their plates. "I'll tell you the secret to this dish. The older the bird, the richer the flavor."

Frieda nodded. "Many things improve with age. There's your proof. Boy, it feels good to be camping again."

"If this is what you call camping, I could get used to it." Her stomach rumbling, Karen watched Mae pour wine from a decanter into three glasses. "Thanks again for inviting us."

"It is my pleasure."

Frieda raised her glass. "To the journey."

Mae swirled the wine around in the glass and sniffed. She looked up at Karen, beaming. "I'm glad I saved this bottle. The vineyard of origin is five centuries old, and very small, near Lyon, France," she said. "I think you'll find—"

"Mae," Wallace called from the motor coach.

"Excuse me." She picked up the casserole dish and hurried inside.

"I wouldn't put up with that," said Frieda.

"Every marriage is different. You can't tell from here."

A few minutes later, Mae returned. "Don't let your food get cold because of me. Eat."

With her first taste of the savory chicken, Karen was transported back to Girard's in Laguna Beach, and a dinner celebrating one of Steve's first big promotions. The diamond earrings he'd given her reflected the candlelight as they held hands in the darkened booth.

But that was very long ago. She reached for her wine, the campfire blurring.

"Mae, you're not eating," Frieda said.

"Really, I am." Mae pushed her food around on her plate. When she saw Karen watching, she shrugged. "Well. I admit, he is anxious that I'm not in there with him. We have forgotten how to entertain."

"Nothing wrong with your entertaining," said Frieda. "This casserole is delicious. You must have gone to some fancy cooking school."

"It's a simple dish."

"Sometimes simple is better."

"Mae."

"Excuse me." She stood and hurried inside again.

"This is beginning to annoy me," said Frieda.

"Maybe it's her tradition. You know, old country."

"Old country, my rear end. Old man, you mean."

Mae returned. "My husband is not himself lately. His back has been bothering him more than usual."

Karen remembered how nimbly Wallace had moved around that afternoon, climbing in and out of her van and hunkering down to chock the wheels.

Frieda wiped up the last of her gravy with a piece of bread and sat back, hands over her stomach. "You two've been married a long time, looks like."

"Yes. Twenty-seven years."

"How did you meet?" asked Karen.

"I am originally from Sweden. One summer Wallace visited my workplace with an American delegation of engineers. I was asked to show them around and explain how our plant operated."

"Because your English is so good?"

"Yes, and also because I had designed the energy system at the plant. I have a degree in thermodynamics with a minor in hydrology." An owl screeched, and they all looked to the forest. "Of course,

I have not worked in that field since I married. Except to raise my family." She grinned. "I could always fix the plumbing."

Karen busied herself with the last bite of chicken.

"Raising kids is work, too," said Frieda. "You have two?"

"Yes, both girls." Mae's face shone in the firelight.

"You must be very proud. I myself have a daughter and a granddaughter and a great-granddaughter. That's where we're going now, to Denver, to see them."

"How wonderful for you. Mine are grown, too, with families of their own. It is more difficult to see them now. Everyone is busy, and there is the distance—one lives in Boston, the other in Texas." Mae stood. "Would anyone care for dessert?"

"That would be lovely." As Mae walked away, Karen snuck a look at her Rolex. The chill she felt wasn't entirely due to nightfall.

"Look there." Frieda pointed at the window. Inside they could see Wallace shaking his head, while Mae's delicate features wore the hint of a frown. "Bet she'd like to whack him with that spatula."

"She must be used to him. Otherwise, she would have left him a long time ago, don't you think?"

"I don't know what to think. She's so smart, and he's such a jerk. It always surprises me, what people put up with."

When Mae returned carrying a tray of glasses, Wallace followed behind with a bottle of cognac. Karen shivered. The camp fire had burned down.

While Mae poured, Wallace put more logs on the fire. When he had the flame blazing, he held a snifter up to the light, turned the glass to and fro, and swirled the cognac before sipping. He rolled the liquid around in his mouth, frowned, and set the glass on the table. "My wife tells me you're going all the way to California."

Karen wrapped her glass in both hands, warming the coppery liquid. "I am, but Frieda is only going as far as Denver."

His thin eyebrows rose. "You'll be traveling alone? Do you think that's wise?"

"Wise or not, she's going, and good luck talking her out of it. She's in a big fat hurry to get back," said Frieda.

"I'll be fine," said Karen.

Wallace scowled. "It's very risky in such an old vehicle."

"Now, that's where you're wrong," said Frieda. "That's a Roadtrek 190, built to last, and my Russell took care of it like nobody's business."

Karen agreed. "The van runs beautifully, and I'm planning to take it around the Divide, through Albuquerque so I can avoid the higher elevations. It's a bit farther, but safer."

"Always play it safe, that's our Karen," said Frieda.

Wallace cleared his throat, but Mae placed her hand atop his. "It sounds like fun."

"Well." He withdrew his hand and stood. "Good night."

Mae watched him walk away. "I'm sorry. He is a little bit not himself tonight."

"At least he has a nice place to rest. Your coach is beautiful," said Karen, hoping to break the tension.

"Yes. We live in it fulltime." Mae put another piece of wood on the fire. "It was Wallace's dream. He sold our home in Boston as soon as our youngest went away to university."

"I've heard of people doing that, selling their house and RVing fulltime after retirement," said Karen. "It seems fascinating. Do you like it?"

"There are plusses and minuses."

"It must be a great way to visit with the kids," said Frieda. "You travel around the country, stop at their place and park your own little house right out on the curb."

"That was our intention. However, we haven't seen either of them for two years, although we speak on the telephone frequently, and I can make video calls on my computer."

"Wallace is the one with wanderlust," Karen guessed.

"He likes to keep moving." Mae glanced back at the coach. "I would prefer to be near them more often. But Wall was raised in difficult circumstances. It has shaped him."

"He's lucky he found you, Mae."

"Oh, no. I am the lucky one. He is a good man." Mae drained her glass.

"Mae!"

She disappeared into the trailer, and Karen stared into the flames. She felt the amber liquid warming her insides, and the embers pulled her gaze into the glowing orange-white fissures in the fire pit. The beautiful destruction of the burning flames hypnotized her. Nothing's perfect, she thought. Regardless of the tension around the campfire, she felt at peace. She had seen so much beauty, given Frieda a chance to visit old sites, and ended their day with a fine meal. Under the influence of the cognac, the news of Steve's legal broadside receded into the background. Aromatic tendrils of wood smoke laced the air, drifting toward her and then away. For years she had reproached herself for not living more in the moment, but in this moment, she felt fully present.

The screen door opened and Mae approached, holding a framed portrait. "This is my family. Four generations."

Frieda took the painting, her hands gripping it tightly. "My goodness. This is a work of art, Mae."

"Yes, it's an original oil."

Karen leaned in closer. In the painting, the two daughters flanked Mae and her mother, who held a great-grandchild on her lap. In the row behind, the sons-in-law stood grinning on either side of an impassive Wallace.

"It was painted in Sweden. That was the last time I saw my mother. She passed away soon after." Mae took the picture back, her eyes locked on the canvas. "She is the one who taught me to cook."

"She's beautiful, Mae, like you and the girls."

"I wish I could have visited her more often. When she became ill, I tried." Mae watched while Karen poured more cognac. "Wallace was uncomfortable flying. We argued for days. Even my daughters fought with him, and he finally relented, but we missed our chance."

Shaking her head, Frieda handed Mae the painting.

Karen capped the decanter and handed a glass to Mae. "I'm sorry about your mother."

Mae stared at the painting on her lap. "It is very hard sometimes."

They heard the sound of pots and pans clanking together, and Mae glanced nervously at the coach. "I wish he would leave the dishes. He thinks he is helping but he has so little patience." She flinched as a kettle hit the floor.

"Goddamn it!"

Mae jumped up as if sprung from a catapult, her eyes fixed on the coach, forgetting the painting. Too late, she felt the frame leap from her fingertips. The three women lurched forward as one, trying to grab it, but in her panic Mae batted the picture toward the roaring logs. With a scream, she watched as the painting landed in the center of the flames and began to blacken.

Karen grabbed Mae from behind and pulled her back from the fire pit. The three of them watched in horror as the flames licked the canvas and the faces of Mae's family disappeared. When the frame had curdled to a blistered black rectangle, Mae fell back against the table, a strangled sound escaping her throat. Karen wrapped her in a hug. Frieda was speechless. They stared at the fire until the painting was indistinguishable from the rest of the charred logs.

Mae slipped from Karen's embrace. "It was inevitable." With small uncertain steps, she returned to the coach, closing the door without a word.

The camp fell silent except for the snap and snarl of the fire pit. Frieda, her limbs trembling, pulled her coat tight and reached for

Karen's arm. Together the two of them felt their way through the dark woods, the icy pine air burning their windpipes. Night in the Black Hills had fallen with a deep chill.

Chapter Twenty-Two

"We should have brought a flashlight." Frieda clutched Karen's arm. Away from the fire, their teeth chattered.

"I think the moon's full enough, once our eyes adjust." Karen matched her pace to Frieda's, inching back to the security of their camp. In the dark, she unlocked the RV and felt around for the light, then helped Frieda into the van. While Frieda leaned against the kitchen counter and shivered, Karen figured out how to turn on the heater. Then she pulled bedding and pillows from a compartment, and converted the dinette table in the rear into a bed.

Still in her velour track suit, Frieda burrowed under the covers and groaned with relief. "My God, I forgot how cold it gets up here."

Karen pulled the curtains closed over each window. She reconfigured the seats in the front of the van, turning two captain's chairs around to face each other and connecting them with a mattress board. Next she laid down a layer of bedding, and finally a sleeping bag lined with down. Shivering, her skin covered in goose bumps, she changed into a pair of sweats and dove under the covers. She reached for the light switch. "Good night, Frieda."

"'Night."

Silence fell in the pitch-blackness. Karen looked up at the ceiling, or rather, where she assumed it was. The darkness was so complete, a hand could have reached out and touched her nose and she wouldn't have seen it coming.

"Frieda?"

"Hmm."

"I can't get Mae's face out of my mind."

"What a shame," said Frieda.

"I know. That picture meant everything to her."

"It's not just the picture." Frieda moved around, getting comfortable. "I meant her whole life. Here she is so accomplished and educated, and it all goes for what? A lifetime with that piece of garbage? What a tragedy."

"You don't know, though. She's smart, so I assume she weighed it out."

"Life with him? Hard to imagine she knew what was coming."

"Every marriage is a mystery." Karen didn't want to remember the look of despair on Mae's face. Shivering, she tried to focus on tomorrow and the road ahead. One more night on the road and then they'd be in Denver.

"I hate to see women sacrifice themselves. Your mother fell into that trap, I'm sorry to say. Not me. I went right out and got a job. I worked even when I was raising Sandy. Russell didn't mind. Not like it would've mattered. I would've done it anyway."

The van rocked slightly as Karen tried to get comfortable. She hadn't yet mastered the art of sleeping in the narrow bed and feared she'd dump out onto the floor if she weren't careful.

"What about you?" Frieda asked.

Karen lay still. "What about me?"

"How come you're getting divorced?"

"Can this wait until tomorrow?"

"Sure, you don't have to tell me." Frieda sighed. "Well, as I said, I was good to Russell but we were independent. Not like Mae. I think she's like one of those—what do you call them—Stockholm people. Mae's like a prisoner."

"The picture falling into the fire was an accident."

"You can say it that way, but if I were her, I'd take it as a sign. Most people live like that, as oblivious as a frog in a pan of boiling water. It happens slow, over a whole lifetime. You don't notice until you're laying on your deathbed thinking, 'I was such an idiot.'"

The back of Karen's head started to throb thanks to the amount of wine and cognac she'd enjoyed. The older she got, the less she could drink. It wasn't fair.

Frieda, her voice sleepier now, continued. "I believe a person gets good at whatever they practice in life. In this case, Mae's gotten good at settling." She paused. "Are you awake?"

"Yes, but I'm exhausted."

"Do you ever think about what you want out of life?"

"All the time, I guess. I don't know. My head hurts."

"You want me to get you some aspirin?"

"No, thanks." Silence fell in the van, and Karen heard her phone vibrate softly. She grabbed it from the console, flipped it open, and read the text message.

"I miss U 2," she texted back before shutting it off.

Chapter Twenty-Three

The next morning, Karen awoke to the squawks of battling blue jays. The van was still dark, but the edges of the curtains were outlined by the gray light of dawn. She pulled the sleeping bag up around her chin. In the back of the van, Frieda slept quietly.

Karen remembered then that it was Saturday, and felt a reflexive sense of joy. She had worked enough years that weekends always felt special, even if she was currently out of a job. There was always hope she and Steve might be able to spend a little time together, maybe work around the garden or see a movie. In reality, when Saturday morning dawned, he slept in while she rose early to tackle the leftover work in her briefcase. She envied his casual approach, raking in both cash and clients without even trying. If he awoke before she finished working, he'd lean against the sink and watch her, his eyes clear and bright from untroubled sleep. Holding his coffee cup in one hand, he'd run the other through his hair, incredulous. "Why don't you hire somebody to do that?"

"No money."

"There's always money. They're taking advantage of you." He slurped his coffee. "I know you hate hearing this, but you're afraid to delegate."

"If something goes wrong, it reflects on me."

"So you apologize and move on. Tony Robbins says you should make a new mistake every day."

"Tony Robbins is his own boss."

"You could be too." Tiring of watching her, Steve would stretch, shower and head for the gym or golf course. Even now, the memory of his amusement rankled until she remembered he was gone. She tried to go back to sleep, but couldn't quit staring into the black hole of her former life.

He had wanted more of her time and attention, and over the years she tried to find a middle ground between working like a maniac and being a good wife, but the phone always rang, the emails and texts and instant messaging never stopped. That was the way of work in the twenty-first century. Years ago, a person could go home, put her feet up, and forget about work until the next morning. Now with new technology, the employer's leash reached all the way to your nightstand.

Steve used to say he was proud of her, and he enjoyed showing her off at corporate events. My wife, the executive, he'd say. She's my copilot. The sky's the limit.

Was that an act?

She rolled over, trying not to fall out onto the floor.

They were at lunch during a workday, at a fancy restaurant in Laguna Beach, when he told her he was leaving. He mentioned it quietly, when she was halfway through her salad. In order not to scream she had reached for the sweating glass of iced tea and taken too large a swallow, inciting both a severe coughing fit and brain freeze. When she stopped choking she caught him looking at his watch.

Now he was about to start his life over again with a woman half his age and soon, a baby. He'd be in his sixties, kicking a soccer ball around; in his seventies when the child would graduate high school. Karen wondered if the reality of it all had hit him yet.

Not like she cared.

Frieda coughed, and Karen waited, hoping the old women would sleep for another half-hour or so. Karen wasn't ready to start working, not just yet. When silence returned, her mind wandered again, surveying the desolate landscape of her future. She roved back and forth, from welcoming her new independence to fearing it, from wanting to be left alone to a fear she would be completely alone for the rest of her life.

Except there was Curt, and she smiled in the half-light. If nothing else, he had shown her that her body still worked. More than worked. It excelled. For that, she would always be grateful. She wondered whether he was up, and if she should call him, but she'd only just left and didn't want to appear clingy. But he'd seemed happy to hear from her.

Karen wondered if she'd made a mistake in leaving so soon after connecting with him. The guy had so much to offer, but on the other hand, she wasn't even single yet. She had never lived alone. What would it feel like, to have all your free time for yourself, never feeling guilty about neglecting your other? How cool would that be?

The downside, of course, was loneliness. In the right proportion, they called it solitude. But what if she got lonely? To whom would she go to fill that void? She had no real friends outside of her job.

Her ex-job.

She rubbed her eyes. Thinking too much, as usual. Frieda was still asleep. Maybe Karen could sneak out and get a quick shower before they hit the road and headed for a campground in Wyoming, three hundred miles southwest. Tomorrow morning she would drop Frieda in Denver and point the van toward California.

The thought of home invigorated her. She found her sneakers and coat, grabbed a towel and slipped out of the van, quietly locking the door behind her. The sun had not yet touched the tips of the pines, but already the tang of wood smoke scented the air. All around the sounds of an awakening camp echoed through the trees: the chop and rip of wood splitting into kindling, the clank of pot against stove, a car door slamming in the distance.

At the shower building, she removed her clothes and, shivering, stepped into the stall. She ducked under the hot water, letting it stream over her face. The steam enveloped her in a cloud of warmth as the minutes ticked by and the fog built an opaque white wall between her and the rest of the world. Here she could stop thinking, aware only of the heat and the sound of splashing water. No pain hammered against her heart; no ideas permeated her brain. Nothing compelled her to move, to comply with obligations, to assess her guilt or victimhood. She leaned into the stinging droplets, eyes closed, bracing herself against the fiberglass wall of the shower, wishing she could stay under forever.

When the door creaked and another woman entered the building, Karen turned off the faucets, toweled off, and dressed. Outside, her breath fogged in the cold air, but the sun had finally crested the pines and the campground glowed in the morning light. The smell of coffee and bacon made her hungry. When she opened the door of the van, Frieda sat at the table, munching a cold Pop-Tart. "Good, you're dressed. Mae invited us to go see Mt. Rushmore this morning."

"We agreed to leave early. Remember? We talked about this."

Frieda got up and threw the wrapper in the trash. "Your phone rang."

Karen played the new messages from Steve, each one more demanding than the last. She knew him well enough to read stress in his tone. No doubt his girlfriend was applying pressure. "Be reasonable," his message said. "I'm trying to make this easy for both of us." She shoved the phone back in her purse and went outside to roll up their sleeping bags on the picnic table. Frieda pulled on a jacket and sat in the sun while Karen organized and packed.

"Watch your head." Karen unsnapped the van's canvas awning from its metal poles and rolled it up, shaking the fabric slightly to dislodge pine needles and tree droppings without raining woodland detritus on Frieda. When the awning was fastened in its holder, she folded and stowed the poles, cursing when she pinched her finger in a hinge.

Mae appeared. "Good morning. Are you ready?"

"Turns out we can't go," said Frieda. "My friend here is in a big fat hurry."

"You're leaving so soon? That is a shame."

Karen gave a little wave but kept working. She was getting tired of explaining herself.

Mae shrugged. "I was hoping we could spend more time together, but in any case, I have something for you." She disappeared back into the trees.

Karen had been working around Frieda, but now she was down to the chair in which Frieda was sitting, and the rug beneath it. The old lady simply licked a thumb and turned the page in her magazine. "I'm not done yet."

Karen shook her head and went inside for one last look, but she could find nothing else to clean, pack, or store. Giving up, she went back outside and plopped in the chair next to Frieda. "You're dragging your feet on purpose."

"I'm trying to enjoy my story. Did you know that people forget ninety percent of their dreams?"

"Very interesting. Ready?"

"You've got such a burr under your saddle." Frieda looked up, her eyes magnified behind her glasses. "We're free as the breeze right now, nobody telling us what to do or where to go. Why do you want to mess with that?"

Karen stood. "At the rate we're going, the sun will set before we get to Cheyenne. I don't want to be out looking for our campsite in the dark."

"There's nothing to be afraid of." Frieda closed her magazine and looked around the camp, absorbing in one slow sweep the thieving jays, racing squirrels, and swaying pine branches. She held out her hand and let Karen pull her up out of her chair. Mae reappeared carrying two pink flamingoes.

"I never used them. Wallace feels they project a lower-class image, but I think they are cute." Mae handed them to Karen to pack.

"Adorable," said Frieda. "We'll set them up tonight."

Karen put her hand on Mae's arm. "I can't stop thinking about the painting. How are you doing?"

"I am fine, of course." Mae pulled away.

"If you ever need–" Karen began, but Wallace marched toward them, posture erect, arms held firmly at his sides. She hurried Frieda into the passenger seat and closed the door, wanting to avoid another dose of Wallace's smug advice. After one last hug for Mae, she started the van and shifted into gear. The gas pedal stuck momentarily, and when it released, Karen accidentally floored it. Wallace stepped back in horror as the van accelerated sharply, bouncing hard over a rock.

"You don't have to kill him," said Frieda.

Karen steered out of the parking space and onto the dirt lane that curved through the campground. Mae stood in the road, waving.

"So sad," said Frieda, watching in her side mirror. "She's going through the motions, acting like if she stays busy, she won't feel bad. There's something you might think about."

"Thank you, doctor." Karen glanced in the rearview mirror. Wallace was walking back to the campground, with Mae hurrying to catch up with him.

Frieda saw it, too. "The one who cares the most always loses."

Chapter Twenty-Four

Within thirty minutes, the van was tearing down the highway. The unfinished monument to Crazy Horse emerged out of the east, pointing them toward Wyoming. Karen began to feel lighter, and her impatience gave way to excitement. By this time tomorrow, she'd be heading home in glorious solitude.

The grasses had been getting shorter and dryer ever since they left Dickinson. The simple two-lane highway cut through miles of plainsland, strewn with rocks and carved by gullies. It was uninhabited but for small bands of cattle or antelope, and punctuated by the occasional windmill. Karen tried to photograph in her mind the wild openness of it all, saving it for those afternoons when she would be stuck in traffic on the 405.

Frieda sipped from a water bottle and watched the country roll by. "Some people call it desolate, but I always liked this emptiness. If you live here, you get used to it."

When Karen first moved to California, she had been surprised by the crowding. Unlike Dickinson, long chains of cars stretched up and down the freeways. Over the years, she adjusted, even though lately it had gotten so bad that a short trip to the grocery store had become as much of a drudge as her daily commute. The traffic guys on the radio had a term for it. *TMC,* Too Many Cars, each one occupied by exactly one human being, said human busy with electronic toys, food, and makeup while driving.

And heaven forbid if you got a little careless toward a guy with an attitude–say for example, accidentally cutting off a couple of gang members or a crackhead or a pissed-off drunk. You might end up dead just running out for a carton of milk.

During her short visit to North Dakota, Karen had reverted back, accustomed once again to a slower pace and what seemed like a kinder populace. She knew she would adjust back again, that in time a person could get used to just about anything, whether it was having too much money or living in prison. It was a survival skill, something primordial that let humans adapt and thrive.

Bloom where you're planted. She'd heard it and even repeated it to her employees. *Make the most of it. Stay positive.* But could that adaptation go too far, making you numb to your circumstances, good or bad? Could that numbness stretch out and expand, taking over your whole life so you ended up sleepwalking through the length and breadth of it?

She held the van steady in the wind. All day the road climbed in elevation, from the fields of sweet yellow clover around Newcastle to the Rawhide Buttes near the hill town of Lusk, and farther south through farm fields dotted with giant hay bales that resembled jelly rolls.

Frieda read the travel guide, dog-earing dozens of pages as if planning a grand vacation. "It's so flat here. Reminds me of Oklahoma. Did I tell you that's where I'm from?"

Karen squinted at highway sign. "Amazing. We're at four thousand feet."

"Still flat."

Karen had seen the map. Once you climbed down off this high plateau, you had to go all the way east to Appalachia to find land of any real altitude. Between here and the Great Smoky Mountains, the Mississippi River in prehistoric times had carved a valley through almost one-third of the United States, but if all a person ever saw was this road, right here at the top of the plateau, that person might decide the entire world was flat and windblown, and for the most part, lacked trees.

Frieda closed her book and looked out the window. "Can you imagine living out here a hundred years ago? How many months you would go without seeing another person?"

"A lot of them had big families, though. So they'd have people around."

"They had big families because so many of the children died. The mothers, too. You didn't have babies in hospitals back then. Some of Mother's family went crazy from the hardship."

"Sounds horrible." Karen floored the gas pedal and passed a slow-moving semi.

"They took a little time off, now and then. On the holy days you'd pile in the wagon and gather at the church for food and weddings and celebration. It was miles away so everybody'd sleep there, under their wagons, mostly. This went on for days. You had to come or it was a sin. But really it was to keep the farmers from working themselves to death."

Karen rolled her head around on her neck, trying to dissipate the stiffness. The wind had battered the van for the last three hours and the need for constant vigilance was wearing her out. Plus she had a headache and cramping in her abdomen, like her period was about to make an appearance for the first time in months. Naturally, she hadn't packed any gear for it, assuming the one benefit of menopause had finally arrived. On top of everything, the RV had been making a low ticking noise for the past sixty miles.

"It says here, the only American ever convicted of cannibalism was caught right around this area. Isn't that interesting?"

"Fascinating." A highway sign informed them that Cheyenne lay one hundred miles away. Even though Cheyenne and Denver were only an hour apart, they would camp again tonight. Karen had promised. Anyway, she didn't have the energy to deal with Denver's traffic or freeways, nor to meet Frieda's daughter. Grimacing, she flicked on the blinker and took the southwest fork in the road toward their night's rest.

Chapter Twenty-Five

*I*n the early evening they checked in at the Hi Plains RV Park, a dirt-and-blacktop affair devoid of vegetation except for a few determined cottonwoods around each campsite. They paid the scowling manager who barely tore his eyes away from the wrestling match on TV, and pulled into their spot, a pitted concrete pad. The RV park was deserted except for a giant-sized motor coach a few rows over.

"Back in a sec." Karen hurried to the restroom, a bleak cinderblock with sheet metal mirrors. In the stall she was relieved to find the cramps were a false alarm.

Frieda sat at the picnic table, frowning. "You find this place on your internets?"

"Sorry. It looked nicer online." After hooking up the water and electric supply, Karen opened a kitchen cabinet. "Cheese and crackers before dinner?"

"Fine with me."

Karen opened the tiny refrigerator and jerked back at the overpowering stench. The coolant had stopped working, and the milk and other perishables had been cooking all day. She found a trashbag in the cabinet and began emptying.

"There was a café a few miles back," said Frieda. "We could eat there."

"Let me think." Karen pinched the bridge of her nose. "I could open a can of tuna and make sandwiches without mayo. Or how about macaroni and cheese cooked with water, and we could have these brownies for dessert?"

"You decide. I'm going to stretch my legs," Frieda said.

Karen stepped outside and watched the old woman limp off toward the restroom. Even though it was summer, at six thousand feet, Cheyenne was already cooling off. She unrolled the carpet and set up two chairs.

A door slammed, followed by footsteps crunching through the gravel. Karen turned to see a barrel-shaped woman with stick legs and a bleached-out buzz cut.

"Hey, neighbor." The woman's voice was raspy from booze or cigarettes, or both. "Helluva place for a vacation, ain't it?"

Karen smiled. "I think we're too tired to care."

The woman crushed Karen's hand. "I'm Barb. You're probably dehydrated. It's the altitude. You gotta drink your liquids. Where you headed?"

"Southern California."

Barb grinned, exposing a chipped tooth. "At least you can stop in Vegas. Do a little gambling, maybe take in a show. Who's this, your mother?"

"Do I look that old?" said Frieda, returning from the bathroom.

"You look like you could use a drink," said Barb. "You both could."

"Actually, we're—" Karen began, but their neighbor was already walking back to her campsite.

"This place is as ugly as a cow's rear end. Where're my flamingoes?" Frieda eased into a chair. "Is dinner ready?"

"I'll get started in a minute." Karen finished leveling the van just as Barb returned with a pitcher of strawberry margaritas. She sloshed the icy liquid into plastic cups and handed them out, then placed the pitcher on the dirt and plopped into a chair. "Salud," she said, the cheap aluminum creaking under her weight.

Karen sat on the cold cement picnic bench and took a sip. The bright tang of strawberry margarita mix barely dented the smoky tequila. Her stomach warmed and her cramps subsided. Barb had brought the perfect medicine. Karen lifted her chin toward the silver motor coach, as long as a city bus and boasting multiple slide-outs. "Nice rig."

Barb grinned. "You betcha. She is my pride and joy."

"Is there a husband in there?" Frieda asked.

"He's been dead two years. Nah, don't worry about it." Barb fended off their condolences. "I'm happier'n I've ever been in my life. How about you gals? You married?"

"I'm a widow," said Frieda, "and my friend here wishes she was."

Barb downed the remainder of the pink slush in one swig. "Lord, I know what you mean." A trickle of the sugary liquid ran down a crevasse at the side of her mouth.

Karen looked away. The color of the distant landscape changed rapidly from brown to gold as the sun dipped toward the horizon. When Frieda shivered, Karen stood. "Thanks for the drinks, Barb, but I need to start dinner."

Frieda made a face. "With what?"

"You folks hungry? Come on. I've got all the grub you need back in the coach. Let's go over and get warm. I'll give you a tour."

While Karen locked up, Frieda and Barb started across the windy expanse to the land yacht. Over the door, custom lettering spelled out *Bit o' Tuscany*.

"I called her that because I always wanted to go live in Itlee," said Barb.

"Have you been there?"

"Nah, only what I seen in pictures." Barb held the door open.

Frieda drew in a breath. "This place is huge."

"She's a Monaco Dynasty Squire IV. Forty three foot, stem to stern." Barb headed into the galley.

Frieda followed her. "Are these granite counter tops? And you've even got a sofa and a big TV. This is some kind of motor home."

"No kidding," said Karen from the doorway.

"Go on, look around. I'll make some more maggies."

The blender rumbled behind them as Karen and Frieda tiptoed down the long hallway. On the left was a bathroom, almost as large as the guest bath in Karen's home in Newport. "Look at this," she marveled. "The shower doors are made of glass."

"Lot of weight to haul around. Lots more fuel," said Frieda. "Holy moly, look here." The bedroom was equipped with a queen bed, a closet, another television, and two nightstands with reading lamps affixed to the wall.

"You gals ready?" Barb brandished a pitcher from the kitchen.

Karen accepted a refill. "This thing is as big as a house. I can't believe you drive it."

"This is nothing. I used to drive a school bus, a ninety-passenger Crown, back in the hell days." Barb slurped from her glass. "That's three classrooms' worth of kids in case you don't know, and you gotta turn your back on 'em to drive."

"And what's this, a desk and a computer?" Karen sat down in front of the screen. "You can work from anywhere."

"Pretty much. I got a booster up on the roof so the reception's always good. I can get email and keep up with my Facebook. And see here? I got my own website." The homepage featured Barb in leopard print leggings, boots and a cowboy hat standing in front of Bit o' Tuscany. The picture was taken in the parking lot of a casino. "You wanna use it, you're welcome."

Karen sat down at the computer and tapped the keyboard. "Frieda, didn't you tell me you used to work in an office?"

"Ran the whole thing."

"Did you do any typing?"

"That and everything else under the sun."

"Come over here a minute."

"But I just got comfortable." Frieda sat half-buried in a bank of pillows on the sofa.

"Come on, I'll help ya." Barb went over and pulled Frieda up. By the time she reached the desk, Karen had created a free email account for her.

Frieda stared at her name on the screen. "Is this me? What do I do?"

"All you do is start typing, and we can send a message." Karen gave her the chair. "Let's send one to my email address for practice."

"Who's ready for another drink?"

"We're good." Karen took a sip from her still-full glass. "Do you have any crackers or anything?"

"I have all kinds of stuff." Barb found a bag of potato chips in a cabinet and tore it open, spilling a third on the floor. She kicked them toward the sofa, pulled out a fistful for herself and handed the bag to Karen.

Frieda tapped the keys, tentatively at first and then with more confidence. "This is easy. Now how do we mail it?"

"Push here."

"That's it? Holy mackerel. Who else do we know?"

Fifteen minutes and another margarita later, Barb hoisted herself off the sofa. "My turn. Lemme show you my grandkids."

"You can get pictures off this thing?" Frieda moved out of the way.

"Yup. Lookey here. Look how cute they are."

Karen leaned in. "They're beautiful, almost like little fashion models, Barb. You must be really proud."

Barb started laughing, her great bosom heaving a guffaw that turned into a lung-ripping cough. She grabbed a towel, blew her nose, and wiped her eyes. When she could speak, she said, "Are you kidding? Those kids are so homely I hafta Photoshop 'em."

"What is she saying?"

"She alters the pictures to make them look better."

Frieda stared at Barb. "How do the parents feel about that?"

"Hell if I know." Barb shuffled over to the bar and drained the rest of the pitcher straight into her mouth. "Last time I saw 'em they bitched me out. For no reason. Really pissed me off. I don't have to take that. So I got in Bit o' Tuscany and *adios*." She wiped her mouth on her sleeve. "That's one of the great things about livin' in a motor home. Somebody rubs you the wrong way, you just pull up the mat and get the hell outta Dodge."

"I guess that would be one advantage." Karen's headache had started up again. She glanced at her watch. Time to get Frieda back to the Roadtrek and figure out some kind of meal.

"I never coulda afforded it on my own," said Barb, sinking into the sofa next to Karen. "If it wasn't for life insurance."

Karen inched away. "How long were you married?"

"Which time?" Barb lit a cigarette. She leaned forward, elbows on knees, picking a piece of tobacco from her tongue. "Coupla years. I used to do charter runs to Vegas on the weekends. Make a little extra money, you know? Tommy was one of my riders. Lonely, dried up, little old man." Barb squinted through the smoke. "When he died, I sold the house and bought this baby. His kids hated me for it, but hell with 'em. The old man had a shitload of money. Figure I earned it." A length of ash dangled from her cigarette. "But you know it's true what they say. You marry a man for money, you'll work hard every day for it, and I did."

Karen glanced at Frieda, who gave a little shrug.

Barb leaned back, eyes closed. "When he got sick, he didn't want me to hire a nurse, so I did it all. Gave him his meds, cleaned up his puke, and wiped his ass. I can't get the smell of shit off my hands."

Barb's head began to loll against the back of the sofa. When her cigarette fell to the floor, Karen doused it in the sink and helped Frieda out the door, holding her arm as they crossed the uneven ground through the cold wind. Reaching the van, Karen jabbed the key into the lock, her fingers almost numb. Inside, they bumped into each other in the narrow space, shivering as they wrapped in blankets and waited for the heater to work. Karen got some water going for tea, and while it was steeping, opened a box of granola bars.

"I wouldn't want to be around when she wakes up," Frieda said, sipping her tea as Karen converted the dinette to a bed.

"That won't be for a long time."

"Things have really changed. When Russell and I used to travel, people were nicer." Frieda chewed, staring into the middle distance. "I'm almost glad he's not around to see this."

"It was just bad luck. Last night was good, most of it anyway. Mae was nice." Karen forced a smile. She felt bloated and headachey, and her cramps were back.

Frieda brushed her teeth in the tiny bathroom and climbed into bed. "Heck of a last night."

"I know. I'm sorry it worked out this way." Karen put another blanket atop the older woman.

"You did your best." Frieda burrowed under the covers while Karen assembled her own bed, layering a couple of blankets over the sleeping bag and carefully climbing in. She switched off the light and closed her eyes, wishing she had driven into town and found a café instead of subjecting them to Barb. She double-rolled a thin pillow, trying to ease the tension in her neck. "Frieda? Are you warm enough?"

"Fine."

Karen pulled the curtain away from the window and peered upward toward the moon, a sliver in the east. The wind began to die, and the dark campground grew silent except for a distant barking dog. A sodium lamp hanging near the office flickered greenish-white, the camp's only illumination.

She let the curtain fall back and pulled on another blanket. If Cheyenne was like this in the summer, what was winter like? Under the massive pile of cloth, she began to relax in the growing warmth, until she remembered Steve, and the fact that she needed to call him. She wanted to hold him off as long as possible without appearing punitive, thereby losing ground at the negotiating table.

As she thought about her arguments, though, punitive looked more enticing. If not for his wandering libido, she'd still have a home and financial security during her unemployment. Now she didn't even have that.

A cramp made her wince. The thought of wringing cash from Steve didn't feel good even if he deserved to be punished. It wasn't her way.

Maybe it should be. Maybe I'm being too nice.

She needed to stay positive. Good news was just around the corner. One day soon, a call or some kind of referral would come through, and then she'd be back at work. Her lengthy list of contacts would pay off and she'd be working at another big corporation. Another spasm twisted her gut.

Or not. The economy wasn't getting any better. The unemployment lines were getting longer. Maybe she should think about another line of work? She knew a colleague who went from selling corporate print jobs to selling a dozen different kinds of pipe for natural gas drilling, and that woman loved it. What else could Karen do?

She pulled the blankets up higher, frowning. She didn't want to do anything new. She loved human resources. If Steve had only honored his vows, she wouldn't have to think about reinventing herself.

Reinvention. What a load of crap. She didn't want to reinvent herself. She had worked too hard to invent herself. Reinvention might be a fun choice if you were bored with your life, but for Karen it held no appeal. She wanted her old life.

But she had to be realistic. At the age of fifty, it was only due to unbridled optimism that she called herself middle-aged. Maybe she should accept she was on the downhill slope, too old to change. Maybe she should accept a check from Steve, find an apartment somewhere, and start learning how to live alone.

She turned over, feeling too warm now, and fear crept into her heart. The world was a scary place. People got lonely and sick and old. They died. It was hard enough if you were part of a team, taking care of each other. What would it be like if you were alone, maybe in a new place where you knew no one?

She thought of Curt, and threw off a couple of covers. Hot sex—would she have to live without it? At least now she knew nothing was wrong with the way her body worked. If anything, it was better than ever, something she would never have realized were it not for the randy professor. The man shook her right down to her toenails. She would have to give that up, because no way was she looking for male companionship in the pink-hands metropolis of Newport Beach. Nobody there was interested in a fifty-year old woman. At her age, it wasn't going to happen.

The thought pissed her off, or maybe it was the blankets—she couldn't get comfortable, and now she felt sweaty and hot. She kicked off a few more layers, but it didn't help, so she kept peeling off blankets until she was completely uncovered. Her skin was so hot it felt as if it glowed, and the air in the van was barely above freezing. The sleeping bag felt hot against her back, and her face and ears burned. I shouldn't have had that last margarita, she thought, opening the window and letting in a stream of icy air. The sensation gave her relief for five seconds. Then sweat beaded on her forehead, and a furnace roared to life on her chest.

She scrambled out of bed wearing only a tee shirt and panties, tiptoed to the door and went down the steep aluminum steps, barefoot, nearly naked. The lights were still on in Barb's coach, but the rest of the campground remained deserted. A raccoon dropped a trashcan lid over by the restroom, and a pack of coyotes called to each other from the distant fields. In the glare of the sodium lamp, Karen wiped her forearm across her face, slick with sweat.

She pressed her back against the searing cold metal of the van, enduring her very first hot flash and the realization of her own pointless mortality.

Chapter Twenty-Six

The next morning, Karen dragged boxes of mementoes from the van.

"You planning a yard sale?" Frieda stood in the door, blinking.

"I'm reorganizing for when we get to Denver."

"What a mess. Where's my overnight case? I have to go to the ladies' room."

"Right there on the front seat." Karen went back to unloading the boxes of photo albums and paraphernalia. In the two days they'd been on the road, the van had become cluttered and she didn't want to have to repack everything in Sandy's driveway. Plus the spoilage in the small refrigerator had stunk up the place. She heard the distant sound of the restroom door slamming in the crisp, high-desert air.

Karen swathed the poppyseed grinder in a towel and returned it to a cabinet. Outside, dried leaves scrabbled past in the chill wind. Across the deserted campground, the store was closed and the office wouldn't open until noon, today being Sunday. Barb had decamped hours ago in her big motor coach. Karen had been awakened by the slamming of doors and ring of hardware until the rig rumbled past in the dark.

She reached for a box of her mother's needlework, but stopped at the sound of voices. Peering around the van, she saw a pocked and peeling Ford Bronco had pulled into a campsite next to the restroom. A man in a hooded sweatshirt hunched against the wind, firing up a pipe while his friend waited. A third man unzipped his slacks and relieved himself against the restroom wall.

The driver, a shirtless skinhead in a leather vest, hopped up on the table top and began dancing and playing air guitar to the asskicking concert in his brain. He screamed the lyrics, pausing only to finish the beer and heave the bottle against the wall. The urinator jumped up on the table as if to punch him, but the skinhead kicked him in the chest and danced away.

Karen ducked behind the van. After living in southern California for almost three decades, she knew well enough the behavior of urban wildlife. Best to lay low and hope they didn't get curious about the Roadtrek or its occupants.

But what the hell was taking Frieda so long? Karen snuck another look as the skinhead leapt to the ground. He bounded over to an empty metal trashcan and, shouting at no one in particular, picked it up and heaved it against the wall of the restroom. The small building seemed to shudder, the noise echoing through the campground.

Frieda would hide, afraid to come out. Karen wanted to go get her and hurry out of the camp, but what would the men do when she appeared? She touched the edge of her sweatshirt, measuring its length in relation to the coverage it would afford her hips.

Not good. She pulled the hood up over her head, hiding her blond hair. Maybe she could get in the van, drive over, and pick Frieda up.

The skinhead strutted to the back of the Bronco and opened the tailgate. A dozen empty beer bottles fell to the blacktop. He picked up an armful that hadn't shattered, lined them up in the roadway, and pulled a gun from his waistband.

Hiding behind the van, Karen flinched as the gun roared twice. She cursed her stupidity. Back in Dickinson, she had refused when Curt tried to give her his pistol. What would she do with a gun, she'd asked, laughing? She hated guns. A cop friend had taken her to a range one time, intent on teaching her to shoot, but her hands had shaken so badly she gave up.

When the gun's report faded, she took another peek. Having hit everything he aimed at, he was lining up another dozen bottles, and judging from the whooping and yelling, his friends were loving it. Her heart raced as she tried to think of how to get Frieda out of harm's way.

Then the restroom door slammed.

The men stopped what they were doing to watch Frieda limp toward the RV. She walked with her head down and her shoulders hunched forward, picking her way across the uneven blacktop.

One of the men fell in behind Frieda and began mimicking her halting gait. Frieda, clutching her overnight bag, churned toward the van, ignoring their howls and taunts. Karen watched in horror. The old lady was almost ninety, and barely four-eleven.

The man reached for Frieda's bag.

"No!" Frieda held on to one end of the strap.

"Come on, grandma, gimme the purse." The man flashed a knife.

"I will not! Let go, you creep!"

"Ya old bitch!" The man screamed and fell to the pavement as a jet of bear spray hit him in the face. Karen stepped over him and gathered Frieda under her arm, all but carrying her to the van. Jumping into the driver's seat, she stuck the key in the ignition as one of the men emptied a beer into the downed man's face.

"Lock your door. Seatbelt!" Karen started the motor. Thirty feet in front of the van, the skinhead stood in the roadway, his vest blowing open in the breeze. He fondled his bare belly, eyes cold as hematite. Slowly he raised the pistol.

"Get down!" Karen slammed the shifter into gear and stomped on the gas pedal. For one sickening moment the motor lugged. Then it caught and hurled the RV toward the men. She heard the gun fire as the men scattered and the van blew through them toward the gate. Seconds later, she heard a boom and a thunk at the rear of the van.

"Goddamn it! They hit us."

Frieda cowered in her seat. Karen whipped the RV around the corner, out the gate and onto the narrow highway. The road was clear in both directions as she accelerated south. Hopefully they'd take the man for medical help instead of chasing her. She glanced in the mirror. Nothing yet. She took a ragged breath, trying to calm herself.

Nothing in her life had prepared her for being shot at. All she could do was run. In seconds the van reached top speed. Karen breathed a prayer of thanks to Russell for keeping the van in mint condition until the day he died. She glanced at Frieda. "Are you okay?"

"I think so. Where's our stuff?" The back of the van was empty.

"God." Karen's face fell. "It's back there. I had to leave it." The needlepoint. The photo albums.

"Don't think about it. Just drive." Frieda clutched her bag in her lap.

Karen took a deep breath for courage. "Okay. I don't think they'll chase us. That Bronco's a piece of shit, and we got a head start." Fired by adrenaline, she couldn't stop babbling. "We'll find a place with a lot of people. Hide. Call the police."

"We should have gone north."

With sickening clarity, Karen saw that Frieda was right. Heading toward the far-distant Denver, the land was deserted in every direction. At least in Cheyenne, they might have made it to a mini-mart or gas station. She checked the rearview again.

The Bronco turned onto the road behind them.

Her stomach lurched as she saw it accelerate. The front of the Bronco lifted as it raced toward the van. Karen gritted her teeth. Of course it would be fast. They probably did this for a living. She pressed harder on the accelerator, trying to keep the van steady on the narrow road. Luckily she had a tailwind, but so did they. Behind her the Bronco closed in, its massive grille a metallic snarl.

"Get my phone out of my purse! Dial 9-1-1."

"Where is it?"

"Under your seat."

Frieda opened the bag, fumbled around inside, and found the phone. Bouncing around, she flipped it open, squinted at the display, and snapped it shut. "No reception," she yelled.

"Shit!" Karen could not allow them to catch up. If the men forced the van to the shoulder, she and Frieda would be their toys.

Frieda had found Karen's rosary in her purse and now she fingered the beads, praying.

The Bronco was closing fast, the road ahead empty. Karen veered into the middle, straddling the line to block them, but the driver found a wide spot and inched alongside, forcing her back into her lane. A meaty arm waved a pistol out the window.

Karen had the van at top speed. She couldn't possibly pull away. Could she slam on the brakes, maybe turn and head back to Cheyenne before he could recover? No. If she could get away with such a cockeyed television maneuver, he could too, and probably better. The Bronco was much more nimble. It swerved toward the van, nearly sideswiping it. Karen glanced over quick enough to see the bald and bolted young men brandishing guns. One made a "v" with his fingers and waggled his tongue between them. A bottle sailed through the air and smashed against her window, cracking the glass and scaring her so badly she swerved hard to the right and almost overcorrected. The men hung out of the windows, taunting her.

When Frieda screamed, Karen saw the eighteen-wheeler.

The rig had crested a hill and now bore down on them from the south. The driver of the Bronco honked his horn, laughing and pointing at the big rig. He eased the Bronco closer to the RV. His buddies, however, had stopped clowning.

The eighteen-wheeler flashed its headlights again and again. Forty tons of truck would not slow quickly. The Bronco raced alongside the van, inching forward but not able to pass unless Karen slowed, and she would not.

As the road curved slightly, Frieda cursed, and Karen saw what her friend had seen: the eighteen-wheeler led a convoy. Karen would have to choose. If she kept up this pace, the men would have to back off or die. Or she could slow down and let them cut in front of her, avoiding the head-on and letting them live, but endangering herself and Frieda.

She knew what she should do. Karen was a good person. She'd been raised to a life of sacrifice.

Her hands tightened on the wheel.

The van flew down the road shoulder to shoulder with the Bronco. The trucker flashed his lights.

Acid flooded her gut.

The pedal was flat against the floor.

Her hands were numb, death-gripping the wheel.

I'm doing everything I can. I think this is it. There's nothing more I can do. I gave it my best.

As Karen raced toward the big rigs, the roaring in her ears began to deaden all sensation. A cool fog wafted into the darkest remote conduits of her mind, and her heartbeat seemed to slow.

I did everything I could.

But if you give up now, you're going to die, she thought, trying to elicit the sense that this was an important fact and that some emotion should rise from it, yet she felt increasingly detached. What does it mean, she wondered, as the sound of the road receded, and the lights and the horns faded, and she drifted into the silence within, when you've tried hard all your life to do everything right, be fair to people and play by the rules, you take care of your family and don't steal and you lift up your employees and…and you're erased from the earth just for sport?

I don't deserve this. I've been good all my life, and for this? I was a good kid, a good adult. Even when Dad got in his moods. "Try to be good," Mom would plead, as if that would stop him from beating the shit out of both of us.

An epitaph, carved in a chunk of granite, flashed before her eyes: "She was a good girl."

Karen blinked. The Bronco was still beside her, the rigs roaring down on her, horns blaring, lights flashing. Elbows locked, she held the wheel steady, refusing to yield. The men jumped around inside the SUV like wild chimps.

At the last second the Bronco braked and swerved hard to the left, careening off the shoulder and out of control. The convoy roared past, partly hiding from Karen the sight of the Bronco cartwheeling across the prairie, spewing a roostertail of dirt and carving a swath through the sagebrush.

Frieda clawed at the seat and twisted around to see the wreckage behind them. The smoking Bronco lay upside down in the scarred landscape a hundred yards from the highway, its wheels spinning, roof crushed. The convoy slowed, and the last eighteen-wheeler pulled to the shoulder. The driver, holding a fire extinguisher, ran toward the wreckage.

"Aren't you going to stop?"

Karen barely heard Frieda's voice above the roaring in her ears. She muscled the RV into a sweeping curve, too fast.

"Karen."

The tires screamed in protest.

"I think they're dead. Karen?"

The van slowed slightly. "Good," Karen tried to say, but couldn't, because she had no spit left. She began to shake and eased her foot from the gas pedal. Her elbows floated away from her body, and her hands couldn't feel the steering wheel.

"Dear." Frieda's hand reached over, trembling, her grasp warm on Karen's forearm. "Please."

The van rolled to a stop on the shoulder as the first ambulance appeared over the next hill.

Chapter Twenty-Seven

The trooper finished scratching notes on his clipboard and handed Karen's license back to her. "If we need to, we'll be in touch."

Karen nodded, her jaw clamped. Wordlessly, she and Frieda walked back to the Roadtrek, arms linked tightly. She helped Frieda into her seat and rounded the back of the van. Shaking, she rested against the bumper, her eyes blurring the red-dot fence line of burning flares that stretched around the emergency vehicles. A fireman in yellow slicker directed traffic past the mess, traffic that slowed to eyeball the smoking wreck as they headed northward.

Her veins throbbed with the charred remains of adrenaline and emotion, and she wondered by how many years this incident had shortened her life.

Not as much as theirs.

She pushed herself into a standing position, the effort almost too much. Feeling as if her feet were weighted with cement blocks, Karen climbed back into the van, put it in gear, and began driving slowly toward Denver. Thankful for Frieda's silence, she played the decision over and over again in her head, but for all her torment, when she reached for guilt she came up empty.

It was bizarre. Fifty years a Catholic, and she felt no compulsion to race to Confession, no burning need to call out to the heavens for forgiveness. Even though her failure to Put Others First had directly resulted in their death.

Theirs, not hers.

The Karen Grace who went to bed last night in a campground in Cheyenne was not the same woman who now puttered down the freeway toward Denver. This new Karen was less heroic, less admirable in every way, and yet she battled a feeling of pride. She had survived and had saved Frieda's life while she was at it. If she felt any guilt at all it was for her *lack* of guilt.

They rolled south, the strip of road slicing through featureless miles of high desert, browning as they approached the arid steppes outside Denver.

How is it possible to go along every day of your life as one kind of person, and then something happens and you change, becoming your own opposite? When she was driving hell-bent across the desert, she wanted to kill them. How very un-Karen-like.

She drove on, wrestling with it.

It's almost as if there's a piece of fabric stretched out across your life, she thought, and part of you lives above that piece of fabric, and part below. The part above is the capable, nice, everyday kind of person you show your friends and family. The part below is the extreme negative, the part that isn't quite rational, that doesn't cope so well-or, actually, it does, resulting in heinous, unthinkable outcomes. The strength of the fabric determines how often the lower part breaks through, corrupting the goodness above.

You might be neurotic and prone to tearing–silk–or someone sturdier, made of burlap. Then all of a sudden something happens, like the third or fourth time he forgets your birthday or maybe gives you a black eye. Or you find yourself facing down the possibility of death, and the barrier rips, exposing all the writhing ugliness underneath.

"Jesus!" She swerved to avoid a small sedan.

"Welcome back to civilization," said Frieda.

"Sorry."

Frieda stared out the window. "I can't get those boys out of my mind."

"They weren't boys. They were dangerous men, and we did what we had to do."

"I know." Frieda turned back toward the window.

Over and over again, the Bronco spun out across her mind, forcing Karen to reevaluate whether she had overreacted, needlessly causing their deaths. She tried to apply logic. The men had a choice. The decision and consequences were theirs, and she had reacted logically to preserve her own existence and Frieda's. Anybody with a brain would have made the same decision. She and Frieda were lucky to have escaped, and yet, luck had nothing to do with their survival. They had survived due to Karen's determination. Her only remorse sprang from the impact on Frieda.

And from the loss of her mother's precious mementoes, now rotting outside of Cheyenne. Nothing could make her drive back over that stretch of highway. She wanted only to get back home to the familiar.

Karen glanced over at the older woman who dabbed at her nose with a ragged tissue. Frieda glanced back. "Stop worrying. I'll feel better after I see Jessie and the baby."

"Are you going to tell your daughter?"

"Oh, for God's sake, no. If Sandy knew, she'd have me committed. And right after that she'd have a nervous breakdown. No, let's keep our mouths shut."

Karen slowed as the highway became more congested near Denver. The Continental Divide loomed to the west. Soon she would be scooting along their southern tip, heading westward toward home. She took a calming breath, the first in over an hour.

Frieda rolled her window down an inch. "A long time ago, Sandy tried to get me to move to Denver. She and Richard felt humiliated that her dad and I still lived back in Hicksville. Richard's got the money, she said. You can live where it's nice." Frieda shook her head at the memory. "Nice."

"I thought your house in Dickinson was pretty nice."

"Exactly. But she wanted to buy a house in Denver and let us live in it rent-free. I don't know if it was Richard's idea of a tax shelter or they really wanted to help, but I told her no. She kept insisting and we had a fight. We didn't speak for a while. Finally I told her if she wanted to buy us something, make it a Roadtrek and we'll use it to come visit." Frieda smiled. "We got the RV we always dreamed of, and she got to feel like a big shot."

"I'm sure she worries about you."

"She doesn't give me any credit at all." The broad swaths of open land began to shrink into strip malls and subdivisions. Karen paid more attention to the road now as it fed into downtown, the traffic flowing like water through a narrowing chute. She knew how to avoid tailgaters and speeders in her own car, but the Roadtrek wasn't as nimble. She was happy to see their off-ramp coming up.

Once on city streets, she eased off the pedal. They passed an upscale mall with a Saks and Nordstrom's. A brace of gleaming skyscrapers reached into the sky to the south, and Frieda pointed to a silver-blue high rise. "That's where Richard works, up on the twentieth floor. He has his own law firm."

"What does Sandy do?"

"Sandy decorates."

"She's an interior decorator?"

"Not exactly. She does her house, over and over again."

They turned onto a shaded parkway that ran past gated neighborhoods and manicured parks, soccer fields and jogging paths, until they reached the entry gate to a private community. As they were cleared through the guardhouse, Karen felt like she was back in her private community in Newport. Same winding lane, same fairways next to the road, same gigantic tract homes.

They found the address on a sprawling split-level on a corner lot. Three sets of limestone steps marched down the hill to the driveway. A stream cut across the lawn, coursing over fiberglass boulders to a small pond where fake deer nibbled grasses along the banks. Karen parked the van at the curb.

At the top of the steps, a heavy wooden door flew open and a blond woman emerged in a bulky beige pantsuit. She hurried down the steps, her hands at her fleshy cheeks like a kid on Christmas morning. Her chubby arms engulfed Frieda. "Oh my gosh oh my gosh oh my gosh."

Frieda struggled out of her daughter's arms. "Good Lord, Sandy, let go. You're going to crush me."

"Oh my gosh, I can't believe you're finally here, Mom. It's so good to see you." Sandy, her mascaraed eyes resembling twin spiders, turned to Karen. "And you are?"

"This is Karen. You might remember her from the old neighborhood."

Karen reached forward to shake hands. "Hi, Sandy."

"Sandra." She squeezed Karen's fingertips, avoiding an actual handshake. "Would you mind parking your camper down at the end of the street?"

"Yes, we would mind," said Frieda.

"Those are the neighborhood rules, Mom. We can't have old vehicles unless they're in the garage. The neighbors will complain."

"Are you going to stand here worrying about your neighbors or invite us in?"

Sandra blinked. "Forget it. Is anybody hungry? Lucia can make us lunch." She turned and guided Frieda toward the stairs, glancing over her shoulder at Karen. "You can put Mom's bags on the second floor, third door on the left."

Chapter Twenty-Eight

When Sandra and Frieda disappeared into the house, Karen slumped in the drivers' seat, where she was tempted to put the key in the ignition and escape to the Rockies. She watched a gardener working on the property next door and wondered how long she could get away with sitting outside.

Checking her phone, she found Steve had left half a dozen messages, so she called him back.

"When are you coming home?"

"I don't know," Karen said. "I don't have a job anymore so there's not that much reason to hurry."

"What're you talking about?"

"I got fired."

"What the hell? What happened?"

"Other than Wes is insane?"

"Jeez, I'm sorry. What an asshole."

"Exactly." For once they had a common enemy instead of each other.

"What are you going to do?" he asked.

She could picture him running his hand through his hair, thinking hard, trying to fix things. A painful wave of nostalgia washed over her. For all his selfishness, he represented the familiar. Familiarity was comforting, especially after what happened this morning. But comfort could be dangerous, too. "All I can do is get the word out to my friends and hope for a nibble."

"I know people who know people. I can help, if you want."

His data-base was huge, and she needed a job. "Thank you."

"But we need to settle things," he said. "The house is sitting vacant."

"The other shoe drops."

"Karen, I'm just being practical."

"I still live there, remember?"

Then he sighed. "I've retained counsel."

"I know. Jean told me."

"You probably should, too."

Karen leaned back against the head rest. So this is how it worked, one side forcing the other to lawyer up. How quickly he had moved to that option.

"It's the only way," he said. "I'm sorry, but we need to move forward."

"You mean you do." They sat in silence, two separate new humans forming out of the old one. "When is she due?"

"I don't want to discuss it."

"Fine. I have to go."

"When are you coming back?"

She hung up. *Albuquerque by dark. That's all I care about.* Karen unfolded the map and reviewed the rest of her route. After a polite half-hour of visiting, she'd be back on the highway and away.

She unloaded Frieda's bags and checked one last time for anything that might have been forgotten. The van seemed so empty now, cleared of Frieda's bags and her mother's heirlooms. The box of needlework was gone too, back in Cheyenne. If only she had waited until Denver to organize the van. On the other hand, if it had been any heavier she might not have been able to outrun the Bronco.

But the needlework. And oh, God, the family photo albums.

Karen went through several tissues before locking up. Inside the house, she dropped the bags in the entryway and massaged her lower back. All the tension of the morning seemed to have settled there.

The house was huge, but she could hear distant voices. A double set of staircases wound upward to the second floor. To her left lay a sunken living room capable of handling forty people and to her right, a formal dining room table surrounded by a couple dozen chairs.

Following the sound of Sandra's laughter, Karen wandered through the dining room and into the kitchen, past the Subzero refrigerator and Viking range, past the butler's closet and wine racks, and through the door to the solarium.

"Mom, you're here, next to me, and Karen, you sit at that end." Sandra gestured at a distant chair while a dark-skinned woman set out plates heaped with aromatic bread, a half-dozen cheeses, three stacks of deli meat, and a separate tray just for fruits and vegetables. The condiments spun around on a lazy Susan in the center of the table.

After the woman went back in the kitchen, Sandra took the chair at the head of the table, folded her hands and bowed her head. "Lord, thank you for bringing my mother all this way safely, and for the bounty with which you have favored us. Amen. So, Karen, what are your plans?"

"I think I'll have the ham." Karen reached for the platter of cold cuts.

"Funny." Sandra filled three glasses with white wine.

"Not usually," said Frieda.

"To answer your question," Karen said, painting a slice of bread with mayonnaise, "I'll be leaving right after lunch."

"You don't have to go so soon," said Frieda. "Spend the night here. Start fresh in the morning." She poked Sandra in the arm. "Don't you think?"

"Well of course she can stay. We've got lots of room."

"That's nice of you, but I need to get on the road."

Sandra's face stretched into a determined smile. "I think Mom's right. It's a long way to Albuquerque, and a woman traveling alone in the dark is a recipe for disaster. You are more than welcome to stay."

"It's been a long day already," said Frieda. "If anything happened to you it'd be on my conscience." Her eyes met Karen's, and Karen saw the Bronco.

She held up her glass. "I accept. Thank you."

"Good," said Sandra. "Now, tell me about your trip."

"Nothing to tell." Frieda took a bite of her sandwich. In the quiet they could hear her chewing.

"What about you, Karen? Was it worth it, driving such a long way in that old van?"

"I didn't think I would like camping very much, but your Mom made it fun. I'm glad we did it." Karen smiled at Frieda, who rolled her eyes.

"I wasn't in favor of that, not for a minute," said Sandra. "Mom, you could have gotten on a plane and been here in two hours. Now look at you. You're exhausted."

Frieda stuck a finger in her ear and grimaced. "You don't have to shout. I'm fine. Now, when are Jessie and the baby getting here?"

"I'm not sure. More wine?"

"How can you not be sure?"

"She had to cancel and reschedule. They're on standby." Sandra refilled their glasses. "You know how kids are. They never answer their cells."

"They're on standby with a baby? I can't see Jessie going for that program."

"Not literally. I meant they're coming later." Sandra set the wine back in the ice bucket. "I can't wait to show you the house. You're going to love your room. I just finished redecorating."

"I don't need anything special. Any room will do."

Sandra's hand splayed over her heart. "I want you to have the best."

Frieda glanced at Karen, who pretended to be interested in the clearing of the empty dishes.

"Come on. Let me show you." Sandra stood up. "We'll start on the east end of the house."

An hour later, after another glass of wine and an explanation of every design choice their hostess had ever made or considered, Karen closed the door of the guest room and fell on the bed in a coma.

By the time she awoke, the light angling away from the windows told her it was late afternoon. She dressed, noticing for the first time the tastefully appointed furnishings. Sandra maybe could have found a more practical hobby, but she did have talent. The oak cabinetry had been distressed and lacquered in a cinnamon finish, and the hardware brought to mind a prosperous ranch in big sky country. Karen's bare feet were comfortable on the warm wood floor, and the walls were hung with paintings of wild horses racing across wind-scarred mesas.

On the patio, Frieda sat in a patch of sun and watched a foursome finish up at the ninth green. Aspens and pine trees lined both sides of the fairway, and the clubhouse dominated a hill in the distance. Karen dragged a heavy metal chair next to Frieda. "How'd you sleep?"

"I didn't. Couldn't stop thinking about our trip."

"You must be exhausted."

"I feel like crap," Frieda nodded, "but I'm glad we went. I'm glad I got out. Let's leave it at that." They sat listening to the distant voices of the golfers and the clank of food being prepared somewhere behind the closed door.

"Something we do need to talk about." Frieda leaned forward, her voice dropping. "I've been thinking about how to say this. You know I'm not getting any younger. I've had health problems recently, and—"

The door opened and Sandra stepped out, bearing a tray. "Sun's over the yardarm. Who's ready for appletinis?"

"Oh, God. I'm barely awake," said Karen.

"This'll fix you."

Frieda frowned. "I don't like martinis."

Sandra placed a glass in front of her. "You'll like this."

Karen sipped her drink, trying to guess what Frieda wanted to say. She seemed withdrawn as if burdened by her thoughts.

A metal club clinked against a golf ball. Karen watched a foursome chipping up toward the green, and felt a longing to be out there herself. One of the players had a long lanky body, his broad shoulders and nipped-in waist starting a glow of warmth in her belly. Grateful for her dark sunglasses, she closed her eyes, remembering the texture of Curt's face, the light stubble scattered across his chin the morning after. Even if she never saw him again, she was glad for the nights they spent together. The martini went down bright and cold, and she turned away from the course. "Do you play, Sandra?"

Sandra shook her head. "Why waste a perfectly good day?"

"It wouldn't take all day if you played with the niners."

Sandra looked up from her martini. "The whatters?"

"Most clubs have women's groups that only play half a round—nine holes. Niners. It's a good idea if you're new to the game or don't have the time for a full round. You get a little bit of fun and socializing."

"Have you been talking to Richard? He's always on me to join some group. I did all that when he was just getting started in his career, but now I don't have to."

The housekeeper set a tray of appetizers on the table.

Sandra leaned in close. "Thank you. We'll call if we need you."

The woman untied her apron. "Mrs. Bonner, I have to go pick up my daughter from day care."

Sandra, dismissing her with a wave, reached for a cheese-topped cracker. "So tell me about your wild adventures, Mom."

"We saw a lot of beautiful scenery and met some nice people."

Sandra took a nibble and shook her head. "This *crostini* is too done."

"Mine's good," said Karen.

Frieda poked at a limp carrot. "Let it go, Sandy."

"I pay a lot of money for her services."

"The food is fine."

"It's not up to my standards."

"Anyway." Karen looked from one to the other. "I enjoyed Dickinson."

Sandra stared at her. "Then maybe you can tell me, what is the attraction? That dump has such a hold on Mom."

"I guess that's why she never visits," Frieda said to Karen. "Last time she came home, Jessie was a teenager. I took her down to the old pool and she found a bunch of kids to play with. I love that girl. If Jessie knew I was here, she would have come."

"They're coming. I told you."

"Tell me this," said Frieda. "What exactly do you do all day?"

Sandra stared at her mother, and Frieda stared back.

Karen inched her chair back. Maybe she could sneak up to her room and read.

"I'm busy all the time. For Pete's sake." Sandra crunched a cracker smeared with cheese. Part of the cheese stuck to her lip.

"Busy's not important. Being happy is. Remember that time you and your friends went to Mexico for a week?"

"I was young and stupid back then. I'm lucky I didn't get in trouble." A timer sounded from inside the house and Sandra jumped up. "Dinner's ready. Richard said to start without him."

Karen pulled Frieda's chair back and together they trudged toward the kitchen. Inside, they found chicken enchiladas in *verde* sauce, with black beans and sweet corn cake on the side. Nobody spoke as they loaded up their plates. Soon Sandra was off on some tangent about redecorating the master suite, something about the Renaissance period.

Frieda dawdled with her food, nodding as Sandra talked. Then she put down her fork. "So Jessie and the baby aren't coming."

"They are coming, I just don't know when. We have a wonderful *flan* for dessert." Sandra scooped up the last bits of tortilla from her plate.

Frieda gripped her plate. "What's your best guess?"

"A couple weeks?" Sandra bolted toward the kitchen.

"Stop." Frieda's voice rang out across the room. She folded her napkin and threw it down on her plate. "Don't play me for stupid. They're not coming, are they?"

"It's not on purpose. Jessie said she would try, and I can't tell you any more than that."

"You told me more than that to get me to come here."

"I said Jessie might be here and you should come and visit. Show a little flexibility for once in your life." The kitchen door swung shut behind her, sweeping back and forth and finally stopping.

Frieda folded her hands in her lap. "I feel like a fool."

"I'm sorry."

"All the crap I put you through, and your mother's stuff and all..." Frieda shook her head.

"Don't beat yourself up. Why don't you make the best of it? Hang around for a few more days, smooth things out between you and Sandy, and then go home. Or if you're too pissed off, I can take you to the airport tomorrow."

"That's what I was trying to tell you."

Sandra interrupted, carrying a silver tray loaded with dessert. "Here we go. Coffee and *flan* with caramel sauce."

"I'll just have a little decaf," said Karen.

Sandra set the tray on the table. "Why do you have to be so negative, Mom? No matter what, everything is always bad."

"I was happy back home in North Dakota before you tricked me into coming out here."

"I didn't trick you."

Karen wondered if she could make a move for the hallway unnoticed.

"How can you be happy? You're all by yourself in the middle of nowhere. What if something happened?"

"Nothing's going to happen."

"If you lived here, I could help you."

"I don't need your help, or anybody's. But if I did, I have neighbors in Dickinson, and lots of friends, too. It's not like I'm a hermit. Which you would know if you ever came to see me."

Sandra looked at Karen in frustration. "You know how it is. Tell her."

Karen shrugged. "She does have a pretty good social network, and the people in Dickinson watch out for each other."

"Great. Now you're both against me." Sandra turned back to Frieda. "This is the first time you've come to see me in fifteen years.

You always say it's too hard for you to travel but here you are, driving cross country and camping, for God's sake."

"Karen took real good care of me the whole way."

"And how well do you even know her?"

Karen finished her coffee. "Think I'll turn in."

"You don't have to go," said Frieda.

"Maybe she should."

Karen left the kitchen but their voices followed her up the staircase.

"Very hospitable of you, Sandra. Thank you very much for treating my friend so rudely."

"She's had three heart attacks," Sandra hollered after Karen. "Did she tell you that?"

If those two didn't back off, it would be four. Was Sandra trying to kill her or was she just plain stupid?

"Leave her out of this," said Frieda. "My health is my own business."

"It's my business too, Mom. I care about you."

"And you show it by tricking me into coming all this way to see you?"

"That's right. That's what I'm reduced to, tricking my own mother to get her to come see me. And you know what? I was stupid enough to think you might like it here and want to stay. But no, you'd rather live in the sticks and be all by yourself when you die." Sandra began to cry.

"Don't be so dramatic."

"You're ninety, goddammit." Sandra's sobs continued.

"So what? Nobody lives forever. I'm not afraid." Frieda's voice lowered. "Come on, Sandy, toughen up."

"I'm not like you. You go where you want and do whatever you want. You always have."

"You act like you're half dead, and you're only sixty. You're a very capable girl, there's no reason you can't do whatever you want."

Sandra broke into a wail.

Karen closed the door to her bedroom, wishing she were in Albuquerque. Morning couldn't come soon enough. She put on her nightgown and checked her phone, shrugging off the disappointment over not finding a message from Curt. Peggy called, but Karen wasn't in the mood to hear about the fabulous world cruise her old friend was taking. Maybe tomorrow.

She snagged a book from the bottom of her suitcase, a hot bestseller on corporate leadership in the new millennium. Propped up by pillows, she was soon immersed in new tips and tactics.

The knock on her door startled her. She'd lost track of time. It was late.

Frieda, wrapped in her ratty pink robe, closed the door behind her. "I saw the light." She limped across the room and eased into a chair. "I'm so achy tonight. These old bones. What are you reading?"

Karen set the book aside. "It's about work."

"I imagine you're excited to go home. What do you figure? Three, four days?"

"Or less."

"Um hmm."

Karen kept her finger in the book, wishing she could get back to it.

"Sandra could've gone into business herself. Richard offered to bankroll her if she wanted her own shop." Frieda glanced around the room. "She's good enough. She could've made a go at it."

"You can't control the way kids turn out."

Frieda nodded, but she didn't answer. Karen heard a branch claw against the window. The old woman's head dipped, and for a minute she seemed to have dozed off in the big wingback. Karen stole a glance at her book. If she were careful, she could read without disturbing Frieda.

On the mantel, a clock began chiming the hour and Frieda flinched awake. Her head bobbed around unsteadily on her stick neck.

"You okay?" Karen asked.

"Never better."

"Good."

The old woman nodded, her gaze in the far distance. "I was thinking."

"I think you were sleeping."

"Very funny." Frieda pointed a wavering finger at Karen, a thin smile on her old face. "No, I was thinking I'd like to see the ocean. I never have, and you're going that direction."

Chapter Twenty-Nine

*K*aren set her book on the night stand, excused herself and went in the bathroom where she locked the door and sank down on the marble steps leading to the sunken tub.

This was not good.

Even if she wanted to take Frieda all the way home with her to California, which was a crazy idea in every way, the trip would probably kill her. How to say no without crushing her?

If she were Frieda, she would rather throw herself in front of a train than live with Sandra, even if only temporarily, but Frieda was very elderly and her choices were limited. She could stay here or go back to North Dakota and live alone until one morning she keeled over on the way to the bathroom, and how she'd get back to Dickinson wasn't even clear.

Frieda was trapped, but it wasn't Karen's problem. She had to think about her own future. Dropping her head in her hands, she thanked God she was still young enough to have one. Frieda's last days were becoming more tragic by the minute, but it wasn't something Karen could fix. All she wanted to do was get in the van tomorrow morning and haul ass out of here. The feeling of guilt would fade in time, and she would never have to see Frieda or Sandra again.

It wouldn't be nice, but she was tired of being nice. If the incident on the road out of Cheyenne had taught her anything, it was that here in middle-age, life was short and she'd better make the best of what was left. She splashed water on her face, flushed the toilet for cover, and opened the door.

Across the room, Frieda waited.

Karen walked slowly across the floor, hands jammed in the pockets of her robe. She sat down on the edge of the bed.

"Frieda, I'm sorry."

"You sure?"

"Yes."

"Fine." The old woman started to get up.

"Wait. Think about it. Sandy means well. She's proud, like you. Don't let one argument run you off. Make your peace with her, and stick around so you can see the baby. You know that's the thing to do."

"Do you think it's that simple?"

"Unless I'm missing something."

"You're too damn young to understand."

"Okay, let's say you came with me. Once you got to California, how would you get back home?"

Frieda's gaze was direct. "Think about it."

"Come on. You'll be around for a long time yet. I don't see you slowing down any."

"Well, I am. You don't know how bad it is because I fake it. That's what you do when you're old. You lie to yourself and keep going. Either that or give up." She slumped in the chair.

"You're a good actress."

"Russ and I used to talk about what it was to get older, and that made it easier, but now with him gone there's nobody as old as me, and I don't want to do it alone anymore. Everything is harder. I feel like hell all the time. My body is falling apart in a million little ways. Like, look at this. See my right ear?" Frieda tilted her head toward Karen.

"The edges look red."

"It's irritated because if I lay on my right side for too long at night, the cartilage gets infected. But if I turn over and lay on my left, I get congested and can't breathe. And I can't lie on my back very long because my heels burn."

"Isn't there some kind of medicine you can take?"

"I'm already taking so many things they're destroying my stomach."

Karen didn't know what to say. She felt guilty for being young.

"All my friends are dying or dead, Russell's dead, my sisters are all dead. There's nobody left."

"You still have family."

"That's her, right there downstairs. There's no one left and no point in living."

Karen pushed her hair back over her forehead and exhaled. Common decency required a response. "A scientist friend of mine—she's an atheist—once told me she thought the point of her life was to have fun and feel useful."

"Back home I had a certain amount of fun, and up until a few years ago, I felt useful. Now, I don't."

"Never? Not one single minute of any of your days? What about when you let that kid mow your lawn and he was so proud he hugged you?"

Frieda nodded. "That was nice."

"And at church. Weren't you on the finance committee?"

"Still am."

"Well, don't you think they're going to wonder where you are?"

"That's pretty pathetic." Frieda planted her cane and started to get up, but then stopped. She stared at Karen, her eyes watery and red. "All I'm saying is, I'd like to see the red rock country again, and the Pacific Ocean. After that, I don't care. You can put me on a Greyhound bus and I'll go quietly back to North Dakota. But if you leave me here you may as well kill me."

Karen felt a tickle on her arm. The cuff of the robe was fraying. "How did you and Sandra leave it?"

"We hugged. She's hurt and I feel bad, but that's beside the point." Frieda rubbed her eyes. "She used to be independent like you. Now she's afraid of her own shadow and bored out of her skull."

"She has Richard."

"Where was he tonight? He had to know we were here. No, his work comes first. If something happened to him, I don't know what she would do. She's very unhappy, down deep."

"Maybe you could help her. Show her how to be more independent."

"Don't be naïve. I came here to die." She shrugged at Karen's shock. "I figured I'd come here and wait, but I wanted to see the baby first." Frieda pulled a paper out of the pocket of her robe. "Here. I signed the van over to you."

"No, Frieda."

"Go on. You need the money more than she does."

Karen took the pink slip. "I'll sell it and send you half."

"Don't bother." The door closed and Frieda's footsteps faded down the hall.

Chapter Thirty

Karen lay watching the walls lighten, until the first clang of a pan and slamming door freed her. After a quick shower, she collected her things and went downstairs to the kitchen, where Sandra bustled around in a black velvet track suit, her hair knotted on top of her head with ebony chopsticks. Frieda sat at the breakfast table, wearing yesterday's clothes and reading the local paper. She didn't look up when Karen sat down across from her. Sandra clattered and banged, pulling a sheet of breakfast pastries from the oven. "Richard had to leave early, Mom, but he said to meet him at Zen's for lunch. It's the hottest new restaurant in town. They have the best sushi."

"I don't eat raw fish." Frieda's eyes remained glued to the Denver Post.

"And he says afterwards I should take you to Saks. Our treat. About time you went on a big-city shopping trip."

"What would I need from Saks?"

"There's always something pretty to buy." Sandra set the pastries on the table and put one in her mouth, licking the frosting from her fingers.

Frieda folded the paper. "I'll probably just lie down after Karen leaves."

Sandra bustled out of the kitchen. Karen tore apart a cinnamon roll and smeared a chunk of butter on the hot surface.

Sandra came back a few minutes later with a thick photo album, which she dropped on the table next to Frieda's plate.

"What'm I supposed to do with that?" Frieda asked.

"I thought we could look at it later." Sandra stood next to her mother's elbow. "It might make you feel better. You can tell me all about the old days."

"You were never interested before." Frieda pushed the heavy album a half-inch away.

"Well, I am now." Sandra sat down next to her mother. "Or we could look through my catalogs to find a wall color for the game room. I'm thinking something red with navy accents. Don't you think that'd pop?"

Karen snuck a glance over the edge of her coffee cup at Frieda. Their eyes met. Karen looked away.

"And I thought I'd have the housekeeper move one of the computers into your room. It's crazy. We have five of them." Sandra held up her hand, fingers spread like a starfish. "Five. Can you imagine? And I don't use a single one. I'm so behind the times."

"Frieda just learned how to do email," said Karen.

"Fantastic. She can teach me." Sandra's acrylic nails tapped Frieda's arm. "Earth to Mom. Hello in there."

Frieda had been sipping coffee, her eyes frozen on an indeterminate point across the kitchen. "Oh. I don't really know that much about computers, dear."

Karen finished her coffee, set the mug down with a definite clunk, and sighed loudly.

"So soon?" Frieda asked.

"I'm kind of anxious to get going," Karen said. "It's a long way across the desert."

Frieda looked down at her plate.

"Hey, Mom, I got a call from a gal yesterday at the club," Sandra said from over at the sink. "Belinda something or other. The social committee needs volunteers to help with their big Fourth of July barbecue. I told her to count us in."

"I don't know, honey. I'm not much of a joiner."

"But what a great way to meet people, doncha think?"

Frieda blew her nose on a cloth napkin.

"I'm always begging Richard to go with me but he's so busy," Sandy said. "But now I have you. We're gonna have so much fun." She glanced over at her mother. "What's the matter? You haven't touched your roll."

"I'm not really that hungry, dear."

"Well, we're gonna change that in a hurry. I am going to fatten you up."

Karen pushed her chair back, trying not to make any noise.

"You're going to see some beautiful country," said Frieda.

"Not really. It's desert. Very boring. And it'll be hot. You're just as well off sticking around here." Karen inched toward the door. "Thank you for breakfast. The pastries were delicious."

"You are so welcome. I get most of my ideas from Rachael Ray. You know she has a house here, right on the ninth fairway? Maybe we'll even run into her at the clubhouse." Sandra danced back to the sink with the empty plates and began rinsing.

"Have a good trip," Frieda said from behind her newspaper. Sandra flicked on the garbage disposal. The roar obliterated all sound in the kitchen.

Karen slipped back toward the table and tapped the newspaper. Frieda lowered it. "What?"

Karen leaned toward Frieda's ear. "I'm going to load my suitcase, then I'll be back."

"You'll never be back." Frieda raised the paper.

Karen glanced toward the sink. "How soon can you be ready?"

Frieda, her mouth open, processed it for about three seconds. Then she tossed the paper aside, scooted her chair back, and hurried out of the kitchen.

Sandra shut off the disposal and the faucet, wiped her hands and looked around. "Where'd Mom go?"

Karen held up a saucer. "You know, your china is exquisite. I love the pattern."

Sandra's eyes narrowed. "Don't bullshit me. What're you two cooking up?"

Karen remained silent.

"Is she leaving with you? I swear to God, she's not leaving with you."

"Sandra."

"No."

"It's her decision."

"My ass. You take her out of here, I'm calling the police. I'll tell them you kidnapped her at gunpoint. And you stole my mother's van." Sandra leaned against the sink, arms folded against her chest. The dishwasher clicked on, started chugging through a cycle.

"She's here because she wanted to see you and the kids. She even talked me into this crazy trip just so she could come. It wasn't that cool of you to lie to her."

"Fuck you. You think you're some kind of hero, but you're gonna kill her if you take her across that desert. Look at her. She could go any time."

"It's her decision. She's old, but she's still got her marbles. Frieda's one of the most alive people I know."

"Oh, for Christ's sake. You think you've got all the answers." Sandra glared at Karen. "Did she tell you she almost burned her house down last fall? She was cooking and a pot holder caught fire. It's a miracle she didn't get hurt. I tried to get her to move then but she wouldn't even listen. We went back and forth for days, and finally she stopped answering the phone. I gave up and hired a man to go in and clean out the smoke damage and repaint everything. She was even mad at me for that. Said I was meddling."

Karen walked over to the sink and stood by Sandra. Outside, the trees waved gently, but the closed window barred the fragrance of pine. "Don't you think it's her choice, though?"

"No I do not. At that age, they're like children. You can't leave them alone to do whatever they want, any more than you would a five-year old."

"She's sharp enough to be pissed off about you using Jessie and the baby as bait."

"I did what I had to, and she'll thank me for it. Or she would have if you hadn't interfered." They turned at the sound of the door opening.

"You're wrong about that, too." Frieda stood in the doorway with her coat and purse.

"Mom, you can't traipse off across the country like this. You're not well. It's not safe." Sandra's face crumpled. "Please don't go."

"Karen, would you mind getting my bags?"

Karen picked up the photo album and left the room, Sandra's voice ringing in her ears. "You don't even know her. What if you get sick?"

"She's a good girl. I'm not worried."

"You should be! What's the plan, Mom? Are you going to let her stick you in some ratty rest home in California to die?"

"Sandy, you're overreacting."

Karen tiptoed past the kitchen, carrying Frieda's bags. She saw Frieda reach out and grasp Sandra's hand.

"We all have to make up our own minds, Sandy. I want to see the ocean before I die."

Karen closed the front door as quietly as possible, went down the stairs, and loaded the van. A gardener pulled up on the other side of the street, *banda* music pouring from the truck. Sprinklers went on in the garden, their spray creating a rainbow in the morning sun. Her phone rang but Karen kept her eyes on Sandy's door, waiting for the two women to emerge. If she were ninety years old, assuming she lived that long, she wanted to live life on her own terms. The risk was Frieda's choice.

The massive door closed on Frieda. Karen helped her down the steps. "Will she be okay?"

"She's got Richard." Frieda stared at the house as Karen started the engine.

"Are you absolutely sure this is the right thing to do?"

Frieda nodded, her chin trembling. Karen put the van in gear and pulled away from the curb. The guard waved as they passed through the gate. "I know it's your decision, but I feel terrible."

"Then don't."

"I spoke with Sandra while you were packing. She's difficult, but she cares about you, and she means well."

"Guess that makes me a bad mother," said Frieda.

"I didn't mean that."

Silence fell between them as Karen drove toward the freeway, where she turned west toward the Rockies.

"Thought you were taking the southern route to Albuquerque," said Frieda.

"We're spending the night in Aspen, it's my treat, and I don't want you arguing."

Chapter Thirty-One

Karen rechecked her mirrors and stepped on the accelerator, sending the van up the first part of the grade that would take them up and over the Continental Divide. Cool air rushed in the window, and the traffic dropped away behind them as they left the city and its pedestrian concerns. As she urged the van up the grade, the clicking in the motor returned. Karen tilted her head. The sound seemed to come from beneath the floor, between the driver and passenger seats. When she accelerated harder, the noise remained the same.

So she put it out of her mind. They were off to a late start and already a summer storm was taking shape over the pass. Clouds turned the mountains gunmetal-gray, and a light drizzle spat at the windshield. Behind her, the skyscrapers of Denver shot heavenward, a handful of glass spires punctuating the high plateau. Up ahead, the steep roadway gained in elevation.

Frieda cried out and pointed to a small herd of buffalo grazing amid patches of snow. Mining equipment from the last century lay rusting alongside the highway like giant yard art. Lush pine forests marched up the slopes on both sides of the road, and Karen felt happy with her decision.

An hour out of Denver the Eisenhower Tunnel appeared, cutting through the Continental Divide. The narrow chute bored through the mountains at eleven thousand feet, well-lit but tight. She kept to the right, working to stay ahead of the grumbling parade of trucks while trying not to push the van too hard.

After almost two miles, the van shot out of the tunnel into a light snowfall, and the women gasped, for the terrain had changed as dramatically as if they had passed through a time warp. Snow lay deep across the landscape in every direction, unmelted even in early July, the glacial crags cloaked in white. One peak, taller and steeper than the rest, resembled the fabled Matterhorn.

"How are you doing with the altitude?"

"I feel fine," said Frieda. "I'm glad we came this way. I never would have imagined."

"Me neither." Karen drove carefully, avoiding holes in the weather-worn blacktop as she started downhill on the rain-slick roadway. She dodged a small boulder in the middle of her lane, and passed two runaway truck ramps, their gravel surfaces groomed and ready to capture brakeless eighteen-wheelers, whose wheels could spew rock with the velocity of shotgun pellets.

As the elevation dropped and the roadway widened, she began to relax. The snow gave way to grass again, and small mountain communities appeared. She wondered what it would be like to live in this wintry Eden. Surely there would be snow storms that trapped the residents for days on end, and the late-summer monsoons would be horrific, but the spectacular beauty of the place would compensate.

The clouds parted, exposing cobalt sky. Rivulets of snowmelt poured off the rocky hillsides, creating ponds on both sides of the highway. Wildflowers blanketed the western slopes in hues of yellow and blue and white.

They passed Vail, its condos and cafes swarming the base of the ski lifts. In Glenwood Springs they saw multi-colored tulips decorating every front yard, and stopped at a restaurant warm with the aroma of freshly baked bread. The waitress brought sandwiches and iced tea, and by the time they had satisfied their hunger, it was mid-afternoon.

Karen spread the map on the table. Aspen lay less than an hour to the southeast. When she asked for a recommendation, the waitress tore a page from her order pad. "The best place is the Hotel Jerome. It's pricey, but you're in the off season. Call and ask. You might even see a movie star. I heard George Clooney was in town last week."

"Sounds like our kind of place." Frieda's eyebrows wiggled.

Chapter Thirty-Two

They followed the Roaring Fork River through meadows of blue columbine and yellow paintbrush until the highway curved against a backdrop of white-tipped mountains. In the town of Aspen they drove past clapboard homes and buckled sidewalks to the Hotel Jerome. When they stopped in front of the hotel, a bellman opened Frieda's door. "Oh, my." She accepted his hand, her cheeks pink.

Karen gave her keys to the valet and followed Frieda through the bronze-clad entryway. Built during the silver boom of the late eighteen-hundreds, the hotel had recently been remodeled to within an inch of its life. The foyer opened to a high-ceilinged lobby where leather armchairs and chintz sofas surrounded a crackling fire. A formal dining room and bar stood adjacent to the lobby, where a uniformed clerk greeted them from behind a burnished wood desk.

"I think you'll like the rooms, Ms. Grace. Both are south-facing, with a nice view."

"Two rooms?" Frieda asked. "Can we afford that?"

"It's my treat, remember?"

After making dinner reservations with the concierge, they followed the bellman upstairs. When he opened the door to Frieda's room, she stepped back. "Heaven forbid."

Two upholstered chairs and a Queen Anne table sat in front of the windows for a breathtaking view of Aspen Mountain. A fireplace glowed nearby, and brocade covered the antique four-poster.

"Karen, come look at this." Frieda stood in the bathroom, which featured a whirlpool tub and a separate shower, marble floors and high-end bath products. Billowy terry robes hung on the back of the door. "I feel like royalty."

"That's our goal, ma'am." The bellman accepted Karen's tip and disappeared.

"I'm going to stretch out," said Frieda. "Call me in a couple hours."

Karen headed for her own room, where she found a minibar stocked with goodies. She mixed a scotch and soda, sank into a plush wingback, and took a sip. The scotch hit bottom, and her stomach warmed agreeably. Alone at last, she felt free. She admired the mountain and let her mind ramble.

Option One was to head back to California as fast as possible and find a new job.

She sipped her Scotch. Jazz wafted up from the street below through the open window, and she leaned back and put her feet up on a fat ottoman. A big sigh escaped from her chest. Life was beginning to feel normal again. Racing back to California was the practical solution, but it did involve a certain amount of discipline, which the liquor was eroding.

Besides, who knew how much time Frieda had left?

Option One began to lose ground to Option Two, which was to show Frieda the time of her life and find a job once the two of them were settled.

Karen took another sip. At the ripe old age of fifty, she had earned the right to find balance in her life, and there was so much she wanted to do. Her termination was a blessing, in a way, because it broke her out of her rut and allowed her to think differently. This would be a part of the Option Two playbook. Relaxation, the arts, creativity, long walks on the beach, showing Frieda whatever delights her fading stamina allowed—that was how Karen planned to live her new life. Even her marriage breaking up didn't seem so bad at the moment. By following his own dreams, Steve had done her a favor. She was now free to create a new life according to her own standards. The thought made her incredibly happy.

After a while she freshened her drink and filled the tub, similar to the one in her house in Newport. As she sank into the deep cloud of lavender suds, the sheer luxury of the hot water and fragrance surprised her. Karen rarely took the time for a bath, tending to hurry through showers on her way to whatever urgent business called her. How stupid to never indulge in such a treat when it had been right at her fingertips for years. She leaned her head back against the porcelain and closed her eyes.

A memory flickered in her mind, and she gasped at the pain knifing through her mid-section. She envisioned the honeymoon cottage where she and Steve had mapped out their dreams, and later, nursery furniture, disassembled along with her hopes, the materials carted off quietly by kind neighbors.

And now, a career had been vaporized, and a family was disappearing into time.

She grimaced. This was not Option Two living. Torturing herself with regret was not the new way. The new way involved more hot water, an appreciation of the fragrance of lavender, and the sight of the suds billowing anew. In the second half of her life, Karen would slow down and be mindful. She tilted her glass for the last swallow of Scotch, but it went down wrong and she sat up, coughing. Her throat burned and her eyes filled with tears.

So much for relaxation. She set the glass on the edge of the tub and stood. As the water and suds coursed off her body she saw that her belly and butt seemed more rounded and substantial. She ran her hands over the warm and slippery curves, feeling almost voluptuous, and her image in the gilt mirror on the opposite wall flattered her. This being the case, why the hell had she worked so hard for so many years to remain thin?

She unzipped her suitcase and dug around for something suitable to wear to dinner, but all she had was her funeral suit and a collection of throw-ons from Walmart. Ah, well. This was Aspen. The funeral jacket over a tank top would go a long way toward dressing up a cheap pair of jeans.

At Karen's knock, Frieda opened her door wearing a polyester top with a butterfly brooch at the shoulder. "Don't we look pretty," she said, taking Karen's arm.

They walked several blocks to LuLu Wilson's, arriving as the mountain turned to gold in the sunset. New grass carpeted the ski slopes and aspens shimmered at the mountain's base. Karen found a small table on the bustling patio and ordered a plate of coconut shrimp for a snack. Nearby, a young man flirted with a tight-faced old woman whose tiny dog snarled and fretted. Two handsome cowboys strolled in, wearing chaps and spurs, and a sulky foreigner pulled up out front in a growling Maserati.

Frieda leaned toward Karen. "We're not in Dickinson anymore."

Three women sauntered onto the patio. One wore a slash of red lipstick and a pillbox hat over thinning white curls. Her friend was well-packed into a pair of seersucker Capris, and the two of them laughed like they were sharing a marvelous truth. Karen wondered if you could get to an age where you look adorable just because you still tried. The third woman was fifteen years younger than the other two, and with her bright yellow hair and frozen eyebrows shooting skyward, she almost looked older.

The hostess waved for Karen, and they followed her inside across scuffed wooden floors. Crystal chandeliers hung overhead, and the tables were covered with linen and silver. Frieda opened the menu. "You paid for my room. I'm buying you dinner."

Karen gaped at the prices. "You don't have to."

"Shut up and enjoy yourself." Frieda signaled the waitress. "Please bring us a bottle of your most popular champagne." The sommelier returned with an ice bucket and bottle, popping the cork with finesse. Frieda watched him pour two glasses. Then she raised hers. "To our roadtrip, with all the ups and downs and in-betweens. It's been glorious."

Karen's hand stopped in mid-reach.

Frieda noticed. "Don't think about it," she said. "Listen. We survived. Now let's celebrate the future. Raise your glass." The old woman's eyes sparkled as she took a delicate sip of bubbly.

"Braised short ribs?" The server placed the platter in front of Karen, and a rack of lamb in front of Frieda. A pianist in a long white skirt and cowboy boots struck the opening notes of a jazz standard as the women picked up their forks. The ribs, dripping with sauce, fell from the bones at the slightest touch. Karen thought again about her new curves, the appearance of which pleased her. Soon she would probably have to embark on a diet to regain her angular frame, but not tonight.

The room filled, and Frieda and Karen fell quiet, intent on the feast. When they finished, they ordered pineapple cheesecake and chocolate mousse, with a glass of cognac for Karen.

"Man, this is the life." Frieda swirled cream into a cup of decaf. "When I'm gone—"

"Frieda, please."

"No, hear me out. We discussed this in Denver. Nobody's immortal, and I'm at peace with my life. But you have thirty, forty years ahead of you. So I have to ask. What are you going to do?"

"Head back to California and get back to work."

"Still?"

Karen nodded. "But I'm determined that it will be different from now on."

"Do you ever think about coming back to North Dakota?"

"I did, seriously. For about a week."

"When you were with the professor."

Karen took a sip of cognac. The man inhabited her dreams nightly, not that she would admit that to Frieda.

"Where do you stand with him?"

"We'll always be friends, but there's no future."

"Here's what matters." Frieda clipped off another bite of cheesecake. "You're too young to go without a man in your life."

"I still have a man in my life. Wish I didn't."

"That's temporary. What comes next?"

Karen scooped up the last spoonful of mousse. She rolled the flavor around on her tongue, formulating her thoughts. "I don't know. But I liked him a lot and I'll miss him."

"You could be making a big mistake. I'm not going to tell you what to do. But don't throw away a chance at love."

"Love is the last thing on my list."

"Work isn't everything."

Karen laid down her spoon. The light had faded outside, but a couple hours west, the sun still lingered over the Pacific. Suddenly, she felt dizzy with homesickness. The Midwest had its own allure, but it seemed like months since she'd inhaled the salt air, watched a crimson sunset or the retreat of the morning fog, or the pelicans skimming the waves like threads of smoke. She remembered the church-bell clang of masts from sailboats bobbing in the marina. "When was the last time you were in California?"

"Never," said Frieda.

"You'll love it. The variety, the energy. Did you know if California were a country, it would be the eighth largest economy in the world?"

"Just because a factory makes a lot of widgets doesn't mean you should live in it."

"California's like a kaleidoscope. You have the liberal big cities like L.A. and San Francisco, but you've also got the Central Valley. It's a conservative farming area, a lot like the Dakotas. Then you've got sandy beaches down south, but up north, it's rocky, and the water's so rough the surf can break your neck. We've got barren deserts and the glitz of Palm Springs. We've got alpine lakes—I mean, think of the pictures you've seen of Yosemite."

"So visit once in a while. You've got family in North Dakota. You just got reacquainted. Lorraine and all of them. Don't give them up."

"I'll visit. I promise."

"Long as you're clear about things."

"I'm clear."

"Because there's nothing worse than waking up at ninety and realizing it's gone."

Chapter Thirty-Three

The next morning, Karen zipped up her suitcase and took one more look around the room, but she couldn't drag herself to the door. The room was too beautiful, and the solitude too rich. Sheer curtains billowed from the windows, framing the waving grass slopes of Aspen Mountain. She sank into the plush chair and tried to memorize the contours of the mountain and the color of the sky, a special shade of heartbreak blue dotted with cottony-white clouds. Perhaps she would come back some day, maybe even in winter with her skis.

No, not *perhaps*. Work was fine, work was essential, but idyllic escapes had their place, too. A person couldn't be just one thing. She had been too narrowly focused. In the future she would remember this place, and this feeling. The days ahead would challenge her as she worked to carve out a new groove, and she would need meditation and silence. Her mental health would depend on it.

Before leaving the room, she checked her voicemail one last time. Phone reception could be spotty on the road ahead as they crossed the desert southwest. She clicked through the menu and waited for the first message to play.

Stacey had left several. "Thank God," she said when Karen called back. "Are you home?"

"I'm still in Colorado. What's wrong?"

"We're being sued. We, as in the company, for allegedly not protecting the confidentiality of our medical files. There is no flippin' way I'm going to jail for this company."

"They can't come after you personally."

"It won't matter because when they do, I'll be dead. They are working me to death. The lawyers keep demanding all these documents and I already have my own job and now I'm doing your work, too." Stacey took a breath. "Wes keeps asking me for stuff from your files and I keep dodging him, but he's getting pissed and I don't care. I'm not going to let him screw things up."

"Kid, you're going to have a heart attack if you don't slow down."

"I'm not going to have a heart attack. I do my job and then go home and get drunk with Jason. In my spare time I send out resumés. So how's your vacation?"

Karen winced. "Is there anything I can do to help?"

"Yes. Do you remember that time when the manager at the Citrus Family Clinic—"

Karen listened until Stacey finished, and then suggested actions Stacey hadn't thought of. Her assistant was grateful.

"You're welcome. Now, how's Peggy? Have you heard from her?"

"Just a couple days ago. She sounds depressed."

"Isn't she on a cruise?"

"Yes, and she keeps sending me emails about how bored she is and how the food is crap and the ports are too busy. Some people are never happy."

"You know Peggy. She likes to bitch."

"Yeah, well, send me on a cruise. I wouldn't complain," Stacey said. "Can I call you again if I get stuck?"

"Absolutely." After deleting several more messages, Karen got to Steve's. "Please call me back right away," he said. "I know you're checking your messages." His voice stopped and she almost pressed delete, but then he continued.

She replayed the message. This couldn't be happening. She played it again.

She was losing her mind.

It couldn't be true.

And then she hung up, turned off the phone, and went to meet Frieda for breakfast.

Chapter Thirty-Four

She drove without speaking for an hour, trying to puzzle out Steve's news. Frieda seemed to get the hint and busied herself with her travel guide and the passing scenery. The highway cut through the twisting curves and terraced cliffs of Glenwood Canyon. Tough little trees clustered at the base of the canyon walls, and sage and scrub oak clung to outcroppings farther up.

When the mighty Colorado River appeared alongside, Karen was jarred from her thoughts. On impulse, she turned off the highway and found a rest stop at the river's edge.

"You need the bathroom?"

"No, I just want a closer look."

Karen parked the van, got a loaf of bread out of the pantry, and helped Frieda to a bench on the river bank. They threw pieces of bread to the ducks while shore birds darted on stick legs before them. As Karen tore the bread into bits, she could feel her hands shaking. Before long, the bread was gone and the ducks went to forage further afield.

A couple of women approached, one old and one not. Between them they swung a giggling toddler. Their men followed behind, hands jammed in pockets, ball caps on heads. One wore a camera around his neck. The group called out a greeting and moved on.

Karen watched them go, mindlessly fiddling with her wedding ring. It was a modest band with a small chip, all that Steve could afford when they got engaged. Later, when they had more money, he wanted to buy her a lavish replacement but she had declined. It had been with her at the wedding, and she had never wanted more. Now she studied the small, dull stone. If a diamond's theoretical power to bind life partners turned out to be false, then what was a wedding ring but an overhyped bit of jewelry? She pulled it off and rolled it between her fingers, steeling herself to flick it into the river.

"There's a million pawn shops between here and California." Frieda looked away, as if she weren't the one who had just spoken.

Karen stuck the ring back on. "I've never lived alone in my life."

"I didn't either until Russell died."

"How long were you married?"

"Sixty years, and I loved him every day of it. Even now, I start to say something to him and then I remember he's gone and I feel sad all over again."

Karen threw a rock at the water. Instead of skipping, it dove straight in.

"Didn't you ever think about it?" asked Frieda. "Make any plans? At your age, women start to lose their husbands. You knew that was a possibility."

"I figured it would happen way down the road, not when I turned fifty. I thought we'd get old together and then he'd die and a couple years later, I would. Beyond that, I didn't think about it. I never expected to get divorced."

"Death, divorce, no matter what, you have to keep moving forward," Frieda said. "It helps if you stay busy, most of the time anyway. But sometimes you just have to wallow around in the pain a while. When you get sick of yourself, you get up and go back to your normal life."

The river rippled by, carrying bits of brush and branches, and occasionally something more interesting, like a wooden door with the knob still attached. A great blue heron took flight, its wingtips touching the water as it lifted off.

"He reminds me of a pterodactyl," said Karen.

Frieda nodded. "Something to be said for dinosaurs."

Around one o'clock they crossed the state line into Utah, and stopped for gas in the farming village of Fruita. When Karen restarted the van, the ticking sound turned into a chattering growl. "Great," she said, turning it back off.

"That used to happen to me and Russell sometimes."

"What is it?"

"I can't remember. Look, there's a garage right over there." Frieda pointed up the street. A bright yellow banner, decorated with peace signs, hung out front. In the service bay, Karen smelled solvent and patchouli. A pair of blue-jeaned legs stuck out from under a battered green truck.

"Hello?" Karen said in the direction of the legs.

"With you in a sec." A young woman rolled out from beneath the truck and stood, unfurling to six feet. Long, blonde dreads swept back into a ponytail and she wore silver rings through lip and nostril. She cleaned up with a rag and followed Karen outside. After a few minutes of poking around, the girl closed the hood. "Give me a couple hours."

"Is it bad?"

"I don't think so, but I want to make sure. There's an organic lunch place two blocks over. Why'nt you go over there and relax, have a bite, and then come back?

"Do those things hurt?" asked Frieda.

"We'll see you after lunch." Karen put her arm around Frieda and moved her in the direction of the restaurant.

When their food arrived, Karen removed the bun from her veggie burger and set the two halves on the side of her plate. "I'm outgrowing my clothes," she explained when Frieda looked at her like she was crazy. "Aren't you hungry?"

Frieda hadn't touched her sandwich. "Whatever happens, I'm not going back."

"Don't worry. I get a good feeling about the girl. I think she can fix it."

"It's an old van."

"I promised you'd see the ocean, and you will. Once we get to California, you can stay with me as long as you want. Now, why don't you eat that sandwich before it gets cold?"

When Frieda picked up one half and took a small bite, Karen felt relieved. "I had this idea. After we get back and settled, we might take one more little trip, up the coast. We could see Santa Barbara, or maybe even go as far as Monterey. I'd love to show it to you."

"What's up there?"

"Have you ever seen those car commercials where they're driving on a winding road on a cliff overlooking the ocean? That's Highway One. It's the scenic route. There's this restaurant called Nepenthe's where you sit on a patio a couple hundred feet above the water."

"I don't know if it's smart to plan that far ahead. Besides, you have to sell your house."

"No problem. We'll find a rental in Corona del Mar or somewhere. We could have coffee on the patio every morning and read the paper like we did at the Hotel Jerome."

"You're a good girl, but don't go and get your hopes up. You know I have medical problems."

"Who doesn't? Enjoy life. Isn't that what you've been trying to tell me?"

Frieda managed half a smile.

Karen reached over and patted her hand. "Don't worry. Even if you need a doctor, I know all the good ones. At least I got something out of all those years in the field."

Frieda picked up a French fry. "What about your work?"

"Things will get busy soon enough. Finish your lunch and let's go see some country."

The young mechanic explained the problem as she closed the hood as they walked up. "So I did a few adjustments and a lube. You shouldn't have any more trouble. She'll run for years if you keep taking good care of her."

Karen opened her wallet. "Is this your garage?"

When the girl smiled she looked all of twenty. "I won it in a poker game. Place was a dump. Nobody thought I could do it, but I did."

"Good for you, young lady," said Frieda.

When Karen started the van, it ran quietly. She unfolded a map. "Moab's about two and a half hours, a nice drive right along the river. I'll bet we could find a place to camp tonight, if you're up for it."

Frieda sat up straighter in her seat. "Tomorrow we could go to Arches National Park, where they have all those red rock formations. We could pack a lunch. You know there's a road all through the park. You don't ever have to get out."

Karen stuck the map back in the visor. "Moab it is."

Chapter Thirty-Five

Karen turned off the main highway onto a stretch of bad road that carried them into a bleached-out stretch of stark desert. There was no sign of the storied red cliffs, and she wondered if she had taken the wrong turn. However, the van was running well and the afternoon sun stood high in the sky.

"Let's give it another twenty," she said. "If we don't see anything then, we'll turn around and figure out Plan B."

"I'm sure we're on the right road."

"How do you know?"

"I just have a feeling. Now drive."

Ten miles south, Karen came to a stop sign and turned right, relieved to see the Colorado River once again racing alongside the roadway. Soon the distant hills drew nearer, taking on the color of rust and the shape of mythical castles. Colorful rafts appeared, bristling with the arms and legs of riders paddling furiously in the fast current. Yellow daisies lined the river's banks, and clumps of red salvia laced the rocks near the roadway. The canyon walls became steeper, their sheer red sides splashed with iron-black desert patina.

Frieda leaned forward, squinting through the windshield. She pointed at a dirt road where a limping buckboard advertised a campground just past the wood gates. "Turn here."

Karen paid at the adobe camp office and followed the manager's directions to an open site. Trees shaded the campground and oleander bushes screened them from visitors. Across the canyon, massive red rock cliffs soared into the sky, their walls blackened by leaching iron and scored by wind and weather until they resembled Ionic friezes on ancient Greek temples.

"I had no idea it would be this beautiful."

"God's country." Frieda opened her door. Arm in arm, they crossed the uneven ground to the far side of the camp and the river, where deep rapids whispered of danger. "Will you look at that? How fast it runs. And over there," she said, pointing a wobbly finger upriver, "over there is a path down to a little beach where the fish hide under a rock just off the shore."

"How would you know that?"

"Came here with Russell. I remember now. It was before Sandy was born." Frieda stared off across the river. "Can you imagine how long ago that was? I was maybe twenty, twenty-five. Hard to imagine now. I feel like I've always been old."

"You're just tired. Let me get a couple chairs. You relax while I set up. Then take a nap and when you wake up, I'll start dinner." Karen brought out two folding chairs and helped Frieda sit where she could watch the river from a safe vantage.

"I do appreciate you," said Frieda.

Karen leaned over Frieda's shoulder and wrapped her in a hug. Then she went back to the van, where she unrolled and staked the awning, shook out the rug, and hammered the surviving flamingo into the ground. She converted the dinette into Frieda's bed and helped her into the van.

While Frieda napped, Karen plunked down in a camp chair and stared at the river. She fell silent as the arguments in her head started.

You ruined our marriage. Why should I trust you?

Because I'm sorry and I want you back.

Then she fantasized about hurting him. *How can I torture you? Let me count the ways.* After a few minutes of Inquisition-style fantasies, she realized it was a toxic way to spend her valuable time. She closed her eyes and tried to treasure the moment, savoring the fragrance of desert sage and the damp earth along the river's edge, the quack of ducks and the rasp of a cactus wren calling to its mate.

Just this, she whispered, repeating an old mantra and trying to clear her mind of anything else. She breathed from the belly, forcing it in and out, filling and emptying her lungs as her shoulders relaxed. From time to time, she sensed a fleeting warmth that almost bubbled into happiness.

But then Steve would come back and shatter her peace. She was almost glad to hear Frieda awaken.

Karen put a pot of water on the small galley stove, remembering that her mother threw in salt to hasten the boil. Unwrapping a half-pound of ground beef, she dumped it into a plastic bowl, added chopped onions and seasonings, and squished it all together. The mixture rolled easily between her hands, and soon six small meatballs were browning in a skillet.

"You need any help in there?"

Karen turned away from pouring a jar of spaghetti sauce into a pan. "I'm fine," she said, coming to the door and wiping her hands on a dish towel. Outside, Frieda sat in a folding chair, watching the evening come on.

When the pasta had cooked *al dente*, Karen loaded up two plates and carried them out to the picnic table. Together they dined by the last light of evening, watching the colors change on the canyon walls, and the night birds dart low across the river, chasing insects.

"This spaghetti is delicious," said Frieda. "I feel like a queen, being waited on hand and foot."

"You deserve it."

"Some would say otherwise." Frieda chewed and swallowed. She reached for a glass of water. "I just want you to know my daughter's birth certificate says Sandy."

"It's no big deal."

"It is to me."

"Maybe she changed her name to look more serious," said Karen, "with Richard being an attorney and all."

"One of the biggest in Denver." Frieda poked around at her meal. "She's a grown woman. I know she's unhappy but I can't go live with her because of that. Anyway, it would only be a short-term fix. And when I kick the bucket, what's she going to do then?"

"She'll be fine. You did your best. It's all you can do."

"I tried to raise her to be independent, but when she married Richard, she changed. I tried to give her advice, but at a certain point you can't help anymore. You have to let people be. Oh, fiddlesticks. The pollen is horrible here." Frieda pulled a tissue out of her pocket and wiped her eyes. "After Russell died, there were times I wanted to call Sandy and talk about it, you know, mother to daughter, but she kept changing the subject and I didn't want to be a burden. Hell." She dug out another tissue. "Anyway, life goes on. What can a person do? Nothing's perfect."

"It's her loss."

"Well, we still talked, but mostly she complained about her neighbors or Richard being gone all the time, or their taxes going up. Never asked me about myself, unless you count the 'how are you' at the start of the phone call. Then she'd cut me off with some inane tripe. She didn't really want to know." Frieda tucked the tissue in her sleeve. "Sorry. I'm not normally such a whiner."

"It's okay. Let me clean up and then we can sit for a while. Do you want a little sherry?"

"No more than a swallow or it'll keep me awake."

The evening grew chilly, and when she went back inside, Karen found matches and an old newspaper for kindling. The previous campers had left two logs in the fire pit, and the wood started right up. She moved Frieda from the picnic table to the more comfortable camp chairs.

"Warmer now?"

"I am." Frieda took a tiny taste of her sherry. "That's the secret to a happy life. Even if you're sad about something, don't let it take over. Try to have good times, too. Like this night. I'm very happy you allowed me to come along, my dear."

Karen raised her glass to Frieda, and they sipped their sherry and watched the fire develop, its orange-white flames reassuring in the deepening night.

"Even after your kids grow up, you never stop being their mother. I tried to show Sandy how to not lose yourself once you marry and have kids. People think I'm selfish but I tried to be true to myself. A mother doesn't stop being a person. But it's hard to keep things even." Frieda glanced at Karen. "Are you okay with this line of talk?"

Karen nodded. "I never had kids, but at work I felt like a mother. HR takes a certain kind of person, and you're always listening to people, trying to help any way you can. So I got a lot of satisfaction from that."

"I'm sure you were excellent at it." Frieda watched a twig flare and curl, finally falling into the coals.

Karen saw the lines on Frieda's face seemed to deepen in the firelight. "You were a good mother."

"Don't give me too much credit. I made plenty of mistakes."

"But you did your best."

"Yes." Beyond the fire, the oncoming night had changed the colors of the red rock cliffs from bright crimson to rust to dark gray to invisible.

"I always felt bad about leaving Mom," Karen said.

"No need."

"There was no work in Dickinson. I had to leave if I wanted to do more than clean hotel rooms, and things weren't so good at home."

"Each generation finds its own way. Lena knew you loved her with all your heart."

"But the older I get, the more guilty I feel. At the end, I worried she needed me or felt abandoned."

"That's my point. I can tell you right now, she didn't." Frieda looked over her glasses at Karen. "We always think we know what's going on in the other person's mind. Like I get these little mental pictures of Sandy curled up in a ball, crying her eyes out, and it kills me. But after she uncurls herself, she's going to stand up, dust herself off, and say, 'Well, I'll show her, the old bitch.' And that's the way it should be. You have to go on."

Chapter Thirty-Six

The next morning, Karen cleaned up the breakfast dishes and helped Frieda out to a sunny spot by the river. Back in the van, she set up a temporary office on the dinette table and got busy. Thanks to the signal beaming from the camp office, she was able to follow job leads, check email, and pay bills. But that was just a delaying tactic. After a while, she gave up and punched a number into her phone.

He picked up on the first ring. "I didn't think you'd call."

"I'm calling." She listened to the silence as they breathed in unison.

"Thank you."

She changed ears. "You said you had papers for me to sign. I'm in Utah and I've got WiFi. If you email them within the next ten minutes, I'll look them over. Otherwise, it'll have to wait."

"That's all right."

"I'll call you when I get back. We can go over the docs together. Goodbye."

"Wait. Can you hang on a second?" A vehicle roared past him. When it was quiet again, so was he, as if collecting his thoughts.

She fingered the button that would end the call.

"Did you get my message?"

"I did."

"So you know. There's no pregnancy."

Karen imagined him rubbing his forehead, eyes closed in humiliation, waiting for her to judge him. "Steve? This has nothing to do with me."

"She was never pregnant. I thought you'd want to know."

"I don't fucking care."

"Karen, please. I was hoping we could talk."

"There's nothing to discuss."

"I know I screwed up. Obviously. Big time. Major. But I'm completely aware of my mistakes in judgment. I mean, she really played me. I was blindsided, but that's not to say I'm not guilty. I am, but I wonder if we might, if you might–."

"Goodbye, Steve."

"Wait, I'm not asking for forgiveness. I know I can't expect that. But could we at least stay in touch, or–hang on." She heard him blow his nose. "I don't know if it matters anymore, but I wanted to tell you how much I've grown from the experience. I wasn't the best husband, I admit. But I was so damned proud of you. Any man would be lucky to have you as his wife. I want you to know I've spent a lot of time in contemplation–"

"Steve."

"No, please. Hear me out. Can you give me that, just out of respect for all our time together? I wanted to tell you I've been thinking of all we stand to lose, and it's major. We know each other, Karen. We understand each other. It would be a mistake to let our marriage go—all those years! So I'm simply asking if you'll do us both a favor and reflect on what we still have. Just out of respect for the love we used to have and hopefully, you might have a tiny thread left for me. I know you, sweetheart, and I know you must have some of the same thinking going on. I mean, it's so logical to stay together. Life is hard, and now I see the risks. I never saw it before, and Karen? I'll be honest, I'm scared. I think we need each other, in spite of everything. We all make mistakes. Will you at least consider talking about it when you get home?"

She stared at the phone in her hand, stared and stared until the display blurred and swam in front of her face.

She hung up.

Her legs wobbled when she stood.

None of it had to happen. Were it not for his stupidity and selfishness, she could be sitting at a sunny kitchen table right now, reading the paper, drinking coffee, and sending out resumes. Outside her window, the gardener would be pushing his lawn mower in neat stripes across the front lawn, and neighbors would be calling to each other along the neighborhood jogging paths.

After dumping her for a manipulative, fake-pregnant girl, after threatening Karen if she didn't move fast enough to grant the divorce, after leaving her to suffer her mother's loss alone, Steve now wanted his life back.

A tiny, hot thread, like an infectious strain of some disease, started to trickle through her veins, delightful in its toxicity, thrilling in its morbidity as she realized how much she could hurt him now, at least financially. She could go through with the divorce, making outrageous demands for support in her new, wonderfully jobless situation, and he would have to pay, because he could and because he owed her.

She wobbled over to the sink and stared out the window.

Or she could skip the games and the lawyers and the bullshit and simply create a new version of the old normal. She could return home to Newport, plaster a smile on her face, and resume her old life. After a period of hateful, silent years, she and Steve would probably get over it. They would work late and avoid dinners and pass each other in the hall with a quick shrug, sharing the house until his mind went and her arthritis took over and they retired from their jobs, their final days filled with doctor appointments and crosswords. Many couples settled their differences in this way. Why not them?

Outside, Frieda sat by the river's edge reading a magazine. She looked up as Karen flopped into the other chair. "I was beginning to wonder if you went back to sleep."

"Ha. I've been inside working my butt off."

"Find a job?"

"Lots of leads." She locked her eyes on the blurring river and tried to settle down.

"Does your husband want you back?"

That snapped Karen's head around. "How can you possibly be thinking that?"

"Men usually don't like to be alone, especially the older they get. Is there really going to be a baby or not?" Frieda chuckled. "Oh, honey, the look on your face. Wish I could take a picture."

"I'll get my camera."

"Don't be mad. You have to accept the fact that nothing changes. We may be from different generations, but people play the same old games. Probably nothing new since back in the caveman days."

Karen looked down at the water. Over the course of her career, she had handed out tissues while one employee after another railed about failing marriages. One woman's new husband stopped working and never went back, and by the time they finally divorced, she had to pay him spousal support. Another woman discovered her husband was a drug user, swearing she'd had no inkling until finding a crack pipe in his shaving kit. At the time Karen had marveled at the women's ignorance, yet now she felt like a member of their club.

"If you want my advice, I'd move on. Divorce him and start over."

Karen watched a baby bird hopping after its mother. Eventually the mother flew away. The baby scrambled to follow.

"You only get one life," said Frieda, "and you're better than halfway through this one."

"You don't have to remind me."

"I'm just saying, there comes a time when you're at an age where you have to look at it rather coldly. Decide how you're going to spend the rest of your valuable time." Frieda opened her magazine back up, and then pinned Karen with a stare. "We all like to think we're going to live forever, but at a certain point you have to come to grips with the reality."

A little later, Karen made lunch using a new recipe. She brought sandwiches to the table, along with fruit punch and potato chips.

Frieda peeled apart the bread. "What is this? Is it spinach? I don't really care for spinach."

"Basil. Do you like it? I got the idea from Aunt Marie."

"Don't we have any lettuce?"

"There's no room in the ice chest. Unless you want me to take the van into town and get the refrigerator fixed."

"No, it's fine."

Karen added a dab of horseradish, took another bite, and scribbled a note on a small spiral pad. When she returned to California, whatever way she went, she planned to take up cooking. It would force her to relax, and serve a productive purpose as well. She would make friends, invite them over for dinners, and create a social life. No more single-minded work, work, work for her.

Over the next few days, their routine took on a comforting sameness as she experimented with recipes and domesticity. At breakfast they ate cinnamon toast resurrected from her childhood, pancakes with fresh blueberries, and a bacon and cheese omelet. A floral cloth from the camp store adorned the picnic table, along with a bunch of daisies and Black Eyed Susans stuck in a water glass. Afterwards, Frieda sat in the sun and read while Karen washed dishes and made up the beds.

For lunches she served homemade soup or sandwiches along with sweet tea and punch. After doing dishes, the two of them would read or talk until Frieda's eyes grew heavy, at which time the laptop came out, and networking and lobbying ensued. Even though the economy was bad, Karen's background made her a valuable commodity, and she thrilled to the overtures from her old familiar world. Everything else might have changed, but in the weeks since word of her firing seeped out, she had become a hot property, with several viable job offers on her plate. She could be employed before she even crossed the state line, and for more money than she'd been making previously.

Steve kept calling and begging, but she hadn't returned his calls. "It's okay," his message said. "Take your time. I'll be here." Except his voice sounded increasingly frantic.

When Frieda awoke from her nap, Karen put away the computer and prepared appetizers. For dinners she had figured out how to cook small portions of fried chicken, meatloaf, and a succulent beef stew, even in spite of the tight quarters. Every evening, she built a fire using wood from the store. As the embers died and the cold returned, they went inside to read until bedtime, listening to soft jazz from Karen's iPod and some cheap speakers she'd picked up along the way. The routine didn't vary, except for the couple times she snuck away to call Curt. "What are you doing?" she would ask, pushing thoughts of Steve from her mind.

"Pining for you. What else?"

"Liar." Karen could hear the sound of surf breaking on a beach. "Where are you?"

"South Carolina. I just climbed this dune and the moon is rising on the water. It's silver. You should see it."

"I'd like to."

"You don't have to whisper," yelled Frieda through the window. "I'm not listening."

On their fourth morning in Moab, Karen tied her hair in a ponytail, noticing in the tiny bathroom mirror that her roots were coming out, and not just a little. These roots were dull brown, surprisingly familiar, like old relatives she hadn't seen in a long time. Their appearance represented a cumulative savings of approximately six hundred dollars in salon appointments since leaving California. She leaned in closer. Those silvery highlights were not from the sun.

When the coffee pot burbled to a finish, Karen filled a mug and took it outside to Frieda, who sat by the fire warming her old bones. "How did you sleep?"

"Like a rock." Frieda accepted the cup and took a careful sip. "Oh, that's good. Nice and strong."

Karen nodded, yawning. She wrapped her hands around her mug and stared into the fire, which she'd rebuilt from last night's unburned wood. What a treat to sleep until almost eight o'clock every morning and have breakfast whenever you felt hungry. For so many years she rose before dawn, ate breakfast in the dark, and commuted to work. What would it feel like to wake up whenever you wanted? A slow start to the day would have to be one of the greatest luxuries of life. And one day, she would have that, but not just yet. "How's your dizziness this morning?"

"Hard to tell. Might need a few more days."

"I found a group to walk with this morning. Will you be okay?" A sign had been tacked to the bulletin board at the store: *CRS Ladies: 9 am hike*. "It's just for a couple hours."

"Go have fun. I'll be here." Frieda looked off across the river.

Karen walked away slowly, but once out of sight she broke into a trot. Soon the trees thinned to reveal the camp store. A baby-faced ranger wearing a brown campaign hat stood on the wooden porch. He held a clipboard in his armpit since both hands were busy thumbing his phone. At the foot of the stairs, a dozen women jabbered, waiting for the walk to start. One hiker wore a matching pink blouse, socks, visor, and sunglasses. Another, her back bent from osteoporosis, wore a green straw hat with pastel flowers. Almost every hat sported a rhinestone CRS pin.

"'Can't Remember Shit'" the woman said in answer to Karen's question. "That's the name of our club. We're a bunch of widow ladies. You alone?"

"No, I'm traveling with a friend."

"I'm Fern. The pins are five bucks."

Karen dug the money out of her pocket and stuck the pin on her jacket collar. Fern adjusted it for her. "Next time bring a hat. You'll get old and wrinkly if you're not careful."

"Too late."

"Oh, spare me. When you get to be my age, then you'll have something to complain about."

"Ladies, can I get your attention?" The ranger called out from the porch. "I hope you all remembered water and proper hiking shoes. Today's trek will last about two hours. With any luck we'll stumble across some arrowheads."

"If I stumble across anything it'll be the end of me," said one elderly hiker.

"If I stumble I hope it's where he can catch me." A skinny old lady with big boobs winked at Karen. The ranger began walking, his hiking stick striking cadence on the hard dirt. "Ooh. Gotta run," she said, chasing after the ranger.

"That's Gina," said Fern. "She's our cougar."

A woman in a blue-flag travel scooter led the pack. The rest marched along in groups of two and three, talking and laughing. Karen fell in beside Fern and her friend Belle, whose sweater was covered with photo buttons of her dogs. "I hope that young man isn't going to run like that all morning."

"At this rate, I'll lose my shapely behind," said a rotund hiker.

"You can reload at lunch. I'm bringing home-made tortellini." Fern glanced over her shoulder at Karen. "We always do pot luck after the walk. You're welcome to join us."

The path narrowed, forcing them into single file, and the conversation faded as the hikers watched their footing. Mares' tails feathered across the cobalt sky. Karen took a deep breath of the clean air and broke into a grin. It felt good to be alone in the midst of strangers, listening to their chatter without the need to join in. Here she had no obligation to anyone but herself, free to enjoy some exercise and a few hours away from camp.

A half-hour later, the ranger called a halt when they reached the campfire circle at the one-mile point. The women sat on split-log benches arranged in a crescent under a stand of cottonwoods. After a short speech on wildflowers, the ranger wandered off, working his smart phone.

Karen leaned over and stretched, her hips and lower back protesting. "Are all of you traveling alone?"

Fern nodded. "We RV as a group. We've been all over the country more times than I can count."

"Sounds like fun."

"It's fantastic," said Belle. "You can do as much or as little as you want, take a nap, read, or go for a hike, but you're never lonely. We're kind of like a commune on wheels."

"What do you drive?" Karen sat down on the log next to Fern.

"Pretty much everything," said Fern. "I've got a Class B van, but some of these gals drive all the way up to the big old Class Cs. That's your fifth wheels, your motor coaches."

"Amazing."

"What, you think we're too old?"

"No, I'm impressed. You guys are awesome."

"That's right. We are awesome, aren't we?" Belle laughed and high-fived Fern.

Karen had needed a few days adjusting to the Roadtrek but these women, twenty years her senior, were driving rigs as big as a city bus. Then she remembered Barb. And the Bronco. And Sandy.

She shook her head. *Breathe.*

"That woman over there," said Fern, gesturing, "she and her husband used to own a trucking business, and she drove a Peterbilt for years. Now that's a tough assignment."

"All of us drive," said another. "It's either that or stay home. And I am not about to stay home. Might's well bury me then."

"Amen."

The ranger waved and the hikers fell in.

"Look at him go," said Fern. "I wish I was that young."

Belle whacked a pinecone with her walking stick. "What matters is how you feel. I feel young in my head."

"Me, too. I'm always doing something new, and I think that keeps you young. Gal over there last week bought a new twenty-four foot Prowler fifth-wheel. You don't do that if you have an old lady frame of mind."

They passed along the far edge of the campground where the RVs thinned out. A shovel clanged against a rock, and a white-haired woman stopped working. She wiped her forehead with her sleeve, leaned against the shovel, and waved. The hikers waved back.

"That's Eleanor. She's always fixing something," said Belle. "Until her husband died, she never even drove a car. Now the RV is her fulltime home."

"She doesn't look sturdy enough to handle it," said Karen.

"Don't write her off. She's tougher than she looks."

The group passed by, waving. A gray-faced dog sat leaning against the woman's leg. Karen wondered what it felt like to fall asleep by yourself at night in your own house on wheels, after puttering around during the day and then cooking whatever you wanted and reading and listening to music until you felt like sleeping. With internet, you could stay in touch with the world, and with your RV, you could go anywhere, all over the country, by yourself or with friends. A woman alone used to be a scary proposition, but if you stuck with a group of fellow travelers, it might be fun.

Karen didn't have friends in her Newport neighborhood, although she had helped out with fund-raisers and fashion shows. The neighbors were nice enough. They smiled and waved before pulling into the garage and closing the door behind them. Without her work, Karen might have felt lonely, but most days she was too busy to notice.

The unfamiliar exercise began taking its toll on her leg muscles, and she was happy to see the camp store come into view. It was high time she got back to make lunch. Frieda would be waiting.

"You sure you don't want to come by?" asked Belle. "It's no trouble. We can always make room for two more."

"Thanks. I would, but my friend is kind of shy." Karen waved goodbye and trotted away. The hike and companionship had served as a welcome break, but she couldn't risk lunch. If Frieda met these ladies, she'd want to spend another week here in Moab, and Karen needed to get back and face her future.

Back at camp, Frieda sat in a dappled patch of sunlight, her large-print Readers' Digest open in her lap. "I was beginning to think you got lost."

"Give me a minute to make ham sandwiches." Karen saw Frieda make a face. "What?"

"Ham again?"

"It's all we have left." A truck stopped at the end of their driveway and Belle leaned out the window. "Hey, Karen, we're on our way to lunch if you and your friend want to change your minds."

"Somebody invited us to lunch?" Frieda asked.

"I thought we should stick around camp and start packing."

Frieda planted her cane. "Nothing doing. This is why you camp, girlie. Make new friends and create memories. Come on, help me up."

Karen knew she had already lost the argument, but the idea of not having to eat the ham took away the sting. Besides, if she let Frieda win this one, they could probably start packing this afternoon. The thought of breaking camp tomorrow excited her. She was homesick. It was time to return to reality. She helped Frieda into the front seat and climbed in after her.

Belle drove to the far end of the campground where a group of RVs were parked in a half-circle. Wind chimes danced from their awnings, and a row of chairs lined the edge of the river. Two picnic tables had been dragged together, end to end, and covered with red-and-white checkered oilcloth. A dozen women had already started on the hot casseroles, salads, and sweets contributed by everyone. Bottles of wine and a tub of beer stood at one end of the table.

"This is fantastic," said Frieda, settling into a chair at the head of the table as Karen brought her a full plate. "You ladies do this every day?"

"Twice a week," said Belle, pouring a splash of wine into a paper cup for Frieda. "Stick around. After lunch, we play cards."

"Count me in." Frieda grinned at Karen. "Have some more wine, honey pie. We're not going anywhere soon."

Chapter Thirty-Seven

"What I like about being old is, I don't care what people think about me anymore," said Fern, gnawing on a fried chicken leg. "I'm free to express my opinion."

Belle chuckled. "When did you ever not?"

"And that can go too far. Some old people use age as an excuse for bad behavior. Like this old fart at church," Gina began.

"When do you ever go to church?" asked Belle.

"I do every Sunday."

"I've never seen you there."

"Because you're asleep," said Gina. "Ask the rest of them. But anyway, as I was saying before I was so rudely interrupted, seniors often feel entitled to act belligerent just because of their advancing years."

"Works for me," said Fern.

Karen helped herself to another plateful of casserole. She was enjoying the back and forth between the old ladies, and she could see Frieda nodding and smiling along, completely relaxed.

"I heard it's the absence of hormones that makes you mean," said one woman from the end of the table.

"They took away my hormones and baby, let me tell you, I got mean," said another.

"When you're younger you hold back, trying to be nice and all. I heard it's the hormones make you pliable. Any truth to that, Doc?"

A woman with spectacles and a long white ponytail nodded. "Some think it's nature's way of encouraging a woman's receptivity to breeding and nurturing."

"Too much information," said Frieda.

Doc continued. "But after menopause, you break out of the fog and start to feel more independent again. Some say you return to the person you were before puberty, and that person is more true to who you really are."

Karen felt that way herself lately, as if she were getting in touch with her inner eleven-year-old.

"I've been the same from Day One," said the Cougar. "No man is safe around me." She scrunched up her shoulders and squeezed her eyes shut in a girlish grin.

"That's just too much trouble," Fern said. "Comes a time in life you should kick back and stop worrying so much. Some things I just don't care about any more. You've heard of the Bucket List? I made a Fuck It List."

"Fern, we have guests. Watch your language," said Belle.

Fern grinned at Karen. "Fuck it."

"So, what's on your list?" asked Karen.

"Well, I figure I'm never gonna bungee jump, or run for President."

"Or win the Miss America Pageant," said Frieda.

"You don't know that." The Cougar scowled. "They have older categories all the time."

"What about you, Karen? What's on your Eff It List?" asked Belle.

"I don't have one."

"How old are you?"

"I just turned fifty."

"Fifty's the minimum. You are now officially old enough for a Fuck It List," said Fern. "Pour me some more wine, and let's make her one. Anybody got a pen?"

Chapter Thirty-Eight

The hoarse cry scratched through the darkness, reaching into Karen's dreams. She sat straight up, listening and wondering if the horrible sound was real, but in the next second she bolted to her feet, flailed at the light switch, and threw open the flimsy dividers. Frieda lay twisted in bedding. Her mouth drooped and one eye remained closed. The other roved the room, the white showing. She struggled to speak but could manage only garbled sounds, more painful than any cry for help.

"Shh." Karen grabbed for her phone and knelt down on the floor next to the bed. Hands shaking, she punched the keypad. "It's okay, Frieda, I'm getting help."

"This is the operator. What is your emergency?"

Karen blurted out the van's location twice. Then she hung up and covered Frieda with a heavy blanket, putting a pillow behind her shoulders and raising her up so she could breathe more easily. "They're sending somebody. You'll be okay. We're going to get you to the hospital." She turned on the heater and sat on the edge of the bed, gently pulling socks onto Frieda's small feet.

"You'll be okay," Karen repeated, slipping her arms around Frieda, warming her. "We're only ten minutes from Moab. I'll call Sandy as soon as we get to the hospital."

Frieda shook her head. "Home."

"We'll go home later. First we're going to get you to a hospital. Hang on." A few minutes later, Karen saw headlights bouncing down the dirt road toward the van. She eased away from Frieda, yanked open the door, and ran outside.

"Over here!" She waved her arms over her head as the lights hit her in the face. The ambulance braked in a cloud of dust, and men in dark shirts and heavy boots piled out. She felt the hot breath of the ambulance's motor as the paramedics stomped past, piling into the van with their equipment. As soon as she could edge herself in, she peered over their shoulders, straining for information.

Minutes later, the men carried Frieda out of the van and onto a gurney, her face nearly swallowed up by an oxygen mask. They collapsed the legs of the gurney and slid it into the back of the ambulance with a great clatter. Karen tried to climb inside, but an EMT blocked the door, his face sympathetic.

"Can't do it, ma'am. I apologize."

The camp host, a thick woman in a plaid jacket, watched from sidelines. Karen hurried over. "I need a ride."

The woman ground a cigarette butt under her heel and gestured toward her truck. According to the clock on the dashboard, it was almost two when they pulled out of the campground entrance and began chasing after the ambulance. The flashing red lights ricocheted off the canyon walls as they raced toward Moab, the frieze-like etchings ghostly in the darkness.

At the hospital, Karen jogged alongside the gurney, pawing through Frieda's wallet for her medical card and answering questions as best she could, but when they arrived at triage, the nurses booted her out and pulled the drapes closed.

She returned to the waiting room and slumped in a chair. Then she thought of Sandy. Whatever was going on with Frieda, Sandy would need to know immediately. Swiping at her wet cheeks, Karen searched Frieda's purse for the address book. The phone rang twice, three times before being picked up, and as soon as Karen said hello, Sandy dropped the phone and began screaming. Seconds later, Karen heard the phone being jostled, and then a man's voice. Richard listened quietly, asking only for logistical clarifications while she explained.

"I have a plane," he said, his voice calm. "We'll be there in three hours." He gave her his cell number before hanging up. Karen stared at the phone. She didn't even know these people and now she found herself shepherding their mother in her last moments.

Sandy had been right in predicting disaster. Karen tried to console herself with the knowledge that Frieda, ever independent, had chosen to make this trip. It was her decision, and the decision had made her happy.

Karen hugged the purse. The cold air in the waiting room smelled like dirty sneakers and pesticide, and the chair was all hard angles, its arms sticky. She leaned her head against the wall and watched the images on a muted CNN. The stories jumped from the latest setback in the Middle East to anorexic supermodels to a commercial about steak knives.

Nothing changes, Karen thought. People you love go through all this suffering, they fall out of love and hurt each other and fight for life in a hospital room. Life and death. Nothing changes and an oblivious world keeps rolling along.

Rolling. She grimaced, remembering the Bronco cartwheeling through the sagebrush.

She would never know exactly what had happened, and told herself for the hundredth time there was nothing else she could have done, but the memory wouldn't go away. Alone in the waiting room, she couldn't find the easy wisdom that had seemed so accessible on the open road, and now the only other person who could help her deal with it was probably dying.

She closed her eyes.

After dinner last night, she and Frieda had talked for hours, of men and children and love and work.

"Don't be afraid to live your life," Frieda had said, staring into the flames, "because if you don't, someone else will."

Someone else had. A whole trainload of somebodies, from her family to her teachers, to her husband, her job, her coworkers—all in the interest of being good. Thinking of herself as doing the right thing.

"Ms. Grace?"

Karen opened her eyes. A nurse stood before her.

"You can join Mrs. Richter now."

Karen gathered her things and followed the nurse into the land behind the door of the ER, where the ill or maimed lay in un-private rooms and moans emanated from behind thin curtains. She found Frieda in a green-draped bed, around which various machines chirped and sighed. Lines and tubes connected the old woman to the machines, but her chin nestled on her chest, and her eyes remained closed. Karen pulled a hard chair over next to the bed and put her hand over Frieda's.

When a doctor looked in, Karen demanded information, but when the young man rubbed his face, she tempered her voice, wondering how many shifts he'd worked.

"Mrs. Richter has had multiple strokes since they brought her in," he said, consulting a chart. "The last was about an hour ago. It was a pretty strong one. We're keeping her comfortable. Beyond that? We'll have to see." He apologized with his eyes and hurried away.

Karen studied Frieda's face for a creased brow or a flicker of anguish, but she saw no movement to indicate whether the old woman remained in this room or if her spirit had already moved on, unburdened. Loneliness swamped Karen, and her forehead dropped to Frieda's arm. It felt cool, but a pulse still fluttered under her papery white skin.

An hour later, she heard footsteps and crying, and the drapes flew back and Sandy rushed in, followed by a tall man in a windbreaker. Karen stood up, offering her chair.

"Oh, Mom," Sandy wailed, but the monitor registered no change as she threw herself across her mother's body. Richard put his hand on his wife's back, making small, useless circles while she sobbed. Sandy straightened up and dug in her pocket for a tissue. "What did the doctors say?" she asked, her eyes still on her mother.

"All they can do is confirm that she's had strokes."

"Strokes plural? Oh, my God. How bad is she?" When Karen didn't answer, Sandy glared at her, her face slick with tears. "Are you happy now?"

Karen took a step back. "I'm sorry."

"How sorry can you be? You got what you wanted. You got somebody to keep you company while you went gallivanting across the desert."

"I am so sorry, Sandra. Please know this. Your mom was happy at the end. Last night, at dinner, she talked about you. She really loves you, and she wants you to be happy."

"Happy! Get the fuck out of this room. Now. NOW." Richard pulled his screaming wife into his arms and nodded at Karen.

"I am sorry," Karen said again. She parted the drapes and let them fall shut behind her while Sandra sobbed. The ER staff barely noticed as Karen left, pushing through the door to the waiting area and disappearing into the waiting room.

In the hours since she arrived, the room had filled with wailing children, hikers with swollen ankles, and trail bikers who tried to fly. She waded close-mouthed through the crush of coughing, drippy-nosed humanity, cutting a path to the door and bursting outside. In the light of late morning, she sucked in a cleansing lungful of fresh air. Past the entrance she found a sun-baked cement bench, and sat against the warm back rest, letting the heat soak into her muscles.

Alone outside the ER, Karen felt the great weight of impending grief, but both of them had known what might happen. Frieda would die the same way she had lived, on her own terms, trying to gentle her family along but in the end, making her own decisions. To Karen, it seemed a great privilege to have been with Frieda at the last, and she thought again of her mother and said a prayer of thanks to Aunt Marie for filling in.

The sun baked her aching limbs, as Karen wondered where her mom and Frieda were now in their cosmic journey. After so many years spent mastering life on this planet, a body would rejoin the earth, but what about the mind and soul? All the wisdom gained, the thoughtful maturity—was it simply gone? The memories of family and farm, dissipated into nothing?

That wouldn't make sense. In high school science, Karen had been taught the earth is a closed system, that nothing is ever lost. Elements change into other forms and recirculate. Water evaporates into the sky, turns into clouds and returns to the earth in the form of rain. If a physical body returns to the soil, then where does the rest of the energy go?

A shuttle van pulled up on the opposite corner, towing a colorful load of kayaks, headed upriver for a day of fun. Today was just like any other for the boaters who would paddle with the current, unaware of Karen's great loss or any other. The world just kept rolling.

She pushed up off the bench, shaking her head to clear it. Maybe the driver would give her a ride to camp. Time was passing and she needed to get back to the RV park and figure out what to do next. She started across the driveway toward the shuttle, her feet moving more quickly, her muscles loosening. Overhead, a jet streaked through the cloudless blue sky, spinning contrails in its wake. Karen looked up, watching as it disappeared, and envious of the pilot who, from his perspective, could see the curvature of the earth.

Chapter Thirty-Nine

Karen thanked the shuttle driver at the campground office and set off on foot down the unpaved lane, her footsteps silent in the powdery dirt. When she rounded a row of oleander bushes, the van loomed into view, waiting for her in the parking space like a tired old horse. Karen unlocked the double doors and pulled them both open wide, leaving them agape to offset her sudden sense of isolation.

She went inside, opened all the windows, and began the process of organizing and cleaning. First she broke down the bed, returning the dinette table to its pedestal and the cushions to their function as bench seats on either side. Then she rolled up the bedding, stuffed it in a cabinet, and hung up Frieda's clothing. In the tiny restroom, she found an overnight kit with toothbrush, hair brush, and assorted pill containers. These items, along with Frieda's clothes, would eventually be packed in a cardboard box and marked for shipment to Denver.

When the back end of the van no longer spoke of the woman whose journey ended there, Karen sat down at the dinette to rest. She noticed a string of amber beads on the floor and leaned down to pick up the rosary. It could only have fallen to that precise spot if Frieda had dropped it from the bed last night, no doubt clutching the beads as her nervous system faltered. How long had she suffered in darkness, alone in her terror, until she had gathered up enough strength to somehow call for help?

Karen lay down on the bench seat and cried, her grief ballooning to embrace the totality of her losses, of Frieda and her parents, her marriage and her work, and mortal life from which she could not regain a single misspent minute. When her head was so congested that she could no longer breathe, she choked off the last of the tears, and standing, felt her way to the towel rack where she mopped her face and neck. She looked in the mirror and saw swollen slits where her eyes used to be. She picked up the rosary, went outside, and dropped into a chair. With the beads laced between her fingers, Karen leaned back and simply listened. The wind rustled through the soaring cottonwood trees and ravens squawked in the distance. The river rushed by, its currents rippling against the rocks. She could smell the damp mud along the shore, and the rich sweetness of decomposing vegetation. Eyes closed, she could be anywhere. Where would she want to be?

She felt the beads of the rosary. The last time she saw it, Frieda was clutching it in one hand and the armrest in the other, praying they could outrun the dangerous men on the highway outside of Cheyenne. Karen wondered what Father Engel would say if he knew about their flight to freedom. Would he blame or absolve her?

It didn't matter. Life had unfolded and caught her up in its danger, and she had reacted in a fiercely logical manner. She and Frieda had traveled many miles together, unlikely compatriots as one of them journeyed toward her end and the other, toward her beginning.

Her eyes opened, and she blinked in the sudden brightness. With no job, no husband, and no reason to hurry back to California, or anywhere at all, she had only to decide her next destination and point the van in that direction.

Duty pulled her home to California where she could make a contribution. The job market would be friendly to her, and she knew it wouldn't be long before she secured another high-paying, powerful position. All she had to do was climb into the driver's seat, turn the key, and return to that which was familiar.

She heard Frieda's voice again, from just two nights ago, sitting by the campfire, talking of the future.

Decide how to live your life, she said, *or somebody else will.*

To hear Frieda tell it, Karen was a youngster with the world at her feet.

"If you were ninety, you'd know what I mean," said Frieda, "but right now, you can't see it. That's human nature. We don't know what we have until we lose it. That's why I'm warning you."

They had sat quietly, listening to the snap of the flames.

"What do you think I would do if one morning I woke up and I was your age, forty years younger than I am right now?" said Frieda. "Let me tell you, girlie, if that happened, nothing would stop me. Nothing."

Now Karen watched a trio of kayakers paddling down the middle of the river, and she marveled at their courage or, depending on how you looked at it, stupidity. If you didn't know any better, you'd think the river was placid, because it was so wide and deep you couldn't see that it flowed dangerously fast. You had to look. If you watched carefully, you would notice objects racing by, here a duck resting on the current, there a log as big as a car, and both of them gone in an instant.

Chapter Forty

The palm trees swayed in the morning breeze, their fronds waving to welcome Karen home. Sunlight reflected like diamonds off the iron-blue Pacific, and the smell of salt in the air filled her lungs. Even the traffic couldn't put a dent in her happiness. It was good to be back in sun-drenched Southern California, relishing the familiar. A wide grin broke across her face.

She parked next to a row of shiny new cars and went up in the elevator. When the doors opened, many arms reached out to hug her, the associates and colleagues she thought she might never see again, and her throat tightened. She broke away from them and walked down the hall to Peggy's office.

"What the hell?" Peggy looked up from her keyboard. "You're not supposed to be here."

"I could say the same about you." The women embraced, and Karen took a seat. The drapes were drawn against the sunlight, leaving fluorescents as the only illumination in the smoky office. "What happened to the cruise?"

Peggy shrugged. "Boring. Nothing but fat people eating. I got off in Barcelona and flew home."

"And Wes let you come back."

"I know where the bodies are buried."

"But you hate him."

"Aw, he's not so bad. Behind that weasely exterior, he's a lot like my kid. The one I never see. Besides, he actually apologized to me. How many people can say that?"

"You've got the magic touch." If Peggy wanted to believe it, Karen wouldn't disabuse her. She stood up.

"What's next?"

Karen glanced at her watch. "I have an appointment with the weasel."

"Age discrimination is a joke. You can't make it stick." Wes sat back in his chair, glaring at the file that sat reeking between them on his desk.

"I can and I will, and you know it." Karen tossed him a business card. "I have a whole firm full of lawyers ready to go."

The file contained the names of eighteen older employees who had been fired in the past twenty-four months. All were over forty. All had acknowledged in writing that Wes had badgered them repeatedly before their terminations, using expressions such as "geezer, old fart and battle-ax," and opining that the company needed an infusion of "new blood" and "young ideas." All were willing to file age discrimination lawsuits, according to Karen.

"Fuck."

"Exactly." Karen sat back, smiling.

Wes scowled at the window, beyond which a small plane chugged across the sky, towing a banner. Something about vodka. "What do they want?"

"Call Peggy. Tell her to bring the checkbook."

Epilogue

Karen stared out across the arid landscape. Other than wheel marks carving through the sagebrush, no sign remained of the Bronco. She hung the rosary on a rusted metal fencepost and returned to the Roadtrek. Without the sound of Frieda's voice, there was only the low whine of the road and a gentle vibration of housewares stowed securely in the galley.

Karen got back in the van, holding it steady as an eighteen-wheeler blew past. She ran through a list in her mind, trying on the options. Her golf clubs were in the back. She might follow the Lewis and Clark Golf Trail through North Dakota, or the Audubon through the southern states, or one of the dozens of other golf trails across the country. She could spend a few weeks in Dickinson with her family and friends, check on Father Engel's office situation, and maybe even drop in on the governor, but then she would head south ahead of the snow. The CRS ladies had said they would be in the Florida Keys for Thanksgiving and Karen planned to join them.

Out of a cloudless sky, a blast of wind attacked the van, but this hefty Roadtrek could handle it. It was a 210, the biggest and beefiest of the line, bought with the proceeds from her house in Newport Beach. Heading north on the same highway she'd travelled with Frieda, Karen knew about wind. It never stopped. It only changed direction. On each curve or rise the prevailing gusts might come at her from any point on the compass, blasting first one way and then another. At the top of a hill, she passed a fluttering highway sign bearing a picture of Mount Rushmore. Past that she saw nothing at all except miles and miles of sweeping dry grasslands rolling out to the horizon in every direction.

She realized she was speeding out of habit and eased up. Over the past three decades in which she had reported to work every day in a large corporate building, years in which she had lived cheek-by-jowl with her neighbors in a gated community, in which she had driven slowly down congested roads through frenetic cities, she had forgotten what was meant by the concept of space. Now, unconsciously, she had been hurrying to get through it, but there was no need. No cars rode her bumper. The sun was plenty high and the day would be long. She was free to choose her own speed through this vast park-like space.

The highway, one lane in each direction and narrow like a ribbon, stretched out in front of her for a dozen miles before disappearing over a hill. When she reached that crest, she knew she would see another ribbon reaching out for ten or fifteen more miles and when she finished that and topped the next hill, there'd be yet another ribbon road and another and another, a dozen or more times that afternoon. As the miles rolled by, she became enthralled by how much country surrounded her, and just how incredibly vast it was.

Suddenly she understood something that confounded her for years—how people could look at the sky or the ocean and feel reassured at their own insignificance. She had always wondered how feeling small and powerless could give a person comfort, she who had always drawn security from significance. As Karen had moved up the career ladder, accumulating more money and power, she felt the world was less dangerous.

Yet at this moment, she realized what they might have meant: as you accepted your insignificance, you could also accept that you were not in control of nor in charge of the world. You could go through your days concerned only with your own small world and the circle of people who loved you.

"Room enough, and time." The phrase tickled around the edges of her memory, something she'd read in a book or heard in a movie, a blessing proclaimed by the Native Americans about places such as this. Here on this highway in the vast freedom of the plains, her mind uncluttered by a daily agenda or the demands of a frantic populace, she could permit herself the luxury of thought. She slowed the van until it came to a stop, the highway deserted for miles in both directions. The wind rocked the van, blowing in through the windows, rearranging her hair until she was blind and thrumming past her ears until she was deaf. Karen shut off the motor. Her bare feet touched the blacktop, warm but not hot. She filled her lungs with the dry, clean air, right off the plains and miles from any town. She heard a ground squirrel chirping and saw antelope walking along on the other side of the barbed wire fence, tearing clumps of grass from the rich earth. The rippling grasses were topped by feathery beige flowers that resembled wheat.

Insignificance: for the first time she considered she need not accept responsibility for everybody and everything within range in her world. In taking on that responsibility she had not only overburdened herself, but shortchanged those for whom she worried. Why had she assumed them incapable, taking that weight on her own shoulders? Other people surely carried within them their own strength, their own resources, and she finally saw she had not been responsible for her parents' satisfaction with their lives, nor that of her relatives, nor her former employees at Global Health, nor what happened to the planet after she left it.

Instead, she saw herself as a bright, vivid figure standing on a timeline, her ancestors barely visible behind her, their small, beloved bodies dim and fading into history. In front of her she saw only stick figures moving into the unknowable and impersonal future, as anonymous as the ancestors. As if she slid a magnifying glass along the ruler of history, the figures became larger and clearer as they edged nearer in proximity to her own life. They gained names and identities, but only for that small space in time they shared with her.

In front of the van she stood on the center line of the deserted highway, her arms outstretched, eyes closed. The wind embraced her with its clovered breath, wrapped itself around her waist, between her legs and under her arms, lifting her. She turned in a slow circle, her arms reaching out, her fingertips lengthening to touch all that she could see in three hundred and sixty degrees of solitude and peace.

It was enough. It was everything.

Acknowledgements

Gratitude and love to my family: my sweet husband, Bill, whose kindness, patience and generosity are seemingly without limit; my incredible mother, Marie Kuswa who is still my most ardent cheerleader; sibs Karen, Tom, Verne, Nan, Cynthia and Bob, for never losing faith; and my awesome kids and grandkids: Danny, Amy, Ella, Andrew, Lisa, Carlos, Richard, Jeff, Donna, Mike, Miranda, Sara, Sean, and Baby Spreen, for being everything a mom could want. I am proud of all of you.

To my critique group who made me feel smart when it was warranted and the rest of the time told me when my writing stunk: Ray Strait, Jim Hitt, Harlee Lassiter, Vicki Hitt, Mary Jane Kruty, Peggy Wheeler, JoLynne Buehring, Judy Howard, Kathy Shattuck, Kathryn Jordan, and Jim Parrish.

To my friend Tammy Coia and her unending dedication to helping women capture their memoirs on paper.

To my mentor, Michele Scott, my editors Jennifer Meeghan and Wendy Duren, and my cover artist Damon at Damonza.com for the professional boost I needed.

To all my Hemet and Palm Desert friends who cheered me on without hesitation: the Wolfe Pack, Palm Springs Pen Women, and the Palm Springs Writers' Guild.

To Michael Stephen Gregory and his crew for making it possible for me to learn and grow professionally at the Southern California Writers Conferences.

I feel like I'm standing at the podium at the Oscars, and you're all wishing I'd get it done already, so I'll just end with love and gratitude to all who helped me realize my dream.

About the Author

After a career in human resources, Lynne Morgan Spreen reinvented herself as a freelance writer, webmaster, teacher, and novelist. She also blogs about issues relating to women of middle-age and better at *www.AnyShinyThing.com.* You can also join the conversation by going to @LynneSpreen on Twitter, or to Facebook. Lynne and Bill live in Hemet, California.

Made in the USA
Monee, IL
15 June 2020